Jun 19

ALL WE COULD HAVE BEEN

ALL WE COULD HAVE BEEN

TE CARTER

Feiwel and Friends

New York

A FEIWEL AND FRIENDS BOOK
An imprint of Macmillan Publishing Group, LLC
175 Fifth Avenue, New York, NY 10010

Our books may be purchased in bulk for promotional, educational, or business
use. Please contact your local bookseller or the Macmillan Corporate and
Premium Sales Department at (800) 221-7945 ext. 5442 or by email at
MacmillanSpecialMarkets@macmillan.com.

Library of Congress Cataloging-in-Publication Data
Names: Carter, T. E. (Young adult author), author.
Title: All we could have been / TE Carter.
Description: First edition. | New York : Feiwel and Friends, 2019. | Summary: After
her older brother commits a heinous crime, a teenage girl attempts to conceal
her identity as she struggles with PTSD.
Identifiers: LCCN 2018019377 | ISBN 9781250172969 (hardcover)
Subjects: | CYAC: Brothers and sisters—Fiction. | Post-traumatic stress disorder—Fiction.
Classification: LCC PZ7.1.C418 Al 2019 | DDC [Fic]—dc23
LC record available at https://lccn.loc.gov/2018019377

Book design by Rebecca Syracuse

Feiwel and Friends logo designed by Filomena Tuosto

First edition, 2019

1 3 5 7 9 10 8 6 4 2

fiercereads.com

I seek no copy now of life's first half:
Leave here the pages with long musing
    curled,

And write me new my future's epigraph

—Elizabeth Barrett Browning

ALL WE COULD HAVE BEEN

PART ONE

Chapter One

Three men in unfortunately gray overalls stare at the wooden knight.

It hasn't even been up for twenty-four hours. Yesterday they spent the better part of the afternoon trying to get it to stand up, despite the knight's sword constantly pulling the figure downward to the left. We'd all sat around, watching them swearing and arguing about how best to fix it. A whole audience of people with nothing better to do.

They finished just as it was getting dark, and now here they are again, first thing in the morning, trying to scrub a spray-painted penis off the sign.

It had to be expected. If you call a housing complex for people who can't afford housing Castle Estates, and then you think a wooden knight galloping his way toward the squat brick squalor is going to make people feel good about living there, you kind of deserve to wake up in the morning and find a dick on your sign.

"That lasted long," Marcus Cotero says, sitting beside me on the bench.

I've lived at Castle Estates for all of nine days, but I already know I'm supposed to stay away from Marcus Cotero. My aunt warned me he's often in the middle of local gossip, and whether or not anything people say is true, the last thing I need is to be right there in the middle with him. Still, it's early morning, it's the first day of my senior year, and he has nice eyes.

"Not really surprising, I guess."

"True story. You can't stop the dick. Try as you might, you just can't stop the dick." He shakes his head as if he actually feels bad for either the men in gray overalls or the cartoonish knight. No reason to feel bad for the knight; given the graffiti artist's poor sense of perspective, the knight has received a substantial upgrade.

"That should be the motto," I say. "Right under the knight. 'Welcome to Castle Estates. Where You Can't Stop the Dick.'"

Marcus Cotero laughs and takes out a pack of cigarettes. He offers me one, and although I don't smoke, I take it anyway. He lights his, but I just pull mine apart, investigating the strange brown flakes people are always in such an uproar about. No, it's not healthy, but lots of things aren't. Starting with Castle Estates.

"You're new, right? Alexia Lawlor?" he asks.

The name sounds weird. Too much alliteration. I took my aunt's last name when I came to live with her. It's how I've managed for the last five years. Every year choosing to move in with a different relative during the summer so I can start school in a new town or state each fall. I have one goal: Survive a full school year—180 days—hiding behind a new name, new home, and new persona. Sure, it hasn't worked for me yet, but this year I only have to last 162 school days. Seniors get the privilege of needing only 90 percent of an education, I suppose.

Maybe this time it will all turn out okay. I'm nothing if not hopeful. Despite everything, I can't seem to give up on the hope that maybe, just once, it won't end up the same. I mean, hey . . . percentages are with me this year, right? Fewer days mean fewer chances to screw it all up. Again.

I shake off the thoughts and turn to Marcus. "Lexi. Call me Lexi. And, yeah, I just moved here a few days ago."

"I'm Marcus."

"I know."

"Already been warned?"

The way he asks bugs me. It's like he's expecting me to confirm it. I have a serious antipathy for taking another person's version of someone else to heart. One of those things I've picked up these past five years.

"No," I lie to Marcus, because I'm determined not to let anyone else define him for me. More so now that I know he expects different. "I just have a good memory, and my aunt gave me a tour when I moved in."

He doesn't seem to believe me, but he nods and looks back at the three men, who are now arguing about the best way to remove spray paint from a wooden sign. I wonder what kind of emergency hotline you have to call to get grown men out of bed on a Monday morning to scrub genitalia from housing-project signs.

"So, *Green Arrow*, huh?" Marcus asks.

I look down at my shirt. I've never seen the show, but the shirt's green, and today's Monday, and Mondays are green days. They've been green days for a while now. I don't remember anymore when I chose which day went with which color, and I definitely can't recall the rationale I hope I had at the time. All I know is that, in all my iterations of myself, Mondays stay green. Mondays and green never change. No matter where I'm living or what name I use, that's something secure. Constant.

"I've never watched it," I tell Marcus. "I just needed something green."

He looks at my green Chucks, olive-green army pants, green T-shirt, and dark-green hoodie. "You really like green, huh?"

"On Monday."

He pauses, takes a last drag from his cigarette, and stubs it out. "Want to tell me about it?"

"Not really. It's complicated."

"Isn't it always?" he asks, picking up on my cliché refusal to talk about myself.

We don't get to say anything else because the bus pulls up.

It's embarrassing to start a new school and ride up on the crappy old school bus, but I didn't have time to meet anyone in the neighborhood in the past nine days. Besides, the neighborhood seems to consist of Marcus Cotero, a phallus-obsessed graffiti artist, a bunch of old people, and Mr. Simmons, who fell asleep drunk in the community fountain on my first night here. He'd been trying to build a device to make the fountain dance to music, but all he'd done was nearly electrocute himself. Oh, and now we permanently get to hear the opening of Beethoven's Ninth at approximately 3:17 p.m. *and* a.m. So there's that.

When you live in shitty public housing and you take the school bus, you get stuck at the beginning of the morning route and on the end of the afternoon route. I guess no one cares if you have to get up before five or if it takes you more than an hour to get home. I'm not surprised. I might be new here, but that's the way of it all, isn't it? If you're poor, people just expect you to be irrelevant.

I watch Marcus head to the back of the bus, looking brooding and intense. I almost go with him but decide instead to settle into the front seat. I'm not here to create anything permanent.

I can't say I'm nervous about starting at a new school. I mean, I'm terrified, but not more nervous than I usually am. About life in general. But this . . . this is what happens every year. School starts, and I try to blend in. As well as I can, despite everything about me that just seems to beg for attention. I do my best not to get involved with anyone, to keep my head down, and to just get through one damn school year. Maybe people will look at me with my weird wardrobe, but if I say nothing or give them nothing of myself, there's not a whole lot they can do with that.

Or there shouldn't be, but of course someone always seems to find out. Someone says something to someone else, and then there's a connection, and suddenly I hear Scott's name one day and it's all out there again. Then off I go to find another place to hide.

No, I tell myself. *Not this time. Every year you tell yourself you won't get close to anyone, and then you let down the walls a bit at a time, until you can't get back behind them. Not this year.*

I sigh and lean back against the seat, taking in the students as they reconnect with friends they didn't see all summer, despite proximity. I watch the freshmen as they get on the bus, and I recognize my anxiety in them. Even if you're not new, the first day can be awful.

Admittedly, most of the first day is a waste. You start out

nervous, but after you sit through multiple classes where teachers hand you a list of rules they then read to you, it starts to blur together. All the teachers have a breakdown of what they expect. How much everything means.

Sometimes I wonder if I could break my life down so easily: 10 percent participation, 20 percent independent thought, 30 percent anxiety, and 10 percent each fear, lies, guilt, and regret.

But amid the blur of rules and textbooks and seating assignments and grading policies, everything stops when you walk into the cafeteria for lunch. That linoleum-floored coliseum. This is the hardest part when you're new, and I know this school won't be any different. The blood leaves its trail behind you as you enter the den, and the tigers are hungriest on the first day. You know they're looking, and they know you're afraid as you stare down the long, wide room, deciding. You have only seconds to make your choice. That one choice—the table you approach and hope will welcome you—will define you for a year. Or longer.

"Hey, new girl," someone yells. I'm grateful because I don't want to start worrying about lunch. I can get through the rest, but lunch never seems to get easier. It's even worse when you're trying to decide who to trust. Which table of people won't dig into you day after day until they unravel everything you're hiding—and then rip you apart with your secrets.

The boy who yelled out to me is across the aisle and a few seats back. He smiles when I meet his eyes, and his smile isn't cruel. I hate how kindness surprises me.

"What's your name?" he asks.

"Alexia," I say, my voice too loud. I can never find the balance between shrieking and whispering.

I have to remember who I am this year. I have to pause so I don't say "Alexia Grimes" or "Lexi Malcolm" or "Suzanne Halston" (that was the year I used my middle name) or "Lexi Driver." I stop to remind myself that I'm Alexia Lawlor now, and all those other places and people are gone. They're just pieces of me, pushed away for a new version. Anything to pretend the real me doesn't exist.

The boy stands and moves to the seat behind me. He's a bit awkward, but he doesn't carry it that way. He seems to embrace the fact that he's probably too thin and too short to be traditionally attractive, but with his thick-framed glasses and messy hair, it works. It's sort of library-sexy, if that's a thing.

"Ryan," he says, and he smiles again. "*Green Arrow*'s cool."

"Oh." I look down at my shirt. "I don't watch it. It was just . . . it's just a shirt."

He shrugs. "I don't watch it, either. But the comic is great." He laughs. "Sorry. What a weak introduction. 'Hey, I'm Ryan, and you're new. Want to talk about comic books?'"

"I used to like comics. It's been a while, I guess."

"Yeah? I know the guy who runs Galactic Empire. Come with me sometime. It's amazing."

"What?"

"Galactic Empire. It's a store. But not just any store. It's, like, *the* store if you're into comics."

"Oh."

My brother loved comics. One summer, when I was nine, I was obsessed with feminism because Stacey Kitteredge was obsessed with feminism, and Stacey Kitteredge had a Disney show and a YouTube channel, so I figured she knew what she was talking about. Scott and I would ride our bikes to Ray's, the local comic shop, and he'd pick things out for me based on whatever I was into that month. I remember stacks of *Wonder Woman* and *Captain Marvel* and *Betty and Veronica*, the books my brother figured were feminist-ish and still appropriate for a nine-year-old.

"You didn't hear any of that, did you?" Ryan asks.

I look up, meeting his eyes. Apparently, this town is full of boys with nice eyes. Not just nice, as in attractive, but nice as in kind as well.

"Sorry. What?"

"Don't worry about it. It must be really weird starting a new school."

"I guess."

Ryan has nice eyes and he seems genuinely decent, but I'm not here to make friends. I'm here to go to school, do some homework, and hope people don't take my damn picture and post it online somewhere.

"At least you've been other places," he says. "I can't imagine anything worse than never knowing anywhere but Westbrook. That's like my nightmare. Never leaving this town. Always just . . . this. Forever."

"Hmm," I mutter.

"Anyway, I'm a junior. You?"

"Senior."

"Well, damn. I was going to offer to be your escort through the ever-so-thrilling hallways of Westbrook High, but we probably can't have you being seen with a younger man."

A tall guy slides into the seat next to Ryan. "Dude, don't say 'escort.' You'll stir up images of sketchy bars and bad animal-print leggings."

"Just because that's your typical Saturday night doesn't

mean we all swing that way," Ryan says, adjusting to make room for the tall guy.

"Eric," the tall guy says, reaching out his hand. I go to shake it, although he was apparently waiting for something else, and we end up just sort of awkwardly brushing fingers.

"Lexi. Lexi Ste—" I catch myself. "Lawlor. It's Alexia Lawlor, but you can call me Lexi."

Damn it. One slip. One mistake, and it will only take one Google search before everything's ruined. You'd think after all this time I could at least remember which name I'm using.

"I just got Alexia," Ryan tells Eric. "Maybe animal prints are her thing."

Luckily, they don't notice I don't reply, that I turn away from them. It sucks not being able to talk to Ryan or Eric. Not being able to laugh and tell Ryan I don't care that's he a junior, that it would be better to walk around with him than to try navigating the halls with a map. I don't get to say that, because that's how things are.

They recognize none of this change in me, because they're already talking to each other. Mostly about me. They talk about me as if I'm not here, but it's not mean. It's the way people talk when they know you.

I so want someone to know me. I desperately want to be Lexi Lawlor, the random new girl. I want to say I'll go with Ryan to this Galactic Empire place, and I want to know no one will ask questions. I want to be Lexi Lawlor, because she doesn't have secrets. Lexi Lawlor doesn't have to lie.

"And so it begins," Ryan says as we slowly approach the bus loop behind the school. Students spill across the lawn and line up along the doorways at the back of the building. Summer held them in suspension for a few months, and now there's so much that's new and so much to tell and they only have twenty-three minutes until the bell rings.

I hate that everyone has somewhere to be, has so much to fill those twenty-three minutes with, and all I have is needing to find the office. Get a locker. The things that frame every September for me.

"Hey, Lexi, what lunch do you have?" Ryan asks.

"Um . . ." I pause. I don't have classes yet or a schedule. "I'm not sure."

"No worries. I have third, but I'll be in guidance second period anyway. Come find me."

"He's their pet," Eric says, pushing his way out into the aisle to get off the bus.

Ryan grabs his bag and stands, squeezing into the aisle as well and leaving a space for me to exit. "Community service. We all have to do it. But I don't have my own car and my parents work and, you know, a bunch of boring backstory you don't care about. But the fact remains, I'll be in guidance second period. Find me and we can look at your schedule."

"Can you move?" someone yells from the back. Marcus is still sitting back there, waiting, and I try to wave, but he isn't looking at me. I hurry out of the bus.

Ryan disappears with Eric into a circle of people, and I weave through reunions, hoping in spite of it all that 162 days can pass differently from all the other years.

Trying not to notice that I'm all alone again.

Chapter Two

I spend first period in the office, meeting with the principal. He uses most of my "orientation" time filling me in on his philosophy of education ("All students are potential wells, and it's on our staff to make sure you leave this school full of water"). After that I go to guidance for my schedule. It's second period by the time I get there, and I find Ryan in the back office, sorting college brochures.

He's on the floor, alphabetizing his peers' ambitions, but he looks up as I pass. "Alexia and/or Lexi Lawlor. That's a lot of *L*s. Can I just call you L?"

"Sure."

He nods. "Done. Don't you have class?"

"I was late leaving the principal's office, so he told me to come here, and they gave me a map and told me to use the time to figure out where things are, rather than show up late to class on my first day." I pick up a stack of brochures.

"Why do you have so many brochures for the University of Tulsa?"

"That's nothing. You should see the Fresno State collection."

I flip through the Tulsa brochure. It's a beautiful campus, although I don't think college is on my radar. Oklahoma would be something new, though.

"Not that it matters," Ryan says, "since no one ever seems to want to leave Westbrook. It's one of the many joys of living in the middle of New England. You're surrounded by higher learning, so you don't have to actually go anywhere. You can live your entire life pretending high school never ended. Which is apparently the life goal of students here."

"What are you doing with the brochures?"

"The college fair is next week, and it's a really big deal. Sure, everyone just stays around here, but they try. Hence . . ." He gestures to the brochures stacked behind him.

"Sounds good."

"It's weird, isn't it?" he asks. "The college fair is huge. College is this totally assumed rite of passage. We all get by on some kind of cinematic idea of our futures, where our lives are full of frat parties and internships in the city and a wacky cast of roommates. But I guess everything's not the movies."

"No, that's true," I say.

"Well, anyway," he says, and I kind of wonder why he's still talking to me, since I know I'm being rude. I don't want to be rude, but I have little say in my choices. "Since you have time, and the brochures are endless . . ." He puts one of the bins labeled VANDERBILT on a metal shelf and stands up. "Want the grand tour of Westbrook High?"

As he goes to grab his stuff in the main room of the

guidance office, I adjust the Vanderbilt brochures because they're not aligned properly. There's an edge in the back that's higher than the others, and if I don't fix it, it's all I'll think about all day.

I hear him say to someone as he returns, "Tell Gauthier I'm showing the new girl around." The faceless female voice tells him to lock up before he leaves. College brochures are kept under intense security, apparently.

"Ready?" he asks, as I turn and pretend I wasn't fixing the brochures.

"Ready."

It's only when we're in the hall that it starts up in my head. We take the corner toward the gym, and I can hear the sounds of shoes squeaking on the floor, that sad earnestness of gym class and forced team spirit.

I don't know these people. I'll never belong here. It's another year where I'll hope and I'll try, but 162 days is too long, and it's not going to last. They'll find out.

They always find out.

"Where do you go?" Ryan asks.

"What?" His face is only a few inches away from mine, but it's not some kind of romantic moment. Instead he's staring at me like . . . well, like I'm me.

"You disappear a lot. You didn't hear me again, I'm guessing?"

"Sorry. I . . . sorry." I should just wear a sticker that says HELLO, MY NAME IS SORRY.

He shakes his head. "Well, anyway, this is the gym. Down there is the cafeteria," he says, pointing. "We can go through the different halls so you can see all the classrooms that look exactly the same . . . or . . ."

"Or?"

Ryan takes my hand, which makes me uneasy. I'm uncomfortable being treated like I'm human. I look down at his hand over mine, worrying that my rot can be transferred through my palm. That I'll infect this guy with what I am, all because he was nice enough to show me around.

"This is top secret," he says as he pushes through a set of double doors. "You're being invited into something only a select group of people know about—and I'm trusting you not to say a word."

"I don't have anyone to tell except you," I reply, and he laughs, but I'm not kidding.

He takes out a Swiss Army knife (*Is that even legal in school?*) and fiddles with another set of double doors about ten feet farther down the hall.

"Welcome to the Shadows," Ryan announces as he pulls the doors open with a dramatic flourish. I guess his voice is supposed to sound like that guy in the horror-movie trailers, but it's a bit . . . not.

We step into darkness, and he takes out his phone to guide us deeper into it.

"Where are we?" I ask.

"The auditorium." He leads me into the black until we both tumble onto something soft. As he illuminates the area by my knees with his phone, I can see tattered and stained flowers.

"Drama club," he explains. "This is one of our many couches. No one seems to know or care that the doors are easily pried open, so we sneak in here when we just can't deal with school or life or basically any of it."

"You sit in the darkness?"

"Life is nothing but darkness," he says, and I feel a moment of gratitude. *After so many years, maybe someone gets it*, I think, until he laughs again. "I'm just fucking around. But we can't leave the stage lights on, because I'm pretty sure we'd be caught, like, instantly."

"Oh. Yeah," I say, and force a laugh in return. Lexi Lawlor laughs. Lexi Lawlor thinks it's fun and exciting to break into the school auditorium and sneak onto a couch. She trusts people and knows tragedy only as something from Shakespeare.

I hear the bell ring, but Ryan doesn't move.

"I have an idea." He turns his phone so I can see his face. He's a glowing skull against the darkness, distorted by the games the light plays. "You don't really *have* to start today, right?"

"What do you mean?"

"Let's be honest. The first day is pointless," he says, echoing my earlier thoughts. "No one cares about it, and if you don't show up, it doesn't count against your attendance, since you didn't start the year yet anyway. And I'd like to get to know you. That would be a far better way to spend the first day of school than learning which teachers count homework as 30 percent of my grade."

Maybe only 5 percent is regret and 5 percent is brand-new bad life choices.

"I don't know. I don't want to start the year pissing off my teachers."

It's also that . . . the routine and the sameness protect me. They keep me safe. No one pays much attention to a girl who does what she's supposed to. No one cares when you follow the rules. I don't have to think about everything when someone else does the thinking for me.

"Yeah. Fine. That's okay. Hold on and I'll walk you to your next class."

There's doubt in Ryan's voice. It's the sound of wondering why you bother. It's the sound I hear every time I call home and I'm not better. When I beg my mom to send me my green pants or my yellow socks because I don't have anything else. I hate the sound of it. I hate always being such a disappointment.

"Wait." I put my hand out, brushing his leg accidentally. "You're right. It's a pointless day."

I don't want to make my teachers mad, but then again, my teachers don't know I exist yet. I missed my first two classes because I was getting acclimated, and I can probably get away with that through lunch. It's amazing how much time people think you need to find a locker, but it's the same at every school.

Ryan gets up and uses his phone to throw a path of light across the backstage area. "Come here."

I follow the path. In the phone light, I see only pieces of things; the whole is still obscured by the darkness. I kind of like the symbolism of it.

We walk maybe four feet before he tells me to sit, and I do while he rummages through something.

Lights come on around me. We're inside the facade of a house, a full exterior wall with a door and windows and even a porch swing on the other side of it, but where we sit, it's only plywood and wires.

"It's the set from the spring show," Ryan says. "We'll probably end up scrapping it for parts, but for now it's like our own secret world." He settles against the wall of the house and leans over, taking out a tin of Pringles from somewhere. I consider asking if he'll get in trouble for skipping the first day of school, but I get the impression he's done this before. Especially when he leans over again and takes out a can of Coke.

"You into theater?" he asks, holding out the Pringles.

"No, thanks," I say to his offer of a chip. "Theater's all right, I guess."

"You guess?"

"I saw a play on Broadway once," I reply.

My mom teaches drama. I've spent a lot of time seeing plays. Studying them. When I was younger, we had season tickets to the local theater, and I remember my parents teaching us about the elements of tragedy before we saw *West Side Story*. I used to love the way stories played out onstage in front of me, but that was a different time.

I don't want to talk about all that.

"Yeah? What show?"

"*Wicked*. It was a long time ago."

My dress was green, and Scott teased me during the entire train ride that I was a wicked witch. I was eleven then, and he was fourteen. We were excited to go into New York for a show—our first outside the university where my mom taught or the local theater. The entire day was incredible, and we were all so happy. Until we got back on the train to head home. I barely remember the performance, but I can still see the way my brother pressed his hand against the glass of the train window and watched the city disappear, until the skyscrapers gave way to nothingness. When we pulled into the station back home, Scott looked at me and whispered, "I hate it all so much."

"Can you believe I've never been to Broadway?" Ryan asks like we're old friends, bringing me back from that moment so long ago. "I've never been much past Westbrook, sadly."

"I'm sorry." I can hear the longing in his voice. That longing I know too well.

"You're so lucky. Getting to go somewhere new. Even if it's here."

"It gets old," I tell him.

"Were you in drama at your old school?"

Once—sophomore year—I decided to try to be a part of things. That was the best year. I joined cross-country in the fall, and our team went to the Western Massachusetts finals. I remember running and thinking I liked the foliage and I was glad to be back in New England. The year before, I'd been sent to boarding school in Virginia. There were seasons there, too, but they weren't the same. That fall I fell in love with the cold autumn crispness again.

The way fall surprises you in New England is something that can only be captured here; other states have their seasons and their changes, but Massachusetts wakes you up with autumn, and it holds you until the leaves blow away with the first snow. It's funny, because I kind of hate the fall, but then . . . it's painful to live without it.

After cross-country season ended, my teammates all hugged me. I had friends, and I was invited out with them. They even asked me to run track in the spring. And I would have, too, but winter is boring in Massachusetts, and everyone spends a lot of time indoors and online. By April I was in my grandparents' attic, finishing classes through a distance-learning app.

"No, I've never acted," I answer Ryan. It isn't what he asked, but we're not talking about the same things anyway.

He's leaning against the house, against where walls would be if it was real. Where we'd hang wallpaper and paintings and light fixtures and all the things we spend so much time thinking about and choosing.

My bedroom at home was dusty rose. Before my parents

moved into the condo and I left. I wonder what happened to that room.

"Well, there's a bunch of other stuff you could do," he says, "like sets and stuff, but if you want to act, you should totally try out. Auditions are next week. And, really, there are only a few of us, and we're always looking for new people."

"Busy. College fair. Auditions. Lots of things going on here," I say.

I notice I'm holding my arms around my knees. Standoffish. I remember me as a kid. I used to like things. I used to laugh and smile, and everything didn't scare me. I used to love stories about tragic heroines and complicated families because they were nothing like my life.

I guess it's true when people say you should be careful what you wish for. I never should have thought any of that was beautiful.

"Hey, are you okay?" Ryan asks. "I probably should've asked if you have questions or whatever. I'm sorry. I don't really know what it's like to start over. Everything has always been the same for me."

"I'm jealous," I admit.

He smiles and takes out a bag of Skittles from the vortex of endless snacks. "We've got that in common. Really, though. Have some Skittles and tell me the story of L."

"Once upon a time there was a girl," I say. "And they lived happily ever after."

I take a handful of Skittles from him and shove them into my mouth. Fruity excuses not to talk.

"You seem to be missing the middle. The best part. All the conflict and drama."

We sit in quiet, chewing, but not in that annoying way

a lot of people chew. Just in our heads and in our thoughts. After I swallow, I stand up.

"I'm going to class," I tell him.

"But what about the rest of your story?"

I shrug and leave him sitting by the hollow house. I wonder what my parents would say about the symbolism of all the facades that surround me.

Chapter Three

I don't sit with anyone at lunch. I end up going back to guidance, flipping through the same college brochures and imagining a different life.

The rest of the day is just a day. Ryan sits with me on the bus, but Eric sits behind us and they talk for the entire ride. By the end of the route, it's just me and Marcus. We don't talk until we get off the bus and are standing together on the pavement.

"So," he says.

"So."

"Westbrook High. How was it?"

"It was a school."

"Yeah, it's that."

He takes out a cigarette, but neither of us moves toward our apartments. We don't have anything to say, though, so we just stand.

"That looks worse," he says after a few minutes, and nods

toward the Castle Estates sign. The knight now has a dick outline; the scrubbing just cleared the color from the sign behind the spray paint.

"You know what they say. You can't stop the dick."

"No." Marcus shakes his head. "That you can't."

The jingle of an ice-cream truck comes over the sign, and a dark-blue van pulls alongside the entrance. There's a picture of a Spider-Man novelty ice-cream bar and a snow cone on the side I can see.

"They're early," I say.

"Nah. The elementary school kids don't have as long a ride. They'll be here any minute."

As if the universe is simply waiting to prove itself to me, the bus comes around the corner and then drops the kids off on the sidewalk about twenty feet from us. The elementary school kids don't live in our complex; they live in some of the surrounding buildings, but we got lucky enough to have the best sidewalks, I guess.

The kids all run to the van to get ice cream, and I don't know what's more depressing: that we get home at the same time as the elementary school kids or that the shady van serves as our ice-cream truck.

"Want an ice cream?" Marcus asks. He reaches into his pocket and pulls out a few singles, looking toward the van and the line of kids before turning back to me. "My treat."

"Yeah, sure." But I don't move. He waits while I try to make it okay. I sigh. "No. I mean, I do, but no. I should probably get all this first-day homework done. And my aunt will be home soon and dinner and stuff."

I don't have that much homework. I have time to sit with Marcus and eat ice cream. It's not like it's a date or a major commitment to have a snow cone for a few minutes, but I'm already starting to feel my head filling up with thoughts I need to drown out.

You shouldn't be talking to people. Don't pretend this year will be different. You know what happens. Can't you last 162 days without messing this up?

"Yeah, okay," Marcus says. He starts to head toward the van, but I see the look before he turns around fully. He's upset or feeling rejected. Or disappointed. People are always disappointed.

I want to tell him it's not him. I want to tell him everything. I hate how he looks at me, as if he thinks it's something about him that's not good enough. I want to tell him that in a different situation I'd be happy to get to know him, but I can't and I won't.

There's no way to win for me. Someone always gets hurt. My history finds a way to suffocate everyone in its path.

"Hey," I yell after Marcus before I can stop myself. "Friday? Ice-cream date? I won't have to do all my homework right away."

"Yeah," he says, and I catch a flicker of a smile. "Friday. It's a date."

He moves on and I go to my apartment. *It's nothing,* I tell myself. But when I reach my door, I look back. He's kind of cute waiting by the van with a bunch of kids, excited to pay three dollars for ice cream.

You ruin everything, I remind myself. *There's nothing you can keep safe.*

I wish I could avoid hearing my thoughts, but it's too quiet here. Once I get past the entrance and the ice cream and the knight and the fountain, it's just me, some raggedy old lawn chairs, and the silence of sadness. Along with the cacophony of voices in my head.

I drop my bag by the door, grab a bottle of water and some Goldfish, and go to my room. My aunt's apartment is actually a one-bedroom, so my "room" is what's supposed to be a dining room. Before I moved in, she hung tie-dyed sheets across the doorframe to make it feel "young." But it's a room with a cot and some boxes of old dishes my aunt couldn't find another place to store. I haven't decorated yet; I don't know who Lexi Lawlor is, and in the highly unlikely and not recommended scenario where I make friends, I don't know what I want them to think if they come over. I don't know who I can allow Lexi Lawlor to be, beyond an alliterative annoyance.

I lie down and take my cell phone out of my dresser. No one has my number except my aunt and my parents, and I don't take the phone out of the apartment. I stopped giving people my number a few years ago, when I realized that it's better not to give them a way to invade even the quiet spaces. You can't really trust people not to use that access to hurt you.

Of course, being the weird girl at school without a phone is what Heath, the therapist my parents hired for me, calls a "red flag of ostracism." He always says pretentious shit like that. Given that I also avoid social media and wear clothes that scream "Something is wrong with me," I think it's more than one red flag; it's like the goddamn UN around me.

I look at my phone. My mom has texted four times already.

"How was it?" she asks when I call home.

"It was fine."

"What have I told you? I don't like when you say something's 'fine.' It's important for you to express yourself," she reminds me. This is the teen version of being told as a toddler to "use your words."

"It was scrumdiddlyumptious," I say, turning on my TV. I need the low buzz of the Game Show Network to keep me company. It's way too quiet here. There aren't even birds. Just falling acorns from the one tree near my window, sporadic Beethoven, and all the things I think.

"You're being difficult," my mom replies. "Heath told you that you have to differentiate when it's appropriate to keep up walls and when you're just pushing away the people who care."

"Heath's a douchebag."

"Alexia," she says, sighing. "What did you wear today?"

"Clothes."

"What colors?"

I don't feel like going through this. I know she'll take everything I say to her colleagues at the university's psych department, and they'll brainstorm new strategies to engage me. They'll probably even make a spreadsheet. Or a packet. Packets are the worst.

"Green, Mom."

There's a rustle as she covers the phone and mumbles behind her hand. She's probably telling my dad I'm at it again. All summer she tried to weed through my clothes to make it harder for me to obsess over my color patterns. She meant well. She thought she was helping, because her friends told her I'd only get over it if she made me face things. But she'd throw things out and I'd go to Goodwill, stashing clothes in random places around the house. At one point I mailed a box of clothes to Aunt Susie. I figured if she has to deal with me for a year, she might as well be prepared.

"How's Susie?" my mom asks when she returns. I can picture my dad, stoic at the kitchen table, warning her not to draw attention to it. To let it go. That's become his mantra. *Just pretend we're all okay.* If we lived in the Middle Ages, that could be on my family's crest.

"She's fine."

"Alexia," she warns.

I flip over and look out the window. I can see Marcus heading down the street toward his apartment, the Spider-Man pop melting down his hands. I should've gotten ice cream with him.

"I don't know. She seems exhausted."

More hand covering and rumbling. "Tell her I'll call her later," my mom says. Aunt Susie will probably be getting a lecture about maintaining balance in my life and remaining a "calm and peaceful presence." That's Heath's thing, too.

"It's fine, Mom. Really. Before you start in on me or ask for something more than 'fine,' I promise, it's fine. I'm fine. Aunt Susie's fine. This year will be fine. I swear."

"You know we worry about you. We may have agreed to this arrangement, but your part is to keep us involved and informed. We've gone over this."

My parents blame themselves. They probably lie awake at night trying to figure out why they're such bad parents and how everything went wrong. It's not their fault, of course. Not that it changes anything.

I miss what we were, but we aren't that anymore, and it's better to get away from the memories of all we could have been.

"I love you," I tell my mom, which causes more hand covering. She's likely telling my dad I'm getting worse, because what high school senior says "I love you" to her mother without provocation? "Stop whispering. I'm not finished."

"I wasn't whispering," she lies. "It must be the connection. I'll have your dad go to the store tomorrow. Maybe it's time for a new phone."

"Don't try to placate me with fancy electronics. I mean it. I love you. And Dad. Tell him I love him, okay? Tell him I don't need a new phone. Tell him everything is okay. And do me a favor. Try to believe it."

"Alexia—"

"Mom, you need to chill. It's going to be fine. I'll be fine. It's a hundred and sixty-two days. That's it. A hundred and sixty-two days and it's over and I can come home and we can try to figure it all out for real this time, okay?"

One hundred and sixty-two, I repeat in my head. *Actually, one hundred and sixty-one and a few hours.*

"It's just . . ."

My mom doesn't want to say it. She doesn't want to remind me that my record is 134 days. She doesn't want to talk about how bad it's gotten in the past. How she worries that the next time will push me over the edge. I don't want to think about those things, either. I know as well as she does how close I am to being deemed forever unfixable.

Still, it's only twenty-eight days—a February—more. I've got to be strong enough to survive a February. Right?

"I've got this, Mom. I promise."

I know I'm lying to her. Lying to myself. The trouble is . . . it's really easy to believe yourself if you try hard enough.

Chapter Four

Tuesdays are blue, which means my color-coding is less obvious to everyone, because jeans are blue. I like Tuesdays; they're when I feel most like a real person.

It turns out I have third lunch with Ryan, which makes this Tuesday even better. He invites me to sit with his friends, and one of the hardest parts of each year passes just like that. *Only 161 days to go.*

"I am so *pissed* at Hawthorne," a girl says as soon as she sits down at the lunch table. Dark hair, somewhat tall and thin, but still mostly average. Yet there's something about her that draws my attention. Something about how sure she is of herself.

Two girls follow right behind her, flanking her across the table from where Ryan and I are sitting, and they wait for her to speak. The first girl drops her tray and stabs a straw into her orange-juice carton.

"Seriously? Fucking *Romeo and Juliet*? How ridiculously cliché can we get?" she asks.

"Shakespeare's good for your portfolio," Ryan says.

She rolls her eyes. "I have plenty of Shakespeare in my portfolio. What do you even think I do all summer? God."

"Rory, Lexi," Ryan says, flicking a hand between me and the angry girl. "Lexi's new."

"Hi," Rory says. She drinks her whole carton of orange juice and crushes it. "Ryan, seriously. This sucks so bad."

One of the other girls opens a bag of chips, but she pauses, waiting to see what Rory does. The greasy spud hovers in front of her open mouth. It's not exactly fear. I can't explain it, but it's the kind of suspended animation that occurs when you can't decide if your friend's freak-out warrants putting your own basic needs, like hunger, on hold.

"It's not always like this," the other girl—the one sitting on Rory's right—tells me. She's prettier than Rory, but for some reason she fades beside her. "Drama's just a big deal."

"Oh yeah. Got it," I say, pretending to understand.

"Sorry," Rory mutters as she spears a french fry on her plastic fork. Chip Girl waits, and as soon as Rory puts the fry in her mouth, Chip Girl breathes a sigh of relief. Her stomach growls as if to confirm that hunger is, in fact, a bigger situation at the moment. The chip makes its final parabolic arc down her gullet.

"Look at it this way: You're probably guaranteed Juliet," Ryan says.

Rory shakes her head. "It's not that, and you know it. She's always going on and on about how 'theater makes a difference.'" I imagine that Rory's mocking lilt is nothing like how this Hawthorne person actually sounds, but everyone in our vicinity seems to be on board with it. "This was an opportunity. You know she's just capitulating."

"You need to lay off the SAT vocab," Chip Girl says.

Rory glares at her but doesn't respond. Instead, she turns back to Ryan, addressing me as well by accident. "All summer I was emailing her and she was totally into *The Laramie Project* or *The Vagina Monologues*. Something edgy. Something with a purpose. She swore she'd choose something that would *matter*. And we're doing fucking *Romeo and Juliet*?"

"I don't know," I offer, which I probably shouldn't. It's not my place, and I don't know the context. My head voice booms its countdown again, but I shush it and barrel on with my opinion, reason be damned. "It could work. I mean, prejudice, hate, judgment, assumptions. *West Side Story* tackles all the same key themes—"

Rory cuts me off. "*West Side Story*?"

"Yeah, I mean . . ." But the glare from the three girls across from me tells me to just keep my mouth shut.

"We don't do musicals," Ryan explains. "It's a whole different kind of theater."

"Sorry," I mumble, and go back to my lunch. The peas are fluorescent. I wonder if they're irradiated. That could be good.

Everyone complains some more about Hawthorne, who I deduce is the teacher-director of the drama club, but I stop listening. Lunch is only twenty-seven minutes. Twenty-seven minutes of 161 days and it's all over. I can survive this. They're so wrapped up in the play that they don't care about me or what I'm carrying. They won't even notice me as long as I don't talk about musicals.

"Hey, I'll walk you to class," Ryan says when the first bell rings to wrap up lunch.

"Lexi," Rory says as I stand. "I'm sorry we were awful. It was just a lot to take in. Maybe it sounds silly, but this play . . . all our plays . . . they're kind of it for me. This is what I've got."

I nod, thinking of all the things that are worse than what play your school performs during the fall of your junior year.

"Well, it's good to care about things."

"What's your thing?" Ryan asks after we drop off our trays and head into the hall. I don't know if his class is near mine or if he's just being nice.

He reminds me of how, when I was a kid, I imagined boys would be when I was older. He's quiet without being too serious. Sweet without it coming across like he expects something in return. Probably the kind of guy the real me thought would be a boyfriend, when I still believed in things like love. He also reminds me a little of my brother—or at least the way I used to picture how Scott would be.

"What?" I ask.

"You said it's good to care about things. What's your thing?"

"Oh, I don't know."

It used to be trips to the comic-book store, and sitting around talking about books with my family, and summer bike rides with Scott. But all those things belong to another version of me. Right now the only thing I care about is not answering these questions.

In eighth grade, when I lived with my cousin Alicia in her apartment in New Jersey, I tried to make painting my thing. I wasn't any good at it, but I had a lot to work through, and Heath had told my parents that Alicia, with her urban garden and handmade hemp clothes and therapeutic painting, would be good for me. She was, too. It wasn't her fault there's such a thing as the internet.

"You must have a thing," Ryan insists.

"What's yours?" I ask, turning the question back on him.

"I can't tell you. You'll laugh."

We stop at my locker and I grab my books. "I won't laugh."

He looks down the hall at the flowing tide of people.

No one notices anyone else. Everyone lives in their own little existence and believe their own version of life. We may flicker in and out of each other's experiences from time to time, but mostly the world only exists as we see it. I often wonder, since everyone's generally so oblivious, why people always get so caught up in my story when they find out. Why can't I be just another nameless face in the crowd?

"I make lawn ornaments," Ryan says.

Despite my promise, I sort of laugh. Not a full laugh, but the beginning of one. "What?"

"You said you wouldn't laugh," he reminds me.

I close my locker and turn around. We're quickly swept back into the mass of students. "Sorry. Just taken aback. A bit . . . random?"

"I know. But see . . . my parents are really into gardening. And I'm not. I'm not only not into it, I downright suck at it. Like, literally kill any plant I touch. So they always tried to get me into this gardening thing they liked when I was a kid. And, yes, I know it's ridiculous that this was what my week-ends were. But, I don't know, it was kind of nice having a family thing, you know? Even if I was bad at it."

I used to like family things, too. Even the ones no one else would think were meaningful or important. The way my dad refused to grill corn on the cob because he thought it tasted better boiled, so we'd always have to wait for him to bring out a pot of corn floating in steaming water, while the burgers burned. The way my mom made a big deal about school picture day and made scrapbooks of all our mile-stones. If you visited my parents now, it would look like their children disappeared five years ago. They kept nothing of either of us.

"You still here?" Ryan asks as we get to my classroom. I nod, and we duck into the little alcove between the rooms and the blocks of lockers. There are several of these through-out the school, usually where couples go far beyond the rules of appropriate PDA.

"Yeah. Sorry. Lawn ornaments."

"So, well, I started making these gnomes and frogs and silly decorations for my parents' garden, and eventually it became a thing. My mom is really into them. My dad kind of likes them, too, although he also says they're girlie. I think he wishes I played sports or something instead." He pauses. "Not that he's . . . Well, he is, kind of, but he's more worried about me than him, you know? Like, he doesn't really care. I mean, the dude gardens for fun. But I got beat up a lot until . . . well, kind of recently. So he thinks if I acted more . . . not like I do . . . it would fix that somehow. He means well. He's just old."

I nod, and I wonder how Ryan got to be this open. This trusting. I've said what feels like ten complete sentences to him since we met, yet he talks to me like he can count on me somehow. If he only knew . . . But I don't tell him, because I really like how he makes me feel. He makes me feel whole. Worthwhile. Valid.

"Anyway," he continues, "my mom got really into it, and she called all these places, and on Saturdays I go to local craft fairs and sell them. I've been doing it since I was a freshman, but only my parents and, like, five of my friends know. We make sure we don't go anywhere too local, of course. Rory and Eric and them are cool, but, you know, it's not exactly school newspaper–worthy. And, I don't know . . . I guess I just don't want to have to explain things to people. I just want them to leave me alone as much as possible."

The second bell rings, ending Ryan's story, and he runs off, waving, trying to make it to his class on time. I settle into my physics class, where students finish the conversations they've been having since lunch and I hate myself as soon as it begins to grow quiet.

I have one responsibility. All I need to do is blend in. Act normal, don't draw attention, and survive 161 days at Westbrook High. What I don't need to do is become friendly with nice boys who make lawn ornaments, or encourage them to tell me their secrets.

What I don't need to do is believe that it's ever going to stop hurting.

Chapter Five

make a point of staying quiet the next few days. Ryan doesn't seem to notice that I limit all my responses to one or two words or a head movement in the affirmative or negative when possible.

Lunch has become part of my routine. Rory—full name Rory Winters—dominates most conversations, which is actually ideal. On my way to lunch today, I stop in the bathroom first, and while I'm peeing I hear my name.

"No. Lexi Lawlor," someone says. I lean forward and peer through the door to see who it is. It's Chloe Parker, previously of Chip Girl fame, and she's with Rory. Lauren Baruch, their other friend, isn't with them. She's probably already at lunch with Ryan.

"Don't start, Chloe," Rory says.

"Seriously, though. Yellow? What's her deal, anyway?"

Wednesday is black, Thursday is brown, and Friday is

yellow. Saturday is pink and Sunday is gray, but Fridays and Saturdays are the hardest. People notice most on those days.

I wish I knew how to stop it, but it's the only thing I know. It's the only control I have, and I have to tell myself it's okay. I try not to feel ashamed or hurt that people are already talking about it.

In Chloe's voice, though, I hear my mom and Heath and everyone else who's had something to say about it. *When you stand out or set yourself apart, people can't ignore you, and that's when they pay attention. If you want to stay off their radar, you have to make an effort to blend in and follow the rules, Alexia.* And I want to, but when I stand in my bedroom and try to mix the colors, I can't breathe. The last time I tried it, I got to the front lawn before lying down on the grass and nearly chewing a hole in my forearm.

Heath's tried to help me get over it. He says it's "attention-seeking behavior," which is sort of the exact opposite of my goal, but his theory is that a part of me wants to be noticed. He thinks there's a part of me looking for someone to see past the other things, and I'm doing everything I can to draw attention away from it by making the clothes "the focal point." I don't know if he's right. I don't know what my brain is doing. I just know the idea of wearing something else makes me feel sick, and even though it means everyone stares at me, I can't seem to stop.

"She's fine," Rory tells Chloe. "You're just jealous because Ryan seems really into her."

"Ryan doesn't even *know* her," Chloe argues.

"And neither do you."

Rory takes out her purse and starts fixing her makeup. I don't think there's much difference between my need for my clothes to match and her need to make sure her eyeliner is perfect between every class. We all have our demons.

"You just feel bad for her because she lives at Castle Estates," Chloe snaps. "You like befriending the poor girl. You think it makes you look good."

Rory drops her eyeliner. She doesn't turn to face Chloe, though, instead holding on to the sink and staring into the mirror. "Shut up, Chloe."

"No, it's ridiculous. It's been, like, four days, and you're defending her. You don't know her, either. She could be a fucking serial killer for all you know."

I don't hear the rest of the conversation. All I can hear is crying and the police and the way they said it like it was inevitable. There was so much blood, and all I could think was that it couldn't be true, because no one had done laundry for days. This made no sense, but I couldn't connect the dots logically and it was just the first place my mind went. We didn't have clean clothes. Everyone should have been where they were supposed to be, or at least at home doing the wash. They wouldn't have any reason to be anywhere else, because we had so many dirty clothes.

NO. Not now, I tell myself.

"Hello?" Rory asks.

Shit. I didn't mean to say it aloud. I didn't want them to know I was here, but now they will, and now they'll know I heard and they'll see I was crying and then they'll start to ask questions. They'll start wondering what kinds of things I'm not saying when I'm quiet.

But you can't just sit inside a bathroom stall and hope people will go away, so I walk out like nothing happened.

"Oh, hey," I say. "I didn't realize anyone was in here."

Chloe gives me a look that says she doesn't believe that for a second, but Rory tries a little harder.

"Oh, Lexi, we were literally just talking about you."

"Yeah?" I say, and Chloe glances down at the floor.

Because, of course, it's all fun and games until someone comes out of the stall after you call them a serial killer.

"Chloe was saying how . . . unique . . . your style is, and I was thinking you'd probably be awesome at costumes. You know, for drama?"

"Right. Having a unique style inherently means I can sew and design Renaissance gowns for your Shakespeare production. Or I'm just really bad at dressing myself. Either one."

Rory laughs. "Stop. You look great. I think it's interesting how you own it. Like no one would usually dare start at a new school and just say fuck it all to the rules, and you don't even care. That's pretty badass."

"Uh, thanks."

"But about the costumes . . . they won't be elaborate at all. The show's a contemporary take on the story."

"Fresh," I say, cursing myself for my snark. But I'm still upset about the whole talking-about-me thing. And the comments about my clothes and the idea that I'm some kind of poor-girl pity party of one. Mostly, though, I'm upset that they were so close to the truth about me.

Rory rolls her eyes. "Oh my God, Lexi. I know." She drags this bit out like she can't even believe it herself. "But we have to do *something*. It's such an overdone play, but we're going to set it in the heart of the upcoming gubernatorial election. Each of the characters is going to represent groups of people being slowly marginalized in our culture. We're going to make people look at the world and talk about injustice. Because we're in the middle of something massive with this election, and I don't think anyone gets it."

"I don't really follow politics," I tell her.

This invites a lecture, but it also sweeps away the awkwardness of their talking behind my back and my discovering it. Somehow I end up at lunch with them both, and none of it mattered or happened and everything's just fine. And I let it be, because somewhere in that moment, I remembered, and that's worse.

•••

Ryan invites me to Galactic Empire over the weekend, but I claim homework. It's a good thing people don't talk to each other; they'd think I had seventy-five hours of a homework a day.

When I get off the bus, I don't see Marcus, and I figure he forgot about our "date," so I start heading back to my apartment. I'm by the fountain when I hear him.

"Don't tell me you forgot," he yells.

He's across the road, on the other sidewalk. He says something else, but I can't hear him. It's 3:17. Beethoven drowns out whatever Marcus is saying.

"I thought *you* did," I yell back, hoping he can hear me over the fountain, and I cross the street toward him.

He leans against the streetlight, and it's absurdly sexy. Dark hair, dark eyes, brooding look, and a sexy lean. *Stop it*, I tell myself.

"A promise is a promise," he says.

"I didn't see you when I got off the bus."

He shrugs. "I got a ride, but I told you I'd be here."

"We might have missed the ice-cream van. It's too late, right?"

"What kind of date would it be if I showed up only to let you down?"

"I'm accustomed to disappointment," I say.

"Well, yeah. You live here," he says, taking my hand.

Marcus's hands are callused but not rough. They're comfortable. It's odd how some people make holding your hand feel like such a chore and it's always awkward because nothing fits right, but then with other people, it's like your hands know something you've been missing.

The music from the van flickers in the air, coming around the buildings, and when we get there, it's already waiting, with a line of kids in front of it.

While we stand in line, we don't talk. I'm not sure if Marcus is quiet, nervous, or just uninterested, but of course it makes me wish he was talking. There's something about standing near someone when you feel like you should be saying something but you don't know what to say exactly. I open my mouth a few times to speak, but everything I can think of to say feels wrong. Being surrounded by a bunch of little kids doesn't help.

I like Castle Estates; everyone is old, and I don't have to see all the faces of children who look like the ones in my nightmares.

"What do you want?" he asks.

"Um . . ." I'm not sure how to answer, until I realize the kids have all moved on and we're ordering. "Oh. Uh . . ."

It's a pretty sparse collection. Of the maybe twenty things, half have duct tape pasted across them with the word *Out* written in black Sharpie. "Batman?"

"Okay," he says, and he orders a Batman for me and a Spider-Man for himself.

"Big Spider-Man fan?" I ask once we're away from the kids and we're trying to keep the ice creams from melting all over ourselves.

"Nah, it's just the only one that doesn't have some kind

of weird-ass flavor in it. It's just cherry and blue raspberry. That's normal shit."

I look down at my Batman pop and see that it's blue raspberry with banana. I immediately regret my bad choice. "You should've warned me."

"Hey, it's not my responsibility to make your terrible decisions. Besides, maybe you're into banana ice cream."

"Is anyone?" When I reach the banana-flavored bat shape, I swallow it quickly. It's not really that bad; it tastes more like Yellow 40 or whatever than an actual banana.

"In all my travels, I didn't really develop a list of the flavors of ice cream people like."

"Well, you should have," I tell him, and he smiles, revealing blue teeth and a purple tongue. I laugh, which makes him start laughing.

"My tongue is purple, isn't it?"

I nod. "Me too?"

"Yup. It's one of the risks you take."

We head toward what was once a playground in the complex, though now it's a metal bar and some chains where swings used to be. Marcus sits in the dirt carved by children's feet ages ago, when kids still lived here, and I join him, taking his Popsicle stick and wrapper and tying them up with mine. Once they're smoothed down and placed perfectly even on the ground, I sit back.

"I haven't seen you around school," I say.

He grabs a stick and starts to draw in the dirt. "You wouldn't."

"Why not?"

I watch as he makes shapes in the ground. It's like watching art happen in real time. First there was nothing, and slowly lines and shapes become something. I don't know what it'll be, but I find the process fascinating. Almost more interesting than the eventual result, because the pieces could have all fallen together in so many different patterns. But this is the one they chose.

"I have 'behavioral problems,' they tell me. So they keep me and people like me in a room in the back of the building. Away from all the normal people."

"What behavioral problems?" I ask. "Like, anger or something?"

He pauses, stares at the half-complete image, and wipes it away. I feel sad for all the things that could have been created.

"I don't know. They tell me I do, so I guess I do, you know?"

"They told us my brother—" I stop.

I want to tell him that people say a lot of things they don't really know. How they said Scott was sick. That he had emotional issues. Everyone said my parents weren't good enough. But all those things don't hold up. I don't have those problems, and we had the same parents.

"You have a brother?" Marcus asks.

"I did."

"I'm sorry. Past tense . . . yeah. It sucks, right?"

I look away from him, out across the complex. So many stories. So many people who don't have the right way of doing things, forgotten because they're somehow the wrong people.

"I guess. A lot of things suck."

"Where'd you come from, Alexia? I mean, before two weeks ago?" He starts to play with the trash from our ice creams, taking the wrappers and drawing them tighter around the sticks, trying to see how small a space they can fill. That's how I feel most days—I want to become as small as I can and fill nothing, so no one even notices I'm there.

"All over, I guess. I've lived in a lot of places."

"And this is where you ended up? That's too bad."

I sigh. It's really not a terrible place. Definitely better than the perfection of boarding school or the cold dullness of Maine last year. Better even than my cousin's apartment in New Jersey. But it's not where I should be, and that's the worst part. It's not home, and it's lonely.

Not that there's anywhere to call home anymore. My parents' new condo isn't our house. It's just a generic reproduction of the other hundred or so exactly like it. And the room where I sleep when I visit is an off-white, empty square. My mom tried to get me to decorate it, but why bother? No one goes in that room except me and my parents.

"It's just a place," I tell Marcus. "I don't know. It's just a lot to talk about or explain. Forget it, all right?"

"You can tell me," he replies. "Anytime. But it's okay if you don't want to. I get it." He pauses, about to say something else, and then shakes his head. "Let's get out of the dirt." He shoves the ice-cream wrappers and sticks into his pocket, then takes my hand again, helping me stand.

I follow him back to his apartment. There's a pile of broken planters out front, some still with dirt and rotten stems of flowers in them. The little patch of grass is too long, but not long enough for anyone to complain yet. It's just long enough to be sad.

Inside, all the curtains are drawn. A woman sits on the couch, watching TV. She looks toward us, and her eyes meet mine. She's not old, but she looks like she is. Realistically, she's probably only about thirty-five, but her clothes are all wrinkled and too big. She's wearing a wig, except it's uncomfortable to look at. The color doesn't match the tone of her skin, and it's too thin to look natural.

"Hey, Mom. This is Alexia. She's Susie Lawlor's niece," Marcus says.

His mom smiles. The effort is almost palpable. She wants to be friendly, but I get the impression she's tried too hard for too long to fake it, and she doesn't remember how to mean it anymore.

"Your aunt's a nice woman," she says. "There aren't a lot of nice people."

"There really aren't," I reply, and I look away from her, into the room with its dust and its darkness. I wonder if this is what happens to people when they give up.

"We're going to my room," Marcus says. His mom nods and turns back to the TV, exhausted from the effort.

"She's sick," he explains as we cut through the kitchen to grab two cans of soda and a bag of pretzels. "I'm sorry. This was probably a bad idea."

"You don't need to apologize to me. I'm sorry she's sick."

"Yeah. Thanks."

His room mirrors mine, since the apartments at Castle Estates are pretty much all the same. This one is a two-bedroom, though, so our dining room (where I sleep) is their second bedroom. If I peer through Marcus's blinds, I can see the edge of my window behind one of the few trees in the complex.

Marcus has lived here awhile—maybe his whole life?—and his room looks like it. He's got a bunch of movie posters on the walls, but they're all starting to fade, and the tape has been covered over several times. One—*Taxi Driver*—is falling down, the multiple layers of tape not enough to keep it in place.

"You can sit on the bed," he says. "I'll sit here."

He leans against his window, hovering a bit but not really sitting. I settle onto the bed, which is made, but in that way where you simply throw a blanket over the bed. Not really making it, but it'll do.

"We can share," I tell him.

"I don't want you to—".

I scoot a bit to the side of the bed and put my hand down on the blanket. "Really."

He shakes his head and stays by the window, sipping his soda. I'm not sure if I should be flattered or offended.

"You like old movies?" I ask.

"I do. My dad and I used to watch them together all the time. He was really into *On the Waterfront* and *Taxi Driver* and *Raging Bull*. You know. Stuff like that."

"I've never seen any of those."

"Really? You can't be serious."

I stare at the poster falling off his wall. "I was twelve when . . ."

I don't know what to say. What parts of it I can tell him.

When I was a freshman, I had a friend. My roommate. I told her things because I thought I could trust her, and it turned out I was wrong. I don't know if I'm wrong about Marcus, too.

"The first time I moved, I was twelve," I continue. "I never had time to catch up on movies."

"I have most of them. We should watch one sometime."

I almost tell him I have time now. There's a definite invitation in his voice. He watches me, and I can feel his eyes on me, but I don't look at him.

I want to stay. I want to ask him to go make some popcorn, and I want to curl up beside him and spend the afternoon here. It doesn't even have to be romantic. I'm not sure that's what this is. Sure, he's cute and I could see myself being interested in him, but it's just the way that being here feels like possibility. I simply want to be *here*. Present. I don't want to go home and be lonely for another night. But that's not his problem.

Besides, wanting things doesn't turn out well for me. For anyone. I should go back to my blank space of a room and decide who Lexi Lawlor is. Maybe call my parents and do some homework. Because Marcus doesn't need all the things I carry.

"I should get home, actually," I say. "But yeah. Sometime would be great."

"I'll walk you home," he offers.

"That's okay. It's not that far."

I leave him leaning against his window. It isn't far to my apartment, but it's far enough that I have to think about the acorns under my feet. About the sign with the knight. About Chloe and the things she said in the bathroom.

I think about everything except Marcus and his old movies. About the way he leans.

The opportunity brushes past me as I walk, disappearing into the early evening.

Someday, I tell myself.

Chapter Six

My aunt puts a bucket of chicken and a giant salad on the table before heading to the bathroom to wash her hands. We've eaten nothing but takeout and sandwiches since I moved here. I stare at the salad, hearing my mother in it. I can imagine the conversation she had with Aunt Susie. Or the lecture, more like. My mom telling my aunt that vegetables are important for my recovery. That I need vitamins and minerals, salad instead of Chinese food. Like my problem is merely poor nutrition.

"How was work?" I ask when my aunt finally sits down. Her hair clings to the sides of her face, a symptom of working too many hours for too little money. She yawns in response while I divvy up salad and chicken on paper plates. "If it makes you feel better, that's pretty much how school was this week, too."

"Is it a lot different than your last school?"

I poke at the salad but don't eat it, twisting my fork so it tears holes in the pieces of lettuce. "Not really. It's kind of the same thing every time. People aren't much different regardless of where you go."

"You aren't kidding," Aunt Susie says. "I guess it's better than the alternative, though. At least they're leaving you alone, right?"

I drown the salad in dressing. I don't even like ranch dressing, but I know it's exactly what my mom would consider a bad decision. I wish I had a reason for being angry at my mom. Besides the fact that she's my mom and she's not here and I need to be mad at someone.

"For the most part," I agree. "They're not awful or anything. Not at all. Some are kind of nice, even. I don't know. I'm just not sure who I'm supposed to be here, and it's hard. Every year I have to figure it all out again, and I just feel like I'm lying to everyone."

"Maybe it's better that way," my aunt says, passing me the bucket of chicken. "Just get through the year. High school is almost over. Things will be different later."

"Maybe."

"They will."

I shrug, eating my salad and feeling sad about how wilted it is already. It probably sat near heat lamps all day in a fast-food restaurant, not sure why it was even there, and feeling a lot like I do most of the time.

"Have you thought about college yet? The college fair is coming up next week, right?"

"It's that big, huh?" I ask.

"What do you mean?"

"One of the guys at school . . . he mentioned it was a big deal. I didn't realize everyone knew about it."

Aunt Susie nods, taking a bite of her chicken. "All the school reps usually come through the restaurant."

"I haven't thought a whole lot about it. I probably should, since I don't have much time, I guess, but Mom said I should try getting the basics taken care of online first. She figures once that's out of the way, we can talk long-term. I'd kind of rather just go away, to be honest. Far away. Maybe Estonia or something."

My aunt laughs. "I don't think they'll let me take you on that campus visit."

"Yeah, I don't think they'd let me go to Chicago, never mind another country. They're convinced I'm broken."

I catch how she looks at my yellow skirt and yellow sweater, pretending she isn't. She doesn't comment on my clothes or on the scars that sneak out past the cuffs of my sleeves. She doesn't need to. I know everyone thinks it. How could I possibly be trusted to go to college? What happens if everything follows me there, too?

"I might try out for the drama club," I say, changing the subject. I hate thinking about the future. Especially when, in my head, it's just more of the same.

"Are you sure that's a good idea?"

"Why not? It'll be good to be social, right?"

"I don't know. Your parents really want you to keep a low profile, and I'm not sure drama club is the way to do that. Maybe you can see what they think first?"

"Yeah, I guess. I'll ask them."

And they'll say no. And they're right, but it's still annoying. I don't even want to join. Not really. But sitting here feeling like I can't makes me want to fight for it. Even if I know better.

"By the way," I continue, already irritated and suddenly

feeling argumentative, "I met Marcus Cotero. He's really nice. And his mom thinks highly of you."

My aunt puts her fork down and takes a sip of water, forced casualness in her voice when she responds. "Oh? How'd you meet his mom?"

"I went over there this afternoon."

"Huh. I thought I'd told you, but I guess I didn't. Marcus Cotero is probably a bad idea. Dianne says he sells drugs, which may or may not be true. They say he's likely to end up in trouble. You definitely don't need to be wrapped up in that. At the very least, you don't need people speculating about you, too."

"I don't think he sells drugs," I say, even though I have no idea if that could be true. "Who's Dianne, anyway? Do I care what Dianne thinks? Why would Dianne think that?"

"Dianne's no one in particular, but she's a person, and people talk." My aunt sighs. "It doesn't matter if what they say is true. All they need to do is say it, Lexi. All they need to do is put it out there. You don't want to be the next person people come in talking about."

"Maybe people need to fuck off," I snap.

"You're doing it again. Please don't lash out at me. You know I'm only thinking about you."

I do lash out. Always at the wrong people, and always when they're trying to help. Heath says it's because I need a "safe rage receptacle." I tried telling him how gross that phrase is, but he simply nodded and made notes about my rage.

"I know. I'm sorry. I wish . . ." But I don't finish. Because that's not why I'm here. I'm not here to wish. I'm here to hide.

My aunt nods, but she doesn't say anything else. There's nothing else to say.

"I'm heading to bed," she says after she finishes eating. "Do you mind cleaning up?"

"No problem."

I get up and clear dinner, thinking of Marcus's mom and his movie posters and the things he tried to say in the dirt this afternoon. *Just 157 days*, I tell myself.

I don't know why, but each year feels so much longer than the last one.

Chapter Seven

"Maybe you should start smaller," my mom says. It's Saturday and my aunt's at work, so I called home. I decided to lead with drama because last night, I stayed up for hours thinking about it. The idea grew inside my head, an obsession, and I wanted to prove I could do it. I wanted to show them that I can make progress.

"Heath would probably approve. He'd say it was a 'shedding of the other self.'" That's another of the bullshit phrases Heath likes to use. He always makes the things in my head sound so easy. And the solutions even easier. If it were up to Heath, I'd have taken up yoga and eaten lentils for six months, and I'd be perfectly well adjusted now.

"It just seems . . . very attention-seeking." There's that phrase again. I hate how wanting to exist is the same as looking for attention.

"But, come on, Mom. I'm an excellent actress. That's all I've done for the last five years," I say.

"It feels like you're trying to make a point, but I don't think it's a good idea to be making points, Alexia."

"Okay, well, drama club is a bad idea, and points are a bad idea. So why don't you tell me what's a good idea? Should I just come home and stare blankly at the bare walls in my room instead?" I ask.

"Don't do this. If it was something else . . . math club or something . . ."

"Is that a thing?"

"What I'm saying is that the theater is not a healthy place for you, with everything you're dealing with, honey."

"Why? You made a career out of drama. Maybe I want a career, too."

"I don't think you're ready to be thinking about careers."

"Got it. Don't think. Don't make points. Don't do anything. Sounds good, then."

She's quiet for a minute. "What about costumes?"

"They already asked me to make costumes, but I don't know. I'm not really interested in that. I'm not much for sewing."

"No, I mean, what about what you're supposed to wear? What if they give you blue on a Friday?"

It's low, and she knows it. She knows she shouldn't use it as a weapon or an argument. For all the solutions Heath and Mom's psychologist friends have had over the years, one that stuck was to avoid ridicule. To make sure I don't feel ashamed of my fears.

I hate her for a minute. Mostly because I know she's right, and I hate that more.

"I'm sure I can handle it," I say. But I can't. I know I can't handle it. I can't stand in front of people knowing everything is off. I can't even make it to the bus if everything isn't perfect.

"What if they ask you to wear red?" my mom continues. "I just don't want you to . . ."

I imagine it. I imagine standing on the stage, eyes on me, while I'm covered in red.

I don't wear red.

I remember the shirt the police officer had in his hands. The way the blood had soaked through it.

I remember the photographs on the news and the ones they showed us later. I remember everyone saying it looked like paint. Like some kind of Halloween prank.

I can see the leaves as I walked home that day, the shrapnel of fall along the gutters and sidewalks. I should have known right away that something was wrong. Mrs. Cabot was always home next door with Lucy and Miles, but they were only four and six, so she wouldn't have had the music that loud. But it filled the fall air, and I should have noticed then. I should have noticed how heavy the autumn felt, even if it really only does now that I remember it.

"I didn't mean to hurt you, Lexi."

I remember those words. And then I remember them fading under the sounds of the police scanner and all the crying and my mother saying that there had to be a mistake.

She's still talking in my ear, but I hang up. There's nothing I can say in response, and now I can't stop remembering.

Chapter Eight

excel at making terrible life choices, which is probably obvious when I decide to audition for the play anyway, despite my mom's best efforts. Sitting in the back of the auditorium, I watch people study the monologues they've prepared. They all chose Shakespeare or some classic or *Our Town*, but I didn't know there were rules. So I picked something I memorized years ago.

The monologue is from a play I saw with my parents during summer vacation between ninth and tenth grades. We had to go because one of my mom's graduate students had written it. I didn't know why that meant we had to go, but it did, and so we went.

I'd always liked plays, but I hadn't expected to enjoy this one, because we were only going out of obligation. But I did. And I thought afterward that the playwright was probably too good for a small town and a small university, especially when we were only a little ways from Boston. Then again, I don't know what the process is for getting a play produced. I'm sure dreams are a lot more complicated than commuting distance.

This particular monologue was at the end of the play. There was a girl onstage, alone, and she said something that sat in my head all night. And the rest of that weekend. And now, years later, I still remember the monologue, even though I saw the play only that one time. I remember it because the words were so honest and true for me.

Nothing hurts more beautifully than memory.

In those words, I was able to make sense of the pain that I still couldn't speak.

Memory tricks you. The past has talons, and they tear you apart. Whenever you think you're safe, that the moment has passed, there's the subtlest change in the air—a smell, a sound, a whisper, or a look—and everything falls to pieces again. That's what seventeen years have been like.

Or at least the last five. Since that fall when I was twelve.

"L," Ryan says, interrupting the way I've slipped into the past again. I feel the talons retract, and it falls off me, but it brushes against the back of my skull to remind me that it's never very far.

I look over at him. He's sitting beside me, his personal copy of *Romeo and Juliet* already in tatters, open to a page filled with highlights and notes. "Queen Mab?" I ask, gesturing to the monologue he's studying.

"It's only the best part."

"It's not called *Mercutio and Juliet*."

"It should be." He pauses. "Besides, there's the whole Juliet part of being Romeo."

He glances toward the front row, where a contingent of girls sits, each hoping she'll get to be the star. It doesn't matter, because if Rory wants Juliet, she's going to be Juliet. She stands off in the corner by the doors that lead back into the school, pacing with her own memories and fears. But she's something beyond the rest of us, and we all know it.

"Nothing really changes around here," Ryan says. "It's the same group of people for the same types of parts every year. It's hard to fake certain things. I just don't think I can pretend to feel like that about any of the girls here."

"You seem to have missed the memo on what drama club does."

"Yeah, it's just . . . yeah. You're right. But c'mon. Mercutio is pretty awesome, anyway."

"He is," I agree.

Lauren and Chloe arrive, bringing their own monologues with them. Lauren sits on the floor in front of us while Chloe sits in the seat next to Ryan and more than casually presses her leg against his.

"What are you guys doing way back here?" Chloe asks. "Auditions are happening up front."

"I just needed some quiet to run over this monologue," Ryan says.

She leans across him and gives me a death stare. "What about you? What part are you going for?"

"I don't know. I haven't really thought about it."

As she leans back, she brushes her hand against Ryan's knee. I catch how he looks down, how he tries to move his leg away.

"Rory is getting Juliet," she says. "Because, I mean, obviously. And usually the better parts go to people who've proven themselves, but I'm sure there's, like, a servant or something you could play."

I don't generally have the same competitive nature a lot

of people do. But I do not do well with assumptions. I don't like being written off any more than I like my mother suggesting I can't handle being onstage.

"You never know. Maybe I'm secretly a star," I say.

No one says anything in reply, and the silence starts to creep into the space between us. Seconds pass and it grows slowly, expanding until it's all that exists. Suddenly the entire world is the awkward silence, and I repeat in my head the two sentences I spoke. I repeat them over and over until they're not even words anymore.

I try to rationalize. I tell myself it wasn't much of a comment, that everyone else is just wrapped up in themselves, that no one even heard me over their own worries. But that doesn't quiet the sounds in my head. It doesn't make me stop repeating the words, and it doesn't make the silence stop growing. The sounds in the auditorium grow dim under the agitated pleas in my brain.

Why did you say that? That wasn't even funny, and now they think you're arrogant. You say the dumbest shit. Something is seriously wrong with you. Why can't you keep your mouth shut? You're absolutely incapable of not fucking up, aren't you?

I want to leave. I want to run away from the auditorium, from auditions, from Westbrook High School. I want to disappear and pretend I never was, which is what Heath calls my "defensive response to stress." Run, hide, and ignore.

It's easy to blame Scott and the past and my parents and the things people have said for all that I am, but I thrive on the disappearing, too. I love starting over and shedding myself year after year because I don't have to face remembering. I don't have to be me.

Sometimes I think I'm glad it all happened. It gave me an excuse to be a mess.

"I have to go to the bathroom," I say, but grab my stuff. I don't owe these people anything. I don't need to audition. I *want* to, but only because I want to prove something to myself. To my parents. I don't need to be here, and I tell myself as I walk out of the auditorium, toward the bathroom, that I'll keep walking. Who cares? So what if I let Ryan down? If everyone in drama expected me to audition? They may as well get used to it.

"Hey, Lexi. Wait up," Lauren says. "I'll walk with you. I needed to get out of there. It's too much sometimes."

"I thought you loved it?"

She shakes her head, pulling her ponytail loose from the elastic and redoing it quickly so it's more of a messy twist now. "I like everyone in drama, but I *hate* being onstage. I mean, at first, I guess. And auditions are the worst. I can't stand how excited everyone gets. Something's wrong with me, I swear. I've been doing it for three years, and I still feel like I'm going to puke every time I walk onto the stage."

"So why do you do it? Why go through that?"

"Well, I do kind of love it, too. I just really hate it and I love it. I can't explain," she says. "I kind of hate it. I mean, I *do* hate it. A lot. But then I don't. I hate auditions and feeling like I'm not good enough. I hate worrying about learning lines, because every time, I wonder if my brain will run out of space for them. I hate being onstage and having people look at me. But then something happens. After the curtain goes up and the show starts, it all disappears, and there's just me and the words and the lights, and it's . . . kind of everything."

What she says makes me wish I was excited. That I wasn't here only to make some kind of point. I wish I felt that way about anything, because I love the purity of what Lauren's saying.

"Oh. Well, I was thinking of just doing crew instead. I don't think I'm cut out for acting."

"Really?" she asks. "I mean, not that there's anything wrong with crew, but why?"

There's a series of excuses I could give. I could tell her I'm nervous. I could pretend I'm worried I'll get a crappy role, and pretend I'm the kind of person who cares about that. I could tell her my parents or my aunt wouldn't approve, which is mostly true. I could say a lot of things, but I open my mouth and the truth comes out. I hate when it does that.

"I'm afraid of getting a part and then, the day before or the morning of or ten minutes before the show starts, I realize I can't do it," I admit. "Because that's sort of something I do. I flake on everyone."

We've reached the front of the school, and Lauren holds the door open, gesturing toward the bench at the front of the building. I appreciate how she doesn't mention she knew I was running away, not just using the bathroom. It's late in the afternoon, and detention has ended, so a few students wait for rides. Teachers stroll past us all, not stopping, not acknowledging us. Everyone walks out of this place leaving something of themselves behind every day.

"You should still try out, you know," Lauren says. "It's really not a big deal. We'll survive if you change your mind. Why not at least see what happens?"

How do I explain this feeling to someone? I don't even know how to make sense of it to myself. Heath says it's a side effect of what happened. That the trauma broke something in me, and now I handle stress poorly. He says my anxiety is how I work through everything, but I don't know. I feel like it's just something embedded inside me. Like there's blood and muscle and bone and this. That the way I overthink everything is the same as the way my heart beats—a natural physical response. The moods and the way I panic are like oxygen for me.

I know what's going to happen if I audition and get a part. Right now, sitting in the fading sunlight with Lauren, thinking of my parents and how there are only just over 150 days left and how no one thinks I can do this, I want it so badly. I want to walk on that stage and not panic. I want to see my name on a cast list. I tell myself over and over that, yes, this time I can do it. I can wear brown on Friday or wear red or even mix colors, and it will all be okay. I can even see it. I can envision standing up there with all those people looking at me, confident and sure and *different*.

But then, seeing it makes me think about what it will really be like. I know what will start to run through my head as the show approaches. I'll be asleep one night—a month or a week or a day before—and I'll wake up and I won't have the air anymore. I'll see the costume I was assigned, and I'll feel the dread creep in. I'll realize I can't wear it and I can't explain this feeling to anyone, because they'll all think I'm overreacting. They'll tell me to get over it. I'll try to talk myself down through it all, but then the other voices will start screaming. They'll drown out logic and reason, and they'll remind me. They'll show me what I really am—and then opening night will come, and I won't even tell anyone I'm not going. I just won't show up and everyone will hate me and I'll hate me and I'll lie in bed, crying, knowing it's never going to get better. And then the following week, when anyone asks, I'll just laugh and pretend I'm too good for it all and they'll assume I'm an asshole and that will be that.

I see this entire timeline gaping ahead of me, but I can't say any of it. Because I know how it sounds, and everyone always tries to understand, but they can't. Even if they're nice about it, they still think it's fixable.

I look over and Lauren smiles, offering me a stick of gum. "C'mon, Lexi. What's the worst that can happen? It's just one audition."

"You're right," I say, even though I know exactly what the worst is, and I know I can't stop it.

I guess I kind of do understand how she feels about acting. I hate how I hope all the time that it will be different. I hate that I can't stop trying to belong anyway, can't stop allowing people in, can't keep my mouth shut and my head down when that's all I need to do. But I can't. Because as much as I hate it, I like sitting here with Lauren, having her think I'm okay, and I like feeling like someone will care if I don't audition.

So while the worst unveils itself in front of me and the voices echo inside my head, I pretend I don't know. I pretend I see things the same way Lauren does. We sit on the bench, talking about drama and nervousness and school. We talk like real people talk. Real *friends*. And, knowing how bad the hurt will be, I continue anyway, because I'm so sick of being lonely.

Chapter Nine

I get cast as Elaine, who's not actually in the play Shakespeare wrote. She was added as one of the Capulet servants so more people could be involved, and I have three lines. The good news is that if I do end up flaking on everyone, no one will miss Elaine, since she's made up. Kind of like Lexi Lawlor. It's fitting.

Lauren got Lady Capulet. Apparently, I'm the first person she tells. She runs down the hall at me between classes, catching me off guard.

"I'm so excited! All our scenes are together!" she says, grabbing my hand.

"Yay." It doesn't come across as authentic, but she doesn't notice.

"*And* Chloe is starring as Person Not Appearing in the Play, so admit you're a little happy about that."

"Kind of," I admit. "Although she's probably going to be really mad I have a part and she doesn't."

"Eh." She shrugs. They're all friends, but at least she's not pretending Chloe's nicer than she is. "You're coming tomorrow night, right?" She swings my hand, and I feel like we should be skipping or something. It's kind of ridiculous.

"What's tomorrow night?"

"We always do this thing after the cast lists are announced. The whole cast and crew go out to dinner and we bond, because it's, like, family, you know? And it's a new family for each show."

"Oh. I mean, I'll have to ask."

She keeps talking, but I mainly just watch her mouth move. It's all too easy and I hate it. I try to tell myself maybe it can be different this year, that maybe this group of people is different, but I know better. People are all the same, when you get right down to it.

We walk together to lunch, and I spend the twenty-seven minutes we're given to eat staring at the people around me. Wondering. What it would've been like if I'd always been Lexi Lawlor and if this had been my life. Rory talks about something someone said in her history class that upset her, and I try to listen. I try to make her real, to find the details that make her different from me, that identify why our paths diverged. But there's nothing. She's just brown hair and blue eyes and passion about theater and anger about injustice, and I could have been those things, too. But I was born me, and although we look the same on the outside, the inside of me is nothing but rot.

"Hey, you seem upset. What's up?" Ryan asks as lunch is ending.

"Sorry. Just a lot happening."

"Don't take the casting personally. There's a little nepotism that goes on. I won't lie."

"Oh," I say, realizing he thinks I'm upset about my part, which I completely forgot about as soon as I saw the cast list. "No, it's not that. I'll be the most badass Elaine that's ever graced the stage in a production of *Romeo and Juliet*."

He raises an eyebrow. "So you're not upset?"

"No, really, I don't care."

"You're coming tomorrow, right? Someone told you about the dinner?"

"Yeah, Lauren mentioned it."

"I hope you're coming. It'll be nice to get to know you. I mean, outside school."

The last time I went on a social outing was last year, unless you count ice cream with Marcus. It was during my two-week love affair with Ben, the guy who was supposed to take me to prom and is the closest I've ever had to a boyfriend. During the two weeks before Janey Eaton happened across my file in the office when someone forgot to put it away in the right place. That's probably a fireable offense, but I guess everyone decided that was less important than focusing on Janey's tidbit of exciting gossip.

Before Janey, Ben and I had gone roller-skating, which is apparently still a thing in Maine.

"I guess," I say to Ryan, telling myself he's not Ben and the world can function without repeating itself into infinity. "I have no plans otherwise."

"That's an enthusiastic reply."

I'm overwhelmed by a series of "almost" moments. Roller-skating in Maine. The homecoming dance at boarding school. Movie night with my friends on the cross-country team. Every time, I thought it was the miracle. A new chance for something. And now I look back on those choices, those moments, as when I screwed up.

"You should come. I want you to," Ryan says again.

"I want to go. I swear. I do."

"Good. It will be nice to have you be part of the group for real."

I smile, but I refuse to let myself imagine it. I'm not going down the path where I picture a life. All that comes from that is remembering it's nothing but a mirage of what I could have had.

"So does everyone just get dropped off or something?" I ask.

"So, since my parents won't let me have the car for the night, I'll probably be chauffeured by my mom in the sexiest move this side of Ryan Gosling."

"You could always ride your bike."

"Do people ride bikes anymore?"

I shrug. "No idea. I haven't had a bike in a while."

"Well, sadly, I do not have a bike, which means, alas, I will be getting a ride from my mom. But, I mean . . . my mom could take you, too?"

"Thanks, but I can get there on my own. I'll save you the humiliation."

"I will admit I'm relieved," Ryan says, smiling. "Let's not discuss this further. We can just imagine I rappelled in from my helicopter."

"Does your mom fly that, too?" I ask.

"Cold, L. Cold."

Chapter Ten

The cast dinner is at a local diner. It's nothing fancy—just a bunch of old tables, a bar with a lot of shiny metal, and a kitchen that looks way too small and way too hot for the number of people back there. The diner is packed full when I enter, and I almost leave to chase my aunt down in the parking lot.

"L," Ryan yells from a table at the back.

I squeeze through the crowds, only to panic when I notice there aren't any seats at the table where Ryan's sitting. He pushes deeper into the booth, meaning I have to sit with one leg pressed against him and the other half of my body falling into the aisle. I try not to think about it. Try not to get mad at myself about being late, about not planning where I could sit, about not considering this possibility.

"You made it," Lauren says from the other side of the table, but it's hard to hear her over the din. Rory and Chloe are at the table across from us. "Do you know everyone?" I'm with Ryan, Lauren, a girl named Caitlyn I know nothing about, Eric, and the guy who's playing Romeo, Tom.

I nod, even though I don't really know all of them, and no one argues. The waitress comes by to get my order. Everyone else has drinks, so I guess they've already been through this. I ask for a Coke and a minute to look over the menu. She rolls her eyes and leaves.

"Pancakes," Ryan says.

"What?"

"Pancakes. It's their specialty."

"Pancakes are a specialty?"

"It's the only thing they have that doesn't taste like bacon," Lauren explains. "Well, except the bacon."

"Wait, the bacon doesn't taste like bacon?" I ask.

"More like feet."

"We choose well," Eric says. "Very high standards here in the Westbrook Drama Club."

"I can see that. It's pretty crowded here, for a place where everything tastes like bacon or feet."

Eric shrugs. "No one ever claimed people make any sense."

They go back to discussing the show and their set ideas while I consider the menu. I don't really like pancakes, but I like bacon even less.

I'm thinking about food when I hear people laughing and look up. Two guys are in a booth down the aisle from us. The guy facing my direction is pointing. Directly at me. I swear, it's directly at me.

Now, this is where a reasonable person would assume they're misunderstanding the situation. They wouldn't care what some guy with a buzz cut who spends his Friday nights eating in a diner where the bacon tastes like feet thinks, even if said guy *is* laughing at them. But reasonable people are not me.

I feel his eyes on me. I hear his laughter through the sounds of the drama kids talking, through the sizzle on the grill in the kitchen, through the constant beeping of the opening and closing diner door. I hear the laughter and it reminds me. I picture him taking out his phone, snapping a photo, making a comment on Instagram. Tweeting about me. I picture all this in the minute or two it takes for the waitress to return.

"Lexi? Hello?" Lauren says, and I blink.

I try to form words. I try to order something, but all I can hear is the guy with the buzz cut laughing. I look at him, and his friend has turned to look at me, too. I want to scream. I want to beg them to stop. I want to ask what they know, but now everyone at my table is quiet and looking at me, too.

"Um," I say, the menu shaking in my hands.

Ryan takes the menu from me, handing it back to the waitress. "Pancakes. She wants pancakes. Obviously."

"Obviously," the waitress replies, annoyed, smacking my shoulder with the menu when she leaves.

"You okay?" Ryan asks. "You disappeared again."

"Yeah, sorry. I was just zoning out."

Buzz Cut Guy is still staring. I look down, focusing on the dots in the tabletop. There are so many of them. The conversation picks back up around me, but it's nervous. Wondering.

I shouldn't have come. I can't do this. I wanted so badly to believe it could be different, but I can't sit here. The voices and the laughter swallow me up, and I try to focus on the dots so I don't freak out and start crying, but the burning hits the back of my eyes anyway.

"I have to pee," I announce.

The worst is that the bathroom is behind the guy with the buzz cut. I walk past, trying not to look at him. He says nothing when I pass, and I remind myself he probably wasn't talking about me, but what if he was? And if not him, when's it going to happen? When will I be somewhere and someone will remember? How long can this last? I'm under 150 days now, but that's still nearly half a year.

The bathroom is dingy as hell. It's the last place I feel like crying.

I stare into the cracked mirror. People wrote their names and thoughts in lipstick and Sharpie and who knows what else, making my face a reflection of time and other people's memories. It feels appropriate.

There's something about it all that I can't shake. I think it's the shame. Crying doesn't wash it away. All the therapy in the world doesn't lessen it. Heath says I need better coping strategies, but how do you cope with shame? Shame is like your closest friend. Always there. Always at your back. Except it's not a comfort. It strangles you while you try to survive. It rests on me, often just riding along, but at any time, without warning, it comes back. I can't move forward, because it always pulls me into it.

I didn't do anything. I can't feel bad for something I didn't do, but I feel bad because I couldn't make it real. I barely knew them. They were just the people next door. I think my mom got a brownie recipe from Mrs. Cabot once, but that was all she was. Someone who said "good morning" on Sundays before she went to church and we went to breakfast. Someone who talked to my dad about flowers in the spring.

"Fuck you," I say to the guy with the buzz cut. I say it in the bathroom because I can't say it to him.

"Oh, hey," I hear, and I swallow the shame again. To choke on later. Rory Winters, in all her perfection, strolls in. "How's it going?"

"Fine. I was just . . . I'm heading back out."

"Yeah, of course. Chloe took your seat, though."

I sigh. "Really?"

She nods, pulling out eyeliner. "Ryan totally seems into you, so I wouldn't worry. But be prepared for some drama. It's her thing."

"She's your friend."

"She is. But you know. She's complicated. Hey, aren't we all?"

"I guess."

"I'm glad you tried out for the show," Rory says. "It's always good to have new people. Sucks you're a senior, though."

"Well, I can go out in a blaze of glory as Elaine."

She laughs and turns to face me. "Hey, listen, I'm not clueless. I know something's up. Something way beyond this show and Chloe and Ryan and whatever. But you're part of us now. I look out for my people, okay?"

I want to ask if that's unconditional. If she looks out for people when she knows everything there is to know. But instead I just nod and thank her, leaving her to her eyeliner while I head back to the table. I swear there's nowhere on earth that's truly quiet or private.

Rory wasn't lying. Chloe not only took my seat but also is trying to take Ryan's by throwing herself across him. She runs her fingers up and down his arm. He looks terrified. When he sees me, he pushes Chloe away, making her fall into the aisle.

"Why don't you go sit over there?" she asks, pointing to where she was sitting with Rory before. "It doesn't really matter where you sit, right?"

"The waitress needs to know where to bring my pancakes."

She sputters, but the waitress arrives with a stack of pancakes at that exact moment. Most of the time the universe hates me, but right now it's got my back.

"Whatever," Chloe says, and she pushes past me, going back to her table.

"Thanks," Ryan whispers.

The pancakes don't taste like bacon, but they don't taste like much. I use them to cover the shame that's still stuck in my throat and manage to survive the rest of the night. Buzz Cut Guy and his friend don't even look in my direction when they leave.

Chapter Eleven

Being part of something makes the days go faster, and I eventually lose track of how many are left. I don't know when I stop counting, but at some point I do, and it almost feels like it's all going to turn out okay. I check in with my parents daily; even they seem to think I'm doing better. Almost six glorious weeks have passed, and everything's normal, and I practically forget that there's anything to worry about.

It's late October—nearly Halloween. I don't know what the trigger is exactly. Maybe it's the time of year. Seeing the leaves on the ground, and feeling the chill when I walk, and smelling woodsmoke in the air. Maybe it's the morbid displays around the complex or the decorations in our classrooms. Maybe it's the play. With all the violence and the fight choreography and now the addition of blood packs.

We're in the middle of rehearsal when it comes, and it comes with all the force it has in the past.

Mark, the guy playing Tybalt, and Ryan are on stage practicing their fight scene. When Mark attacks Ryan, the blood pack doesn't just splatter his clothes like it's supposed to. It bursts, and the rush of red comes through Ryan's shirt, covering his hands and spilling onto the floor. Under the lights the blood glistens, and it's all there again.

My kitchen. The way the clothes they'd found were bloody and crumpled, resting in the middle of the table like a Sunday roast. The sounds of sirens and feet on dead, crunching leaves. And the crying. So much crying.

I can't stand up. I can't find a bathroom or a place to go, because my legs don't work anymore. I try, but I fall to the floor between the aisles and I lie back, the cold, hard concrete of the auditorium floor against my skin. It's painted light blue to make us think it's not concrete, but it is. And I can feel the ground below it. I don't want to think about what's beneath that.

In all my memories, what hurts the most is that mixed with the after, there's still everything before. Bike rides and comic-store trips. There are the late nights in the summer during thunderstorms when Scott would let me crawl into his bed and we'd make a tent and pretend we were camping and that the thunder and lightning were part of some exciting story, not just a storm outside. There was the time he helped me paint my bedroom, and all our Christmas Eves spent baking cookies.

I don't have any pictures of him anymore. The only times he's anything beyond what I remember is when other people remind me of what happened. When they've tagged me in Facebook posts. Tweeted me their opinions. Reminded me what he was. What I am.

I can't stop the memories and the thoughts, and I curl up on the concrete floor, trying to make it all go away.

"L? You all right?" It's Ryan, but I can't look at him. I can't look up and see the red staining his clothes.

"I don't feel well," I say, which is about as honest as I can be.

He sits on the floor with me. "Do you want me to see if someone can bring you home?"

Home. I don't have a home. We don't have the same house I grew up in, because we couldn't stand walking by everyone's stares every day. Couldn't stand how when my mom needed an egg and sent me to ask a neighbor, no one on our street would answer the door for me anymore.

The entire auditorium is darkness and swimming and sounds and cold concrete, but I'm here and there and now and then all at once.

"I don't know," I tell Ryan. "I don't think I can stand up."

He maneuvers to help me up. I try not to look at him, although the red stains are at the edge of my periphery. "I . . . Can you change?"

He looks down at the blood on his shirt and nods. "Sorry. I'm so used to it, but yeah, it's kind of awful, right?"

Awful.

I play with the word. I think of the letters. Make patterns with them. Turn them around and try to list synonyms. Anything to distract myself.

"Hey, Lexi. You okay?" Lauren comes running over. Ryan's headed to the costume closet to grab a different shirt. He passed her on the stairs, where she was running lines, and I wonder what he told her.

"I'm fine. Just sick."

"My mom just had the weirdest thing. I hope you didn't catch it. She was, like, supernauseous all of a sudden, and she even thought she was pregnant. Which, ew." She pauses. "Oh my God. Are you pregnant? You and Ryan? I didn't realize it was that serious."

"What? No. I mean, we're not even . . . No. Definitely not pregnant."

"That would be so cute. A drama baby. Right?" she asks, imagining the hypothetical child of a hypothetical relationship. I should be annoyed at her absolute and utter ridiculousness, but it's so far from the truth that I'm somewhat grateful. I feel the room expand a bit while she rambles about a fictional child.

By the time Ryan returns wearing a new shirt and holding a set of car keys, Lauren has named our nonexistent child Lexann (she says it's a perfect mix of Ryan and Lexi) and aged her through fourth grade. She's apparently quite the dancer.

"I could totally see us all coming back from college and jobs and stuff to go to Lexann's recitals, right?"

"Who's Lexann?" Ryan asks. He's wearing a pink T-shirt with a sparkly pony on it. I can't help but smile a little.

"Your daughter," Lauren says, and then she pats my knee as she goes to leave, letting me know my secret—which isn't a thing—is safe with her.

"What the hell was that about?" Ryan asks.

"I can't even begin to explain." I gesture to the keys. "Are you taking me home?"

"Yeah. Eric's working on the set, and he said I can take his car."

I follow Ryan out into the parking lot, where the early evening is already settling. The sky has that weird purple-gray, not really night coloring, and the streetlights are on. Leaves blow across the pavement, although there are no trees near the lot. I don't know where all the leaves come from.

Inside Eric's car it's cold, and we wait for the heat to kick in.

"Do you want to talk about it? I completely forget that the stage blood can look real, and you're definitely not the first to get upset by it."

"I don't . . ." I can't continue, so I shake my head and press my cheek against the passenger-side window, feeling the contrast between the chilly autumn air and the car heater on my face.

"Okay," he says.

We ride in silence, and I feel guilty for it. I should tell him something. At least thank him for being here. But the swirling timelines and all my thoughts are a hazy kaleidoscope. We're almost back to my aunt's place by the time I think of something to say.

"How go the lawn ornaments?" I ask.

Ryan laughs, a shattering of the quiet tension. "Good, actually. I have a table at the regional craft fair this weekend."

"Do you now? Tell me more. I have several lawn ornament needs, and that sounds ideal."

"You don't have to come. I know it's random."

"No, I want to. I don't have a car, but hey, there's always rappelling."

"Or your bike," he says.

I swallow the memories and shame again. "Where is it?"

He gives me directions and I promise to go. When we pull up to Castle Estates, to my aunt's apartment, he doesn't say anything else. He doesn't comment on where I live, which I appreciate, but he also doesn't make a move to walk me to the door.

I don't know if we're a thing. Everyone else seems to think so, and I don't know if I'm supposed to kiss him good-bye or something. I don't really want us to be a thing, because I love having him in my life without there being a thing, but the unspoken *maybe it's a thing* just makes it so complicated.

"So . . . I'll see you," I say, the door open only a crack. I wait to see if he moves to kiss me or looks surprised, but he only nods.

"See ya," he says.

I get out of the car and watch him drive away.

I don't want to go inside yet. I'm afraid of my aunt questioning me, of having to admit what happened. I don't want anyone to know it's not getting better. So I walk. The fountain is off now that it's grown colder, but I walk alongside the water and listen to the geese overhead.

I hate the fall. I love it because it's beautiful, but I also hate how beautiful it is. I hate that, underneath the beauty, all it brings is death. It's an entire season that outright lies to us.

"October sucks."

I turn to see Marcus sitting on the same bench where we sat on the first day of school. I haven't seen him at all since our ice-cream date. I looked for him, but I didn't feel like I should go to his apartment, and he didn't come to mine, and time just does that thing it does and now it's been almost two full months.

"It does," I agree, joining him on the bench.

"My dad left in October. Which, I guess, is why I hate it, but it's like it's proud of what it does to people. The entire month is just a countdown to winter."

"I didn't know he'd left. Your dad. I mean, I figured,

since you only mentioned him in the past tense, but I didn't know. I'm sorry."

"Not your fault," he says. "But yeah, he left. Just packed his shit and was out. Like you do."

"People, right?"

"People," he agrees. "So what are you up to? What brings you to this bench on a night like this?"

"Well, I joined drama. You knew that?"

He shakes his head. There's no reason he would know. I don't see him on the bus. His classes are in a different part of the school. And we haven't talked.

It's kind of comforting that he doesn't know.

"Yeah," I continue, "so I joined drama. And we're doing *Romeo and Juliet*, which is fine. But I don't know. It's weird. I'm a part of it all, but not. I'm not really one of them. I feel like this outsider, and they're all nice, but it's . . . something. And today was bad."

"Because of the something?" he asks.

"No, it's more than that. Today was . . . Okay, there's so much story here. But basically before I came here, things were kind of crappy. And today just reminded me of that."

"It's fucking October, I tell you," Marcus says. "It's a month of this. The slow unraveling of everything."

"That's kinda poetic."

He turns to look at me. Those eyes. It's too dark to see his features, but his eyes shine through somehow. I don't get it. "Yeah, I'm a regular poet."

I gaze out at the water. The security lights from the sides of the brick buildings reflect in the darkness and fill the slowly descending evening. A car goes by with the bass too loud. Somewhere, someone is yelling in a one-sided argument.

"I'm sorry I haven't seen you," I say.

"That's okay. I didn't make much effort, either."

Still looking at the water, I tell him, "I wanted to."

"I know. Me too. I really wanted to. I just . . ."

"I don't get it, you know? The world. The way it all plays out." I turn toward him, lifting my leg up under myself. "Why us? Why are we the ones who are here?"

"Here as in *existing*, or here as in *literally on this bench*?" Marcus asks.

"I don't know. Both, I guess. But mostly here as in *on this bench*. Like, this place. Like . . . Do you know Rory Winters?"

He nods, but then pauses and shakes his head. "Kind of. I know who she is. But I don't know her."

"I don't know if anyone does. But, like, she's perfect, right?"

"That's not a thing," he argues.

"No, you're right, but hear me out. That's just it. She's perfect, but no one's perfect. Still, everyone thinks she is. She seems nice enough, and she's not the kind of person who has to remind you that she's perfect. She just is, and we all sort of get it. But why? What cards did she draw? And where was I that day?"

Marcus turns on the bench, too, so our knees are pressed together. "You sound jealous."

"Maybe I am. But it's so much bigger than that. I guess I just don't get any of it. It all seems really fucking unfair."

The streetlights come on finally as the last of the orange sinks below the horizon, and Marcus is bathed in them. I feel his knee pressing against mine. Everyone thinks I have a thing with Ryan, but he's a friend. He's comfortable. He makes sense. With Marcus, I feel like who I am, though. The real me. The one I haven't spent any time getting to know over the past five years while I hid in alternate versions of myself.

I don't want a relationship, but if I did, this is what the one I'd want would be. Someone to sit with in the late autumn evening, knees pressed close, and you just know they get you.

"Do you want to come over?" he asks. "We can watch a movie."

"My aunt will probably freak out. She won't notice for a bit longer, because I'm supposed to be at rehearsal, but a few hours . . . I don't want to upset her."

"Because you're out late or because it's me?"

I don't want to tell Marcus that some women at the restaurant told my aunt things about him, so I pause, trying to decide what to say instead. He knows, though.

"It's me," he confirms. "It's because of what they say, right?"

"Who?"

"Everyone. I know. My mom has to listen to them. Every time she goes anywhere. She doesn't go many places anymore, but it started when my dad left, and now she's too sick, I guess. Or she's just tired of hearing it and pretending not to."

I remember this one time, right after everything fell apart. I was at the grocery store with my parents. My dad had gone to the bakery to grab a loaf of bread, and my mom and I were looking for dish soap. I had the bottle in my hands when the woman came by. She had a kid in her carriage— maybe three years old. The woman looked at my mom, then at me. "You'll never find enough soap to wash yourselves clean," she said, and then she continued on. She'd said her piece, and we were left holding the soap and the memories of Scott and the knowledge that we were changed now.

I stand up. "Let's go. I have time. It's a good night for a movie."

"I don't want to start shit for you."

I shove my hands in my pockets. I keep them there, because if I don't, I'm afraid I'll reach out to him. I want to touch him. Not because of anything romantic, but because I remember how alone I felt in the grocery store that day. How I longed to be held and to be told I wasn't somehow less than. I want to do the same for Marcus, but I can't, because I don't want to taint him with what I am, either.

"Let's go," I say. "Really. It's October, and I don't want to sit at home thinking about what comes next tonight."

Chapter Twelve

Marcus's mom is already asleep when we get back to his place. He doesn't say anything, instead talking around it, and I ignore the darkness and sadness of the apartment.

Once we're in his room, we settle on his bed with a box of snacks. Literally a box. He opened an Amazon delivery and dumped out the books he'd ordered (all good choices, if I do say, because of course I checked). Then we filled it with snacks.

We decide on *On the Waterfront* because it's at the top of his DVD stack and I don't have a preference.

"So, no talking during the movie," he says. "Total attention, okay?"

"Of course." I lean back against his pillows, letting the box fill the space between us. It's good the box is there, because the tension needs something to take its place. As the film starts, I glance over at Marcus leaning back against another set of pillows.

I've had one sort-of boyfriend. And it wasn't serious. I've kissed two guys ever. One was Ben last year, and one was during the summer when I was twelve. It's not that I don't want to date or don't find myself interested in anyone, but it's a lot of baggage to carry at seventeen, and I haven't wanted to share that. Or to drag someone down with me.

I don't want to drag Marcus down, either, but I like the way he looks at me. I like how he makes me feel like maybe it wouldn't matter. It's the first time I feel like something could be possible with another person someday. I know it can't be with him, though, because I'm lying to him. That's not a good way to start any kind of relationship.

Still, he's really cute. And I try to focus on the movie, but I find myself imagining that I didn't have all these secrets and that I could ask Marcus to kiss me.

"Discussion time?" I ask after the movie ends. "Is that the next part?"

He shakes his head, tossing the DVD case onto his desk, where it slides off and lands in his trash can. "No, it's not about that. It's not about what I think you should think. It's about what you do think. And that's for you. I just wanted you to see it."

"Do you want to get into movies? Like, later or something?"

"I don't know. I'm not really getting out of Westbrook. There aren't a lot of colleges that want kids from the behavioral classes. We don't exactly get the same quality education."

"Why'd they put you in there exactly?" I ask, before I realize it's probably not okay to ask. "Never mind. You don't have to tell me."

"Nah, it's okay. I got in a lot of fights when I was younger. And I couldn't sit still in class, so they decided I couldn't do anything. And when I got older and could hold it together more, no one really thought to reconsider."

"You could probably have a meeting or something," I suggest.

"My mom would have to go, and she's . . . It's really hard with just the two of us. It doesn't matter. I could be the smartest guy in school and I can't go anywhere anyway. She needs me here."

I stand up and look through the rest of his DVDs. I don't want to go home yet, although I don't necessarily want to watch another movie. I kind of just want to be near him, even if we're both still stuck behind our pasts.

"My parents are . . ." I try to think of the word I want. I try to find the words to give Marcus something of myself without giving him the parts I can't. "They mean well."

"That's always followed by something bad, isn't it?" he asks.

He takes the box of snacks that neither of us touched and puts it on the floor beside him. The bed's now an empty welcome. The dark sheets are messed up from our sitting on them during the movie, and they peer out from under the comforter.

I don't know why Marcus interests me. I don't know if it's merely that he's supposed to be a bad idea and that appeals to me somehow. Or if it's how oddly vulnerable he is, even though he covers it with disappointment. Or if maybe it's just a lifetime of hormones exploding because he has nice eyes and I can't help looking at the way his shirt is caught in the top of his jeans and we're only a few feet apart in his quiet bedroom. Whatever it is, though, is exactly what I don't need, and yet I make no effort to leave.

"Lexi?" he says, reminding me I'm supposed to be talking. "Your parents mean well, but there's something else, isn't there?"

"I don't know. I mean it, really. They try. They want things to be different. And they do it the only way they know how. It's just sometimes . . . I wish they pushed me more. I wish they didn't let me give up so easily."

I sit on the edge of the bed but leave space between us. I won't look at him. I feel the words as they start to come out, and I wonder if I'll look back on tonight and remember this is when I screwed up.

"I couldn't handle it," I tell him. "I needed to be somewhere else. Everything was a mess at home, but my parents still wanted me there. It was hard for them, too, but it didn't matter. All that mattered was how hard it was for me."

"So you run away?" he asks.

I turn to look at Marcus. I think about this place. How it's shitty and the fountain barely works and how the ice-cream truck is just some guy in an old van. And I realize it's all a lie and I don't have the right to it. This is all Marcus has, and I just come in here and try to pretend it's my life, when I'm the girl who runs away and hides in other people's pain.

I nod. "I run away, and everyone just resets the world for me every time things get hard. Sometimes I wish they asked me to stay, that they made me fight for something."

He sits up and he's right beside me. I can feel him breathing, small bursts of warmth against my neck. Marcus unnerves me as he looks at me. I try to look down at my hands, to break eye contact, but he lifts my face. "Stay this time, Lexi."

I almost say yes. He leans closer, and I feel myself meeting him there, my face only a flicker of space from his. I can almost taste his lips on mine, but then I think of my brother. I think of the after. I remember the things people said about me. Why I stopped going online for months.

I stand up, grabbing my stuff. "I have to go. I'm sorry. Honestly."

He nods, but he won't look me in the eye anymore, and I leave, the full October cold and darkness greeting me on my walk back to my aunt's apartment. I run to my room, yelling to her that I'm home. When I lie down, I peer through the small gap under my shade at the light across the complex. Marcus's room. I wonder if he ever looks over here. If he will anymore, even if he ever did.

I close my eyes and blame October.

Chapter Thirteen

After the night with Marcus, I'm happy to go to Ryan's craft fair. I like Ryan, even if it's not in the same way I like Marcus. With Ryan, though, I find it easier not to reveal myself. It's safer being around him.

He's the only person here who's under 309 years old.

"Now, I should tell you that I'm quite the connoisseur of lawn ornaments," I say, "and these, sir, are far and away the *best* lawn ornaments I have ever seen. In fact, if I happened to have a gigantic lawn, I would fill said lawn with these exact ornaments."

An old lady with a basket full of wreaths stops as she passes, glances at the lawn ornaments, and shakes her head at me. I don't know if she's refuting my lawn ornament expertise, Ryan's work, or just our being here.

"It's been a nightmare," he says. "I've sold two."

"Do you normally do well?"

"I do, but this is the big time, you know. This is where the real crafters make their name."

"And you're not making your name in the record books of lawn ornament creators?"

"Alas, no."

I pick up a small ladybug sculpture. I'm not sure what a person does with these things. I don't have a lawn per se, although I guess the few dead blades of grass in the dirt in front of our apartment might count as a lawnlike space. There's probably room for a ladybug. It certainly can't hurt the aesthetics of Castle Estates.

"How much for this future MoMA piece?" I ask.

"Four dollars."

"Four dollars?" I repeat loudly, getting the attention of more old women and a few men, although I think most of them are just wondering what the high school girl wearing all pink is yelling about. "My God, man. This is worth three times that price!"

"It's a pity you've only got three lines in the show. Your acting skills are sensational," Ryan says.

I laugh, pay for the ladybug, and suddenly realize I have no other plans for the afternoon. I said I'd come, but I'm here now, at a craft fair, and I have to wait three hours for my aunt to come get me.

"So . . . I have come to the unfortunate realization that I've got all day. Want some help?" I ask.

"Well, as you can see, it's been nigh impossible to keep the crowds away. It's very hard to do alone."

"I'll help you fend off your rabid fans, then."

Ryan stands up, opening a random closet behind him. He grabs a folding chair and sets it up next to his.

"How was the rest of rehearsal last night?" I ask after I sit down.

"It was fine. We figured out the blood packs, so no more Tarantino-esque fight scenes. It'll be much less . . . intense from here. How are you feeling?"

"I'm okay," I say. "I got plenty of rest. Drank some fluids. But you were right. I was probably just reacting to all the stage blood. I get so grossed out by stuff like that."

"A lot of people do."

"Yup. Totally that. I feel a lot better now," I lie.

"That's good. I'm glad. I was afraid you were faking it so you could ride off into the night with your secret lover."

I think of Marcus. How we sat on the bench, my knee against his, and how I couldn't look at him completely because of his eyes. I think of how badly I wanted to kiss him, to ask him if he felt the same way, to tell him the truth about me. I think of how I ran away, right after he specifically asked me not to. I think of all of it, but I shake my head. "Yeah, I don't have lovers."

"Well, that's a good thing?" Ryan asks.

I glance over at him, but he goes back to rearranging lawn ornaments.

I'm not interested in being in the midst of some kind of love triangle, although I don't know if that's what any of this is. Still, the possibility of it and the added confusion aren't great for my emotional state.

"So what did you do last night? After you dropped me off and went back to rehearsal and whatever?"

"Nothing, really. I mean, we hung out at rehearsal and went to the diner and stuff."

"Did anyone ask? After? Like, about what happened?"

He pushes some of the lawn ornaments to the side and then puts them back in a new pattern. It's nervous behavior. I recognize it, and I know what it means.

"Were they talking about me?" I ask.

"What? No. Of course not. I mean, yeah, everyone asked, but that was it and . . . hey, do you want a snack? I was thinking of heading to the vending machines." He won't look at me as he bends down toward the jacket he draped over his chair, rummaging through the pockets for loose change. "I've been here since, like, eight. I'm starving."

"No, I'm okay," I say. "I'll hold down the fort."

"Don't go too easy on them. Don't let 'em talk you down on the prices." He jingles the change in his hand. "Listen, none of that matters, okay? People can say what they want. It's not important."

"What did they say?"

He shrugs. "Nothing that matters," he says, and heads toward the vending machines.

I know no one knows yet, but I hate it. I hate that they sat there talking about me. Was it during rehearsal? What did they say when Ryan wasn't there to hear it? Who was it? I can just see Chloe talking about me, making up stories, reenacting my reaction to the blood. Laughing at me. At everything that's happened.

I try not to get angry. I don't want to be angry. Not here. Not with Ryan, who's been safe and nice and a respite from it all. I don't want to lose this. Drama itself isn't important to me—not in the way it is for Rory and Lauren and some of the others—but it's something. It's someplace, and they've welcomed me.

Or at least I thought they had. But I know from the way Ryan wouldn't tell me what they said that they haven't. Not really. As soon as they had something, they sat around and made up versions of me. Sure, those versions are still probably better than the truth, but they did it, and it sucks. It sucks because I just want to be someone people don't ridicule. Someone who doesn't have a panic attack over something normal. Someone who can dress like a person and who doesn't wonder at night why she deserves this. Why can't I be that girl?

"I got you trail mix," Ryan says when he returns. "Sorry. It was that or gum. The pickings are slim." He hands me a bag before opening his own. We sit quietly, eating seeds and nuts and M&Ms, probably both thinking about what was said at rehearsal, neither of us wanting to let it carry into now.

"You know what your problem is?" I ask.

"What do you mean?"

I point down the room to an old lady selling birdhouses. "It's your competition. People keep heading to that woman's table. There's only so much room on people's lawns, and they're filling the space with birdhouses. I think you need to do some deep market analysis."

"That's Mildred. She's been doing this for ages. She's on the committee. I think she might even be president this year."

I look at Ryan in mock surprise. "Egads, Ryan. Are you saying what I think you're saying?"

He nods. "The craft fair circuit is hard-core rigged. It's good you realize it now. It's not a place for the faint of heart." A man coughs loudly as he passes our table. "Well, actually, it literally is, but you get what I mean."

"Well then, I'm glad I've got you to introduce me to the underground world of birdhouses and lawn ornaments.

One could get in with the wrong crowd if one wasn't careful."

Ryan crinkles the bag from his trail mix. A few seeds that were missed fall onto the floor by his feet. "Stick with me, L. I know the ways of the world."

Chapter Fourteen

After the fair Ryan invites me to get dinner. Sadly, it would be with his parents sitting in another booth, so I tell him I have to head home with my aunt. I shouldn't be pretending any of this is real anyway, and I don't feel like meeting anyone's parents if I don't need to.

When my aunt comes to pick me up, she sees me standing in front of the building talking to Ryan, and she immediately starts before I even have my seat belt on.

"Dating is a bad idea," she says. "I knew I should've been paying better attention."

"We're not dating. I don't even like him. Not that way, anyway. He's just nice."

"*Nice* turns into something else," she says, glancing back at Ryan once more before turning out of the parking lot.

"*Nice* can just mean *nice*. I'm not interested in a relationship. And definitely not with Ryan. He's a friend."

"You're not interested in anyone else, are you? Anyone like Marcus Cotero?" she asks. I don't respond and she shakes her head. "Be careful, Alexia."

"That's me. Always being careful."

She opens her mouth to say something else but changes her mind. I feel bad. I shouldn't take it out on her. She's doing her best. She has to hear it from my parents, and if they find out I'm spending time with not just one guy but two, they'll assume the same thing. They almost made me come home last year when they found out about Ben. Luckily for them, everyone else found out about me first.

"Can I ask you something?" I say to Aunt Susie. "About Marcus, actually?"

She looks over at me, trying to focus on the road but making it clear she doesn't like the direction the conversation is going. "I warned you about him. Clearly, that didn't take."

"I know. I know you warned me, and I know I didn't listen. But I mean, why? Why did you warn me? What do people say about him?"

"Like I said, they say he's trouble. That he's been trouble for a while. I heard he almost killed someone when he was a freshman. Got in a fight. He has anger problems. And Louise says he sells drugs, too. Just like Dianne told me."

"Really?" The drug thing doesn't seem like Marcus, although can I really say? I don't know much except his dad left, he seems sad, he has incredibly attractive eyes, and he likes old movies. And I like how he makes me feel normal.

"I don't know," my aunt admits. "Louise has a habit of saying things. I don't know if any of it's true, but people talk, and with everything, you don't want to be the one they talk about. I'm supposed to keep you out of all that."

"They already do," I tell her. "People at school. They're already starting to talk about me."

She tightens her grip on the steering wheel, but her face remains stoic. "How did they find out?"

"They didn't. They don't know anything."

"Your parents are counting on me, Lexi."

"I know. And I'm doing my best. I haven't told anyone. But . . ."

She looks at me quickly, even though she's supposed to be driving. "But?"

"But I freaked out last night at rehearsal. There was blood for the play, and it reminded me. I couldn't stop thinking about it, and I panicked. I told them I was sick. Ryan said I was just grossed out by the sight of the blood, and I went along with it. But no one believes anything. I know they can tell. They know I get distracted and sometimes forget to respond to them when they ask questions. They can see my clothes. They see how I shut down when things freak me out. I'm not fooling anyone. I don't even know how to try to fit in." I look back at her, her face still impassive. "I wish I could just be this other girl. Your niece. The one who transferred here because she needed to improve her GPA."

"You know you *are* that girl, right?" she asks. "Sure, there's other stuff, but that doesn't make you any less *you*. And the real you is pretty great, Lexi. Maybe you don't need to fit in. Maybe you just need to let them get to know all these things you're holding behind some kind of wall."

"But once they find out . . ."

She shakes her head. "People have an amazing capacity for forgiveness sometimes. Not everyone, no, but I truly think you're so much more than the girl you're holding on to. Maybe it's a good time to think about letting her go?"

This feels a bit deep for a car conversation as we pass Taco Bell. And I don't know if that's true. I don't think she's right. Are we able to separate what we *were* from what we *are*? And are we what we are if we're always hiding some of what we were?

The slowly fading summer that's turned to dying leaves and early evenings and bursts of clouds from our breath in the cold is always such an odd time for me. I know I said I hate it—because I do. But I also love it for its tragedy. I feel like there's a lesson in there somewhere, but I don't want to think about that now.

Chapter Fifteen

Somehow, despite the one moment so close to the edge, the next couple weeks until show week go by like the rest. People mostly seem to have forgotten about the blood pack debacle, or at least they're so worried about forgetting their lines or missing a cue that it's not a priority.

I, on the other hand, feel more anxious by the day because I'm three nights from being onstage and I'm seriously doubting whether I can show up. At least the show can go on without Elaine, but I've grown more determined to do this—even though I still can't convince myself I can.

I get away with my plan of changing my costumes every night, claiming a lack of time to do laundry. No one believes me, but the fact that people don't question it aloud makes me feel a little closer to them.

"Three days, people. Let's go," Rory says as everyone filters into the auditorium for rehearsal. Most of us don't have the same sense of urgency she does—and it pisses her off. We're all committed to making the show good, but *good* isn't in Rory's vocabulary. It's either life-changing or it's not worth doing at all.

"Calm down," Eric says. "Give people a chance to breathe. School got out, like, eight minutes ago."

"Yeah, exactly," Rory says. Eric rolls his eyes, dropping his bag into a seat and heading to the cafeteria for a snack. She watches him leave, her eyes wide. "Really?" she calls after him. He doesn't reply.

"Hey, I've been looking for you," Ryan says, coming up behind me. "I'm in charge of the cast party, and I need to get your food order."

"What cast party?"

"Saturday. After the last show. At Rory's."

"Oh."

He looks at me, slowly realizing no one's mentioned the party to me. Sure, it could be because everyone assumes someone else told me, and it's part of the show, and they figure I'll find out and come. They could have figured Ryan would tell me, so they didn't need to worry about it. But regardless of all the could-haves and the likely scenarios, I can't help feeling left out.

For all the ways I want to disappear and not let people see me, it still cuts me every time they don't.

"I'm sure everyone just assumed you'd be going. Since I am."

"Oh, right," I say. "Except, I mean, why? We aren't inseparable or anything."

Ryan sits in the seat in front of me and turns toward me. "Can I tell you something without you getting upset?"

"That question never precedes something that's not upsetting," I point out.

He looks down, eyes focused on the top of the auditorium seat, his hands picking at the fabric on the back of the seat next to him. "I might have let everyone believe we're together."

It's not a big deal. I'm not with anyone else, and while I don't like Ryan that way, I don't really care what people think in terms of my relationships, especially the ones that *aren't* relationships. Ryan hasn't acted like we actually are together, so does it matter if everyone assumes it? In some ways it's probably easier. But there's something kind of . . . well, it's a violation, isn't it? I'm fake-dating someone I'm not interested in, and I didn't even know I was.

"Why'd you do that?" I ask.

He looks up, and his eyes are sad. There's also an odd fear there. "Can we talk about it later?"

"Okay, but I'm holding you to that. Maybe during the dinner break?"

We agree, and it's better we wait, because Rory is losing it onstage now. People are milling around the auditorium, talking about food and dinner orders and calculus tests and the semiformal and basically everything that has nothing to do with star-crossed lovers in fair Verona.

"Can you all please *sit*?" she yells.

Everyone stops what they're doing, and while they don't seem thrilled about being yelled at, all of them move quietly to their seats.

"Thank you," Rory says. "Look, we have three days until opening night. Everything's mostly on track, but we still have some serious issues with the party scene, and Tybalt's death is . . ."

"Awful?" Mark, the guy playing Tybalt, offers. "Horrendous? More comical than tragic?"

"It needs work," she agrees. "And, like, half the English teachers are giving extra credit to their freshman classes if they attend, so it's a big deal we do this well, guys. I don't want to look bad in front of the whole school. This club is very important to me. I've been working on building this program for three years now. It's going to be my legacy."

"It's high school drama. She way oversells legacy," someone whispers from behind me.

I kind of envy Rory. Yes, the mysterious person behind me is right. It doesn't mean a whole lot in the grand scheme of things, but at the same time I wish I had Rory's passion for anything.

After a lecture that's way too long and ends up draining the entire cast and crew of any potential enthusiasm for the first run-through of the show tonight, we start rehearsal. After some script adjustments for time, I now have three lines—all in regular everyday English, so I sound ridiculous. I had to veto calling Romeo a badass. I'm no Shakespeare fangirl, but come on.

By the time the dinner break comes, I've mostly forgotten about the Ryan thing. Until we all stop and I head backstage to return the candlestick I am inexplicably responsible for bringing to Lady Capulet during the party scene.

"I don't get you," Chloe says to me. Lauren is in the prop closet behind her, but the sounds of people fighting with the set onstage and guys yelling out sub orders prevent her from hearing Chloe.

"How do you mean?" I ask, clutching the candlestick and praying that Lauren quickly finds what she needs. I can't see her, because the black curtain over the door covers the inside of the closet. I can only see her feet while she rummages for something.

"You just show up and you think you own people," Chloe says.

"I really don't think that."

"Ryan and I have a history, and you can't just come in here and take it."

You know how you can be sitting outside in the middle of a summer afternoon and a colony of ants can run over your toes and feet while you're dreaming of being somewhere else? How you don't even notice every little brush of ant feet? But then all of a sudden it's one ant too many? And you realize the ants have surrounded you?

That's how it is with people. You try everything you can. You don't hear things. You let them go. They run over your toes and tickle your feet with their words, but there are bigger things to hold your attention. You tell yourself it doesn't matter. You promise yourself to make this year work, that you can last 162 days. And then, during the first week of November, some girl named Chloe, with no real defining characteristics as far as I can tell, just says the wrong thing. And suddenly you realize all your happy delusions are individual ants and the entire ground below your feet is a swarm of blackness.

"I didn't try to take anything from you," I say.

"You better watch yourself. You're not special, Lexi Lawlor. And it won't take much to let everyone know just how not special you are."

She leaves, and I don't let the thoughts crowd me. Not yet. I put the candlestick away, say hi to Lauren, head to the bathroom, and smile at the sophomore girls who are playing random Montague girls in the fight scene. It's not until I get to the cafeteria and see Ryan, not until he leads me outside to the football field and bleachers, that I run through everything I've ever said to Chloe. I replay all the conversations she might have heard. At no point did I reveal anything about myself. My aunt was extremely careful when she filled out the enrollment paperwork, especially after what happened last year. There's nothing Chloe has on me. I don't use social media anymore. There's no phone call or text she can dig up. Nothing about me hints that somewhere inside of me is another girl, with a whole lifetime of secrets that do nothing but hurt people.

Yet she made me feel like she knew. She looked at me like she knew something was wrong with me.

"I got you a coffee," Ryan says, handing it to me when we get to the bleachers. The cup keeps my hands warm.

The moon is big tonight. It's so cold outside now that it's November, but it doesn't stop us from sitting at the top of the bleachers and looking out over the moon-soaked field.

"So we're together?" I ask once we're both sitting.

He won't look at me. I put my coffee down and reach over and take his hand, the freezing cold of it sizzling against the coffee-baked warmth of mine.

"I didn't think you'd care," he says. "I figured you were single and it wouldn't matter if I went along with it."

"That's kind of harsh. Yeah, it's true, but that doesn't make a girl feel good."

"I know. I just . . ." He stops talking. The wind picks up and shakes the bleachers. In my chest, I feel winter pushing back against the last strains of autumn.

"You could have asked me," I say.

"Asked you what?" Ryan continues to stare straight ahead of him, steam coming from his words as he speaks into the night.

"Whatever it was. To date you?"

"It's not like that. I just didn't deny it when they asked. I don't . . ."

I drink more of my coffee. "So I guess you're not interested in actually being with me."

He sighs and looks down, taking his hand away and running his fingers along his knees. "It's not you. It's me. Really. That's not a line. It really *is* me, I promise."

"Why lie about it?" I ask. "And why me? Or at least why not tell me first?"

He finally turns to me, sparkling eyes spilling his sorrow onto the metal bench below us. "I like you," he says. "A lot. And I figured if anyone would be someone I could maybe talk myself into feeling that way for, it would be you."

"You don't need to be with someone. Who cares if you're single?"

He shakes his head. "There's always Chloe, and everyone keeps asking why. They want to know what happened." He breathes in and stares up at the moon. I can feel his desperation. Wishing he could go there and leave all this behind. "We were together last year. But she wanted . . . well, a boyfriend."

"And you wanted?"

"I don't want anything. That's just it. But that's not okay, for some reason."

I nod and look back at the field. I love the stillness of it. I love the way the night and the cold make this place, usually so full of energy, a husk of what it's meant to be. But Ryan and I fill it. Right now, we reach out into the space and make it something new.

"I get it," I say. "It's easier to have what people think is a normal reason. So I'm your normal."

"Yeah. I'm sorry, though. I wasn't trying to complicate things for you. I just didn't want to listen to it anymore. I guess I should've asked you all along."

"Ask me now," I tell him.

He faces me and holds my hands, both of his shielding both of mine from the cold. "L, will you be my normal?"

"If you'll be mine."

"You don't need me. You're already fine the way you are."

I laugh. "Oh man. You have no idea."

"Tell me?" he asks.

"That's okay. I'll save that for the unlucky guy I eventually real-date." I pause and realize that, while it's unlikely, fake-dating Ryan could get back to Marcus. Although I guess I'm so buried in fake me that fake-dating while yearning for a real guy is probably apropos.

"Can I ask you something?" He nods. "Do you just not like Chloe, and it's too much work to explain . . . or do you like guys or something?"

"I don't really *like* people."

"I don't like them much, either, but I mean—"

"No, I mean, that's what I mean. I'm not interested. At all. I don't want any kind of relationship like that. I don't feel any of that. And I'm totally okay with it, you know?" he says. "But for some reason it's a big fucking deal to everyone else. It's completely unacceptable to not be interested."

"Oh. So you dated Chloe because you thought . . ."

"Yeah, I figured I'd come around. I figured I was slow to warm up to people or something. And she was . . . aggressive, let's just say. I thought it would be good for me."

"But instead—"

"Instead I basically led her on, and—I don't know. I'm an asshole, but she's not exactly nice about it."

I think of her threatening me by the prop room. "No, she really isn't."

"I didn't want to hurt anyone," Ryan says. "I don't want to use girls or to lie. I just kind of wanted to be allowed to be me."

"Yeah. I get that. Believe me, I get that."

Ryan stands up and grabs my coffee so I can lift myself up from the bench. It's so cold I feel like my ass has frozen in place.

"I'm really glad you transferred here, L."

"I'm glad you like *Green Arrow*," I say.

"You really should check it out." He starts rambling about some guy named Oliver Queen and vigilantes, and I tune out as we walk back into the school, my coffee as cold as the air around us now. As we come around the corner and head toward the cafeteria, where all the drama kids are, I reach out and take Ryan's hand.

"Listen, if I teach you only one thing in exchange, let it be this: When you want to shed everything you are and live inside a fiction of yourself, you need to breathe it every second of every day."

"You sound like you know what you're talking about," he says.

I cut off the questions in his eyes, kissing him quickly on the cheek as the cafeteria door opens and some of the other people from drama come out into the hall.

Heath probably wouldn't approve of the way I'm digging myself further into a lie, but there's something comforting about the reality Ryan and I can shape for each other. We can create a place where we're both safe from the truth neither of us is ready to confront just yet.

Chapter Sixteen

On opening night, moments before I walk onstage, I still don't know whether I can do this. But then, I do. And I get it. I get everything Lauren said.

Moments earlier the nausea roiled in my belly, and my tongue filled my mouth, swollen somehow and choking me from speaking. And then there was my cue. A word and one step forward.

The curtain slides open, and a whole universe exists inside a moment.

The gasp between breaths is overwhelming. The hard wood of the floor reverberates under my feet as I move through to my mark. The lights burn, but it's a painful dazzling as I look up and meet them. Halos appear—echoes of the light as I blink. Carefully. Slowly. I can't blink too quickly or the makeup will smudge. All that work. Hours of perfect planning.

Behind the lights, in these seconds, is a shadow world. People and ideas and events and all the fears and anxiety I have disappear behind the sharp white.

I am . . .

I am Desdemona, and I ache to be heard. To be believed.

I am Lavinia, with my words stolen from me.

I am Eliza Doolittle, and I fall for words all over again.

I am Elaine, and Lauren asks me a question, but she's not Lauren, and both of us exist as someone else. I am everyone and no one and I breathe and live in these gasps between breathing. The shadow people see me, but only what I give them. I am wrapped in words and beats and motions and blocking.

And I am finally free.

The audience exhales in a collective sound, and the moment passes. I blink again, and the lights don't hurt as much, and now the shadow world is Hawthorne with her script shaking in her hand as she stands backstage. It's Eric flirting with two freshman girls in my peripheral vision, and I can't help but wonder if they're even in drama. It's Chloe watching me and shaking her head, and it's me again, handing Lauren the candlestick, and a moment turns to minutes before I'm back behind the curtain again.

"That was awesome," I tell Ryan later, once Mercutio is dead and we're sitting in the back of the auditorium, watching the rest of the play with the audience.

And then . . . as quickly as the moment filled my life, it's suddenly Saturday—and we're hours from it all being over.

There's a weird feeling among us. Sadness, yes, but also relief. Joy. There's a quiet satisfaction in knowing you did something well and it will forever be a part of you.

Something's different about this place, I tell myself as I get ready for our final curtain, and it feels true. There's something special about these people. I feel like I'm not walking forward through a steady tide that keeps trying to knock me off my feet. I can almost breathe here.

"Can you believe this is it?" Lauren asks. "One more performance?"

"I'm really happy you talked me into being here."

"I'm glad you're here. Especially . . . Yeah, well, I'm glad you're here."

She walks away, and I consider following her, but I know she's running lines in her head. And I know she's upset because no one has come to see her after the shows. After each performance, we've all gone out to the auditorium to meet friends and family. Even my aunt took time off from work to come, but Lauren sat in the cafeteria. Alone. I don't think anyone's coming today, either.

She hasn't said a word about it, and either everyone knows that's just how things are, or she doesn't want anyone asking. I have to respect that, but I wish I could do something. I would never wish that clinging loneliness I recognize on anyone.

During intermission Ryan joins me in the cafeteria again, but today we don't leave when everyone else rushes back to the auditorium after fixing their makeup and using the bathroom.

"Is your aunt here again?" he asks.

I nod. "I didn't see her, but she said she was coming. Did your parents come?"

"No, they came yesterday. My sister has a karate thing today."

"You have a sister?" I feel like this is something I should know, real boyfriend or not.

"Yeah. She's eight. We don't have a whole lot in common, and our paths don't exactly cross most days. But yes, I have an annoying little sister."

"What's her name?"

Ryan rolls his eyes. "Madison. She's not the worst, I guess. I mean, she's irritating, and she's always messing up my stuff, but she's not horrible. I probably should have introduced you last night when they were here."

We haven't talked while visiting with our families, and it's another one of the ways our relationship isn't real. I wonder what he told his parents. How he explains a girlfriend who sort of forgets he's there sometimes.

"But you're lucky," he continues. "Even if she's not the worst, I'd so much prefer being an only child."

"I . . ."

But there's nothing I can say. So I don't.

"L?" he asks.

"We should start cleaning this stuff up," I say, gesturing to the utter destruction we've left in our wake around the cafeteria. The sooner we clean up, the sooner we can go home and get ready for Rory's party.

"Yeah, okay," he says, but he didn't miss it. He's just kind enough not to push.

By the time the show ends, the cafeteria and backstage are almost fully clean. When I'm trying to avoid things, I am an exceptionally motivated person. I have everything organized, until the cast filters out from the stage doors, dropping a bunch of props everywhere.

"I've got it," Ryan says. "And if I don't see you before you leave, I'll pick you up tonight? Six thirty?" He leans over to start boxing up the props that were dropped by the doorway.

"For Rory's?"

"Yup. I can't go to the cast party without my girlfriend."

"Get a room," Eric says, pushing past us.

"There will be plenty at my party," Rory says from behind him, and she taps me on the shoulder. "Don't worry. I'll make sure you guys have all the privacy you need."

Ryan stands up, and the box starts to topple. I wait for everyone to pass, helping him with it. "They really are strangely obsessed with your sex life, aren't they?" I ask.

He sighs. "Seriously. Anyway, six thirty?"

"Perfect. Should I bring a deck of cards? It sounds like we may have a lot of quiet time."

He leans close to me, the box of props stabbing me in the chest, and whispers in my ear, "I'm bringing Pictionary. Don't get too excited, but it's gonna be hot."

I laugh and kiss him quickly on the cheek, then pack up my stuff and a few more props, trying to avoid Chloe as I go to meet my aunt. I see Lauren, already wearing her coat and heading to the parking lot, and again I consider talking to her. Asking if she needs a ride. But I recognize that kind of need: the need to be alone with your thoughts. Your disappointment.

Inside the auditorium people are chatting, the conversations competing for the space of sound. The noise grows louder by the minute. I maneuver through families and friends to find my aunt. But when I get close to where she's waiting, I stop.

"What are you doing here?" I ask, even though I'm not near enough that they can hear me. I hear my voice through the overwhelming noise, and although no one actually notices, it feels like all the spotlights have been turned on me. I feel like the entire world has stopped moving.

In her hand my mom holds one of the programs we made, turning it into a tube between her fingers. I watch as she taps out some kind of code against the script letters of Romeo's name. My father sees me first and he waves, but it's a tired wave.

I watch them with my aunt. Barely looking alive. I can't hear the conversation, but I know it's mundane. It's filled with nothing but the sagging weight of so many years and so many questions, all of it heavier on them than it was even this past summer. I want to tell them they shouldn't feel this way—that they haven't failed. I want to go to them and remind them they're here: Because there's still hope. That I got onstage today and for the last two nights.

I want to remind them that I'm still possible. I want them to believe in me.

"Lexi?"

I walk closer and let my dad hold me for a second. I try not to let the other futures hurt. Try not to remember what could have been. How I could have been here, like the others in the cast, hugging them and celebrating. I could be listening to my mother lecture me on effective staging and interpretation of Shakespearean language, but instead we're all quiet and full of nothing but memories of what we never had.

"I didn't know you were coming."

I look up at my dad. When we were growing up, he was a cliché. A teddy bear with a massive beard, always wrapped in tweed. Now he's a frail old man with gray hair, with only the stubble he forgot to shave this morning. He's wearing a gray suit that hangs on him. He still has patches on his elbows, but they don't look professorial anymore. They just look sad.

And my mom. She smiles when I step away from my dad. She doesn't hug me, because that's not how she is, but she smiles, and it should be light. It should be a smile that says we're okay. But she's always smiling now, and it's somehow wrong. A contrast to the serious literary scholar of my childhood. That could be okay, but it's not the same accidental light that appeared every so often then. Instead it's practiced muscle memory. Years of pretending you're not listening to the things people say when you just want to buy eggs.

"Did you like the show?" I ask her.

"It was wonderful. And you really shone, even in a small part." I listen for more, but there's nothing. It's almost like she's really happy. Like she's proud of me. Like for one instant I finally exist outside the shadow of our memories.

"We wanted to surprise you," my dad says. "Are you surprised?"

"Yeah. I had no idea you were coming. Are you staying? For how long?"

He shakes his head. "Just for the show, and we want to take you out to lunch. To celebrate."

"I'm sure you probably have some things planned with your drama friends," my mom adds. It's weird to hear that phrase. *Drama friends.* Everything about today feels different. But I can't tell if it's a good different or if this is the moment I've been waiting for. When everything falls apart.

"We have a party tonight, but I have a few hours," I say.

"Let's go, then?" my dad asks.

I look to my aunt, who's been quiet. Her smile is tight, and I almost ask her why. I almost listen to my brain when it tells me not to get too comfortable. But I don't want to ask my aunt if something is wrong. I don't want to listen to my brain. I want to believe my parents. I want to think there's nothing to worry about, and for one afternoon I want to go to lunch with them and celebrate me.

Chapter Seventeen

L unch is almost real. For the better part of it, we talk, and
my parents ask questions most parents ask their kids.
They ask about my classes, and they tell me about work,
and they discuss other family members with my aunt. It's
all what happens in other people's lives, and I pretend. I let
it envelop me, a comfortable blanket of another reality and
another girl. I know it's nothing but a stolen moment, yet I
try to hold on to it anyway. Because it's the life I should have
had. The one that another me could have lived and com-
plained about endlessly.

At the corner table there's a girl around my age, and she
rolls her eyes like she's attached to a metronome. Someone
at her table speaks, they pause and look at her, and her eyes
move forward and back. It goes on like this for the entirety
of our meal, and I wish for a moment I was that girl. That
this normal was annoying to me.

But like everything that's happened, it's not real and it can't last. The waitress asks if we want dessert, and my mom says we'll all just have coffee, and while we wait, a lull fills the space between us. It's a lull that's on the other side of words you don't want to hear, and I feel the words forming in it. The seconds move slowly but tangibly until my dad clears his throat.

"There's one thing," he says. "While we're here."

"David," my aunt says, but it's futile. He looks to my mom and she nods, and he clears his throat again. I almost tell them to save it. *Whatever it is can wait,* I want to say, but I don't, and the lull expands until it breaks.

"You know we're coming up to Scott's birthday," my father continues. "Just over a month and he'll be twenty-one."

"Okay," I say. I try to hold on to the girl rolling her eyes or how I felt after the show or anything that's happened here, but those things fade away while I remember him. I see my brother and how he never looked much older than me. I remember his hair and how it grew even longer in that last year and how he forgot to wash it sometimes. I want to think about the coffee that appears somehow through the memories, but I can't, and I feel the talons tearing into my flesh.

"It's just that . . . he's going to have to be moved," my mom explains.

"Moved where?" I ask.

"Well, where he is, it's . . . He's going to be too old soon to stay there."

"What does this have to do with me?"

My parents look at each other, silently trying to find the right way to say it. My dad's the one who does.

"They're trying to decide on his placement. There are

two options for him, but they want to speak with each of us. Get our take before making any decisions."

"You can't . . . No. You can't ask me to do this," I tell them. "How can you ask me to do this?"

My mom reaches across the table and rests her hand over mine. "You don't have to, Alexia. We would never make you do it if you can't. To be honest, I don't even know if you should. We almost didn't tell you. We weren't going to tell you."

"Why did you?"

"We had to. We at least had to mention it. To offer you a choice. Heath says . . . He told us that if you felt we'd kept it from you, it wouldn't allow you control over what you process. He said it would be denying you the opportunity to decide for yourself."

"I hate Heath."

"Do you really?" my mom asks. "Or are you just processing by venting?"

"Did he come up with that, too?" She doesn't say anything, which means he did. "What do you want me to do? Do you want me to do this? Is this what you think is best?"

She sighs. "I don't know, Alexia. Part of me wants to say no. I don't think you should, and I don't want to ask you to even consider it, because I know what it will do to you. I'm not sure anything good comes of it. At the same time, yes. I do want you to do it, because he's my son. He's still my son. And if there's anything we can do . . . If there's a chance for him . . ."

I hear her voice breaking, and I picture them. I picture my mom sitting at their new kitchen table—since they got rid of our old furniture when they moved. I imagine her waiting for me to call when I get home from school every day, wondering about me, feeling me slipping away from her as I live my life without them. I can see the way she picks at the wood on the edge of the table when she's nervous. She'll do it for hours, too, and then she sits in the cafeteria with her colleagues in the psych department, wondering why I have so much trouble coping.

"You couldn't have waited?" I ask. "I'm going to a party tonight. I'm supposed to be going to a party. Why couldn't you wait?"

"We weren't thinking," my dad says. "Lexi, when they called . . . It was sudden. We only found out last night, and we were already planning on coming, and we . . ."

"You were thinking of Scott," I say. He nods. "That's not fair, you know. It's not okay that you couldn't think of me today and save this. My whole life is defined by him already. Couldn't I have had one day?"

"You've had years," my mom says. "For years we've worried about what you need. But he turns twenty-one next month, Alexia. We had to tell you. We needed you to know what was happening. To give you time and . . ."

She starts to cry. Right here in the middle of the restaurant, and she's sobbing so loudly that the girl stops rolling her eyes for a moment to stare.

I feel like shit. I hate my mom. I hate my father, and I hate my aunt for not saying anything this whole time. I hate Scott, and I hate the girl at the other table. I hate everyone else, and I hate myself because of it.

Because I don't actually hate any of them.

I hate that I don't hate Scott. I hate that he needs me and my parents need me and I shouldn't go and I can't go, but at the same time I want to go. I hate that if I don't go, I'll always blame myself.

Even though I don't have anything here—not really—I hate the idea of losing it. I don't want to lose worrying about what kids say about me at drama club or being annoyed by Chloe staring at me for looking at Ryan a certain way. I don't want to lose my pretend relationship with Ryan or falling asleep thinking about Marcus's eyes but being too scared to talk to him again because of how I feel. I don't want to lose any of that, because as petty and meaningless and empty as it all is, it's the most real I've felt in ages.

I kind of love the silly drama about Ryan and worrying whether Rory will lose it if someone forgets a line. I love pep rallies and how annoying they are. I love leaving class and going into the auditorium and knowing there's a group of people waiting there, people who kind of like me but also kind of think I'm weird. I like all the irritating and awful parts of being Lexi Lawlor, and I don't want to have to live the reality of me instead.

"I made friends here," I tell my parents finally, after my mom's sobs subside. "Sure, some kids don't like me, but they don't like the way I talk or the way I act or something I did. They don't hate me for something I was or that someone else thought I was. They only know this person, and they don't see—"

I stop talking because now I'm crying, too.

"You should call Heath," my mom says, drying her eyes.

"Do you still see him?" He was supposed to be my therapist, but it's not like being an adult makes you immune to needing some guidance.

"Not anymore," she says. "Well, not because I need to."

"But you do? See him, I mean?"

"He comes for dinner sometimes," my dad says. "We really like him."

I try picturing that. My mom adjusting the placemats because they're slightly crooked, my dad fighting with the oven, and Heath, in his plaid shirt, stroking his beard and suggesting that my parents are using inanimate objects to demonstrate their need for control. He probably says it while sipping sangria or something and nodding to himself.

"Why do you like him?" I don't mean to sound confrontational, which I'm sure Heath would say I'm being.

"He's not just Heath the therapist, Alexia. Did you know he once backpacked across Iceland?" my mom asks.

"No, it never came up."

"People are a lot more than we see."

"Not Heath. Heath is my therapist. *Our* therapist if you still need to see him, too. He's not a guy who backpacks anywhere. I don't want to know that about him. I want him to be the person who exists to help me when I can't adjust. When I need someone to talk to while I move all over New England. I don't want to talk to an Icelandic backpacker about Scott and the trial and the words cut into my arms. I like keeping Heath in his place."

My mom laughs, although nothing is funny. "You're old enough to know that's not real. You have to realize that . . . well, we're all large. We all contain multitudes."

"Don't do that."

"Do what?" she asks.

"Don't start quoting Whitman at me. Don't go running to poetry because you don't want to talk."

I realize I sound a little like Heath at the moment, but fuck him. Fuck everyone.

"You don't have to go," my dad says, reminding me what we're talking about. What my "celebration lunch" is really about. "You can say no. It's your choice."

"But I do have to go, and you know it. You knew I would, and you knew what it would do, and you knew it would make it all impossible. You knew how I'd feel, and you knew today was the last show, and you knew that this would ruin things. I'm supposed to go to a party tonight, and now I have to decide if I can handle that, but it doesn't matter because it's all going to end up like it always does anyway, isn't it?"

"We're sorry," my dad says.

"Sorry isn't good enough. You should have waited."

"Alexia," my mom says.

"Fine. I'll go. And I'll call Heath or whatever. I can see him when I come home for Thanksgiving. But . . ."

"What is it?" my dad asks.

"Can this thing with Scott wait until then? Can we pretend we didn't have this conversation? Can you at least let me fake it for a little longer? Can you please give me that? A few weeks before it's all over?"

My parents both nod.

Thanksgiving is in nineteen days.

Chapter Eighteen

After my parents leave, I have an hour before the party. I tell myself it's all going to be okay. I tell myself I have to be okay. I have to go tonight. I need to be there for Ryan, because in nineteen days who knows what happens? I may as well enjoy what I have right now.

But all the logic washes away with the stage makeup in the shower. Only a few hours ago, the entire future was open to me. I survived three shows onstage. I had friends. Last night, on the drive home with Ryan, we sang along to *West Side Story* because it's a damn good play. Musical or not.

That feels like a lifetime ago, even if it's been less than twenty-four hours. Last night life felt possible. I thought maybe life could be good.

But that's the thing with life, isn't it? It's give and take. It gave me hope for the last couple of months. And now it's taking that hope back.

"Are you going to be okay?" my aunt asks from the door-way as I brush my hair and put on lip gloss. It's all pretend. I don't care if I look kissable. But I was supposed to be there tonight and look like Ryan's girlfriend. That made sense this afternoon, although now it's like being an alien on a new planet. How did I let myself believe this kind of simplicity?

"I don't know," I admit. But I don't have time to think about it as Ryan pulls into the driveway, his parents' station wagon sputtering in the cold November night.

I grab my bag and jacket, then push past my aunt.

"Lexi," she says. "Wait."

"I have a party to go to."

Ryan's headlights blaze through the glass of the front door, flickering into a kaleidoscope of light. As I walk for-ward, my aunt says my name again, and the colors start to swirl.

Not now. Not tonight, I beg the universe. But since when did the universe give a fuck about me?

My eyes ache from staring into the glare of the head-lights. Burning my retinas to replace the chill in the rest of me. I keep moving toward the door, telling the past to stay away, telling myself to focus and to remember this morn-ing. To stay here and now. Heath's a big fan of "mindfulness," and I try. I try to use everything he's taught me.

As soon as I'm outside, though, I know it's not going to pass. I don't want to be here. I don't want to be anywhere.

The world takes on the haze it always does when the past refuses to let go, and I open the car door, my arms feel-ing like they're on someone else's body and I'm only hear-ing a story about what they're doing.

I can see the night laid out before me. I'll go to the party with Ryan, and everyone will talk about us until we come into a room. Chloe will stare at me, and I'll play this game with her, like any of this is important. I'll give her a million more reasons to hate me, reasons she'll remember later, and it will be so much worse because of it.

Ryan and I will go into some room, and people will think we're doing all kinds of things in there, and they'll talk about those things that we aren't really doing but they want to pretend we are. We'll stay in there long enough for everyone to have a story. And then, after we leave Rory's tonight, they'll talk about me some more. They'll wonder what he sees in me. Call me names. Talk about what makes me better or worse than Chloe, depending on where their loyalties lie.

They'll talk about me later, and I'll be at home with the imagined voices and taunts bouncing off all the things my parents need from me, too. I'll be stuck with my parents' version of me, and these impressions of Lexi Lawlor, and all my thoughts and everything Scott used to be. My head is already too crowded as it is, but I'll have to add the whispered things they'll be saying to that mess.

And somehow, in the middle of all that, I need to figure out what I'm supposed to say about my brother at the end of the month.

I can't be all these people. I can't balance all the thoughts and what everyone needs from me.

I can't do any of it.

"I can't go," I tell Ryan, leaning into the car. "I'm sorry. My mom . . . I mean, my aunt . . . She needs me for something. About my mom."

He blinks but nods slowly. "You all right?"

"Sure. I'm fine."

"Are you sure?"

"What choice do I have, right?"

"Okay," he says, and I know he's trying to decide if he should stay. Should be a good boyfriend and comfort me. But he's not really my boyfriend. And even if he were, this is so much bigger than him and us and drama club.

I shut the door and watch him drive away, but I don't go inside. Instead I turn around and walk toward the broken swing set where I sat with Marcus a lifetime ago. I lie down in the frozen dirt and ruin the pretty pink dress I've never worn before. I bought it at a thrift shop with my aunt last week, something special to wear tonight. To a party. With people. *Friends*. All those things I almost forgot weren't welcome in my life.

I used to be happy. I remember that so vividly, probably because I know what's missing now. Maybe if my memories were the sort that haunted me because they were bad, it would be easier to let go. But things weren't bad. They were amazing and wonderful . . . until they weren't.

Before that one October day, there was the beach in Maine, where Scott taught me how to swim. Where our parents yelled at us to be careful, because we kept pretending the waves were washing us away. But it was always safe; nothing real happens to most kids.

Only months before it happened, Scott and I were still close. We knew it was probably his last true summer, though. Soon he'd be sixteen, and then he'd have to work and he'd probably drive and he'd be an adult. Meanwhile, at twelve, I was still taking on the lives of YouTube stars and fictional characters because everyone else was so much more interesting.

I sort of wish I remembered one important day. One time, maybe, when Mrs. Cabot came outside from next door and said something. That maybe she upset Scott somehow, but I don't remember that. I only remember sitting outside with him, both of us reading comics, and him sneaking sips from my lemonade because he'd already finished his own and he was too lazy to go inside and get more.

I remember the two of us sitting in the backseat of our parents' car one summer evening, looking at the signs and trying to guess where we were going. We always did that—whenever we went anywhere, we created a world outside the car and made it into a mystery that even Agatha Christie couldn't have worked out. And my parents played along because it was fun to make the world nothing but potential.

We drove for an hour, and my parents refused to answer any of our questions about where they were taking us. When we pulled onto a dirt road full of cars, we still didn't have a guess. Across the street was a giant barn and an even more giant crowd, but I couldn't see what any of them were doing.

"What's this?" Scott asked.

My mom giggled, and it was odd. It was the happiest I'd ever seen her—this woman who was so serious about everything.

"Summer's almost over," she said, although that wasn't an explanation.

We crossed the street and made our way through the crowd toward the barn. On chalkboard signs bigger than me were lists of flavors.

"An ice-cream stand?" I asked.

"Not just any ice-cream stand," my dad said. "This is Lendell's."

This meant nothing to me or Scott, but my parents were giddy. They were absurdly excited about ice cream, which made me get absurdly excited about ice cream, and twenty minutes later the four of us were sitting on a bench under a massive oak tree that dipped right over us, eating sundaes the size of my head for dinner. It was childish and pointless, but it was the kind of thing my parents used to do.

It was the kind of thing that should have been my future.

All this is who my brother was. He rode his bike with me to Ray's for comics and he stole my lemonade and he protected me from thunderstorms and he gave me his cherry from his sundae because mine had fallen off. He cleared away the spiders above the fridge—where our mom always left us money for our so-called "adventures" in the summers—because I was scared of them. My brother was my hero and my best friend and the person I trusted with my life.

And then . . .

Two months after we had surprise ice-cream sundaes at a barn on a dusty road, I sat at school one afternoon, wondering why Scott was so late to come get me. I kept calling, but he wouldn't pick up, and eventually I had to walk home by myself.

It was a few days before Halloween.

While I was waiting in front of the middle school, my fifteen-year-old brother came home, and he dropped his school bag on the kitchen table. Then, instead of coming to get me like he did every other day, he grabbed the biggest knife we had, and he walked into our neighbors' house, turning on music for reasons I'll never understand.

After stabbing Mrs. Cabot twenty-seven times and both Miles and Lucy fifteen times each . . . After brutally murdering the woman next door along with her children, he came back to our house, changed his clothes, and put the other ones—the ones still drenched in blood—on the kitchen table next to his bag. Then he called the police, told them everything he'd done, and went outside on our porch and had a glass of lemonade.

I came home to police sirens, Mr. Cabot on the front steps next door crying, and the overhead light in our kitchen flickering off the handcuffs as they led my brother away from us.

"I didn't mean to hurt you, Lexi," he said, but I barely heard him. I was too busy staring at the blood he hadn't been able to clean out from beneath his fingernails.

PART TWO

Chapter Nineteen

Juvenile offenders get a lot of breaks. The system doesn't seem to want to lock someone up for life if it can be avoided. So now, at twenty-one, Scott's up for evaluation. Of course, he'll still be in some kind of correctional program, but my parents said what comes now is about rehabilitation.

They want to rehabilitate him. To make him whole again.

They can't make little Lucy and Miles whole again. They can't rehabilitate Mrs. Cabot.

I don't want to go there . . . to where they keep him. I don't want to answer questions about Scott's potential. I don't know his potential. I haven't seen him since they took him away, apologizing to me while I stared at his bloody clothes on our table and tried to make it not true.

I wasn't even thirteen yet when it happened. After,

someone left a dead squirrel in our mailbox with a note say-ing I was next. Kids at school called me psycho and joked that everyone should stay out of my way because I'd stab them. Even the ladies in the cafeteria looked nervous when I'd take a plastic knife for lunch, despite the fact that the pizza was like stone and I couldn't kill anyone with the flimsy utensil anyway. I was excused against my will from history class when the teacher covered anything violent. The school told my parents I needed to be removed from triggers, but what they really meant was that they were afraid I'd start stabbing people, too.

I haven't gone to see him. I haven't said his name to anyone besides Heath and my family since it happened. Yet now I have to talk about him to a panel of strangers who will decide his fate. No panel was assembled to discuss my future. No one called in character witnesses to decide what options existed for me.

I don't know if I can do it. I don't know if I can see him. The reason I haven't is that I know as soon as I look at him, I'll remember. I'll remember Scott from before. I'll remember him teaching me how to play chess. The way he showed me how to store my comics. His laughter when we'd all gather in the den for a movie. I'll remember how he always looked behind himself to make sure I was okay when we were on our bikes.

They want me to tell them he can be fixed, that he's not evil, but I don't know if that's true. Still, even if I'm not sure, how do you condemn your own brother? How do you deny your best friend for two-thirds of your life a chance?

"I'm going for a walk," I tell my aunt. I slept until nearly two in the afternoon, but I need to get out of the apartment. Out of my head. I stayed in the dirt by the playground last night until it was almost morning, trying to decide what I could say about my brother. Wondering if my life would ever exist beyond any of this.

"Does a walk involve a certain boy you're not supposed to be spending time with?" Aunt Susie asks. She's making jam, even though we already have way too much for two people. But when she doesn't know what to do with herself, she makes jam. Everyone in my family finds a way to pretend they don't feel anything.

"It might."

She turns to look at me, the wooden spoon in her hand spilling blueberry back into the pan. "Okay, well, let's just say I've told you what you need to know, and I'm done worrying about your decisions."

"I have to go home and help them," I remind her. "I have to help with Scott. And I only have three weeks before I have to do that. I want . . . I don't know what I want. But I need this. I just need to remember what it feels like."

She nods. "I know. And you're right anyway. He's a nice kid. Dianne and Louise and the rest of them can kiss off."

I laugh despite myself. "I don't think anyone says that anymore."

"Well, they can kiss off, too. Here," she says, pouring some of the still-hot blueberry mess into a jar. "Take some jam."

I don't think Marcus or his mom needs blueberry jam, but since we certainly don't need a fourth jar, I take it from her.

Marcus's mom answers the door, and I don't know what I'm supposed to say. I haven't talked to him since I abandoned him. He didn't come to the play, although I didn't personally invite him and I don't know if he finds out about school events in the back of the building.

Standing in front of his apartment and holding out

blueberry jam to his mother, I realize I don't really know anything.

"I . . . well . . ."

I hand her the jam.

She takes it and looks it over. "Tell your aunt I said thank you. Marcus is in his room."

"Oh." I stand there in the doorway, uncomfortable about surprising him in his room, and his mom nods, coughing. She walks down the little hallway and knocks on his door.

"Marcus, Susie Lawlor's niece is here."

The door opens and Marcus peers through the crack, those damn eyes meeting mine across the entirety of the tiny apartment.

This is no way to start a relationship, I remind myself. Once he knows, he won't want to be in a relationship with me. People have a hard time empathizing with the family members of child murderers. I consider leaving, but he looks at me and shakes his head.

"Don't go running away again," he says. "What's up?"

"Do you want to go for a walk? I came to see if you wanted to walk."

"Yeah. Sure. I'll be right out. Gotta grab my walking shoes."

He closes the door and leaves me in the hall with his mom, who looks exhausted from walking the few feet to his room. Breathing heavily, she leans on the table by the front door and places the jam down beside a dead plant.

"Can I get you something to drink?" she asks.

"No, I'm good. Why don't you sit down? I'll put the jam in the fridge for you."

"I'll be okay. Just wasn't expecting company. I'm sorry for the mess." She heads to the kitchen, and I watch her put the jam away, functioning in slow motion.

"Hey," Marcus says as he comes out of his room in a black T-shirt and jeans, carrying his hoodie. He's wearing combat boots, which aren't exactly walking shoes, but they're pretty sexy, so I'll take it.

"Hey."

"She brought jam," his mom says, sitting at the kitchen table and putting her head down.

"Yeah?"

"Blueberry. My aunt made too much."

He grabs his keys from the front table with the plant and leads me outside. I already regret being here. I can't stop staring at him, and meanwhile my head keeps yelling at me that this is all a lie.

"So, where to?" he asks. "Where did you have in mind?"

"Nowhere in particular. I just wanted to see you."

He takes my hand, running his fingers along my palm. It's not supposed to be hot, but somehow it's ridiculous. "I'm glad you came over."

"I didn't interrupt anything?" I ask.

"Nothing important. So . . . there's somewhere we can go. If you want to?"

"Sure. Like I said, I just wanted to see you."

He leads me farther into the complex and then out of it, away from the knight, whose penis is now just another thing about Castle Estates that's faded and old. We head toward the woods at the other end of the buildings. They're not exactly woods as much as they're a lump of trees that stops us from being bombarded with the sounds and lights from the gas station and McDonald's on the other side.

Marcus lets go of my hand, takes out a pack of cigarettes, and offers me one. I decline. He lights one for himself.

"I know," he says. "It's bad for me."

"Life is bad for you. For all of us."

He laughs. "I knew there was a reason I liked you."

"How's your mom?" I ask. "She seemed tired."

"Yeah, she's tired. She's always tired. I mean, she's better, I guess. The cancer has been in remission for a while now. Not that you can really tell."

"Oh. I'm so sorry. I didn't realize—"

He puts his arm around my shoulder and pulls me toward him as we walk, him smoking with one hand and holding me with the other. I like how he smells like a mix of cigarettes, bad cologne, and lemons. It doesn't make sense, but I think that's what I like most about it.

"Yeah, I mean, what else, right?" he asks. "Seriously. Fuck cancer. But it's gone. Or whatever remission is. But cancer is only part of it, I guess."

"There's something else?"

He sighs, his warm breath brushing against my neck as we walk. "She hasn't been the same since my dad left. So the cancer was kind of the first thing, and then she just . . ." He pauses, smoking, looking back toward where his apartment is, although we can't actually see it anymore. "I think she kind of wishes she still had it. Or, really, that it killed her."

Right after everything happened with Scott—when I went back to school and the kids ridiculed me and I saw the way they assumed things of me—right after all that and the dead squirrel and the constant news coverage, I started playing with knives myself. I never understood the way Scott had hurt someone else. Instead I found the knives and anything else that would cut deep enough, and I started keeping a record on my skin of the things people called me. That was when my parents sent me to Heath.

I remember one of the first things Heath asked me was if I wanted to die. I just looked at him and asked him why he thought that. I thought it was irrational. Because I never wanted to die. I just wanted to be someone else.

"Maybe she just wishes things were different," I tell Marcus.

"Don't we all."

After he finishes his cigarette, he pulls out a pack of gum, takes a piece, and then offers me one. I accept this time. Spearmint sparkles inside my mouth, filling the small bursts of cold in the air with minty reminders.

We walk for a while, into the woods and then out of them, along the road by the gas station and the McDonald's and past all the warehouses and old stores that aren't stores anymore because no one goes to an appliance shop when they can get everything at a chain store. Finally we come to an old bowling alley, the ball and pins still visible in faded colors on the front of the building.

Marcus walks over to a truck in the back corner of the parking lot, the tires and rims missing on the left side of the vehicle. He opens the door and rummages through the glove compartment. When he comes back, he goes to the door of the building and opens it with, apparently, the key.

"Should I ask?" I of course ask.

"This kid in my class, Tyler. His dad owns the place. I don't know the whole story, but he refuses to sell it, even though they can't afford to reopen it. Not that anyone cares about bowling anyway."

"The school I went to last year—in Maine—people were all into roller-skating. It was fucking weird."

"People are weird. But I don't know. I guess people aren't excited about this, and Tyler's dad is, like, attached to it, so he just lets Tyler and anyone he tells about the key chill here."

We head in, but Tyler's dad hasn't bothered paying the

electric bill for an empty building, so we have to navigate with Marcus's phone. It's still light outside, but the late-afternoon sun only reaches so far into the dark bowling alley, especially given the grime and age on the doors.

"I realize how this looks," he says, "but I swear, I'm not some kind of serial killer."

Flashes of bloody clothes on a table. Bodies being taken from the house next door. My mom crying. Jenny Adams telling me I should be dead, too, because Mrs. Cabot was her Girl Scout troop leader, and now they couldn't go to camp this spring.

I sink to the floor by the shoe-rental desk, crying, shaking, my legs unable to do anything but melt underneath me. I hear Marcus saying my name, asking if I'm okay. I feel the glare from his phone on my face, see his own shadowed face behind it. I sense him holding me and keeping me steady, but it's all happening somewhere else. To someone else. Although I try to find my way back to now, there's no now anymore. There's never a now. There's always only what was and what will be, because now is just waiting for this to happen. Every minute of the present is a lie. A breath between memories.

"I'm sorry," I say, or at least I think it's me, because the words are in my voice. I can't even tell him why. What I'm sorry about. All I can muster are two words that tell him nothing.

"You don't need to be sorry. Just breathe," he says, sitting beside me.

And so I do. I breathe, and Marcus holds me, and I swim through the past to find an anchor here in this dark place. I try to remember how I felt only yesterday and only a little while ago.

I hate this. I hate my mind and I hate being crazy. I hate that I went to Marcus's apartment determined to find a reprieve from everything, but it didn't matter, because now here I am in sawdust, little pieces of it clinging to my corduroys. I hate him seeing this part of me. I hate revealing to Marcus how easy it is for me to drown.

I don't know how long we sit on the floor in silence. The whole time he doesn't move. He's steady. Solid. And I keep fighting for the surface. Every time, when I think I've almost reached it—almost reached him—there's something on the other side. It's Scott or Mrs. Cabot or Mr. Cabot on the news or the reporters or all the kids at school or the principal strongly suggesting to my parents they find a new place for me to go because I'm a distraction to the other students.

But every time I sink back down, I can see Marcus there behind the other faces. And once I fight through each and every one of the flashes from the past, he's still there, lifting me out of it.

"I'm sorry," I say again, when I finally force myself back into now. I don't know how long it will last, but eventually I'm here. On the floor. With a boy from across the street, in a bowling alley everyone forgot about.

"Why?" he asks.

I shake my head, staring into the darkness ahead of us. I push my back against the hard desk behind me, trying to remind myself of what's real.

He continues to hold me, and I continue to breathe.

"Can I tell you a story?" he asks after a while, once my breathing is back to normal and I've stopped shaking a little.

I nod because I don't trust words anymore.

"My dad was really into old movies. You know that—I know—but that's not the story. The thing is, I didn't really like them. When I was a kid, I thought they sucked. We'd watch them together all the time. They were boring then. Who wants to watch a bunch of old people in a black-and-white movie talking about things that don't even exist anymore?"

I just nod again.

"And then he left. I was fourteen. And I was so fucking angry. He was supposed to be there. My mom was sick, and she started disappearing, and suddenly I'm fourteen and I have no one." He pauses. "The worst, though? He left them. He left these movies that I didn't even like. That's it. That's what I had. I'm fourteen, my dad's gone, my mom's dying, and all there is is a box of shitty movies I don't even like. He left me nothing except this giant fucking box of DVDs I didn't even want."

He lights another cigarette and continues. "And a note. He left a note. Do you know what it said?"

"No," I say, reaching out and taking his cigarette from him. I must have swallowed my gum at some point, but I taste the memory of mint on the cigarette as I inhale. I hand it back, and Marcus keeps going with his story.

"It said, 'I'm sorry. But someday, maybe these will help.'" We sit in silence for a minute while he remembers. "Help what? What were they supposed to help? How the fuck are old DVDs gonna help a kid whose dad disappears in the middle of the fucking night while the woman he supposedly loved until death did them part was puking in the bathroom? I didn't even like those stupid fucking movies."

"He left while she was sick?" I ask.

"He left *because* she was sick. He couldn't take it. Seriously, what kind of person does that?"

"I don't know," I say. "I don't know why people do a lot of things."

"No kidding, right? But that was it. My mom kept fighting this fucking disease. And I had no idea if she would survive, but I had to hope she would. I had to think about it all day. Every day. I needed her to stay alive because I couldn't live with nothing but a box of goddamn DVDs if she didn't. So she fought it and she beat cancer, which is a huge fucking deal. I thought that would be the end of it, but then she realized she was alive and she had nothing worth living for anymore. She had me, but it wasn't the same, and between the two of us, we had nothing but memories and a box of DVDs. Because it was hard on him."

I slip down the wood of the desk until I'm lying on the floor. Marcus joins me, and we wait in the darkness, each of us caught up in the past and our anger. Our disappointment.

"Now," he says, his voice coming through the blackness. It's the only sign he's real, besides the little ember of his cigarette. "Now my mom doesn't leave the house. She's depressed, they said. The doctors all said depression is sometimes a symptom of cancer. But they're wrong. It's not a symptom of cancer. Depression is a symptom of people being assholes."

"I'm sorry," I tell him.

"You didn't do it."

I think of going home in three weeks. Of what happens next. Even if Scott is moved somewhere where he'll be forgotten, there's still a chance everyone here will find out at some point. And if they do? If it all ends up the same way it always does? What if I come back after Thanksgiving and somehow they know, and suddenly Westbrook High is the same as everywhere else?

Eventually I'm going to have to go back to the real version of me. Leaving Marcus with his DVDs. Leaving him alone again with nothing but old movies to explain it all, and I can't even tell him why.

He leans over and looks at me, dropping his phone by his side. A beam of light shoots up to the ceiling while we're both wrapped in shadow. I try not to look at him, but I can't help it, and my brain can't stop thinking. I can't stop wanting to tell him, but also wanting to pretend it's not true. I want to be the girl he's looking at this way, not the girl I am.

"Am I an asshole if I kiss you?" he asks, his hand brushing my hair away from my face.

I should say yes. I should give him a reason not to, but I don't. Instead I shake my head and lift myself up onto my elbows, closing the space between us. I ignore the screaming in my head. I ignore images of Marcus alone with his movies, reading in the news or online about me and Scott and all the lies I told.

When Ben kissed me last year, it was just a kiss. It felt like another item on a checklist of growing up. Things people do but that no one really knows *why* they do. There were none of those sparkles people talk about in movies. I wasn't swept away in it. I didn't even want to kiss him a second time.

When Marcus kisses me, though, it hurts. Not in a bad way. It's painful because as we come together, I want so much more than I've ever let myself want. I want to tell him everything. I want to throw away all the lies and hiding and memories that broke me into so many pieces. I want to be here with him, and I want to stop thinking that this can't last. I want to turn my mind off but I can't, so it hurts because I'm caught between wanting to keep kissing him and wanting to stop because I can't miss this. Three weeks or two months from now or this spring, when I've gone back home and finished high school in my parents' living room because I couldn't stop myself from running away, I can't remember this.

I totally understand that monologue now.

Nothing hurts more beautifully than this.

Chapter Twenty

Marcus and I don't end up exploring much of the bowling alley. We spend most of the day by the shoe-rental desk, lying in the sawdust, kissing. A part of me wonders if I should feel guilty. About Ryan. About Scott. About everything I am.

I should tell him. I know I should. Every time he kisses me, I remind myself that I have to tell him. Before someone else does. I hear these things in my brain, and then I kiss him again because I'm somehow incapable of listening to my own mind.

"We should head back," he says eventually, although he doesn't move.

"I don't want to."

"I know . . . but . . ."

"But?"

He laughs. "I don't know. I can't think of even one legitimate reason to ever leave."

I kiss him yet again, and more time passes. More reminders are ignored. More memories are pushed aside while day turns to evening and evening slips into night. We continue lying on the floor until the darkness outside makes it impossible for us to see anything at all. Hours later we're surrounded by nothing but night. Marcus's phone turned off hours ago.

"You want to come over?" he asks. "We should probably go, but I don't really want to be alone. We can watch a movie or something."

"Something?"

"Hey, I'm serious. We can just watch a movie. There doesn't have to be something. I mean, unless you want there to be something."

I don't have a lot of experience with *something*. I know if we stay here, though, I'm going to forget about Scott and rules and time, and Marcus will be lying on top of me, and something is far more likely to happen. We should go back to his apartment and watch a movie. Or I should go home and ask my aunt if there's a good convent she recommends.

"Yeah, we can go," I say, sitting up and fixing my shirt, which has somehow been turned backward. "We can watch a movie."

Of course, we don't go. We sit up and he fumbles for his phone, but neither of us moves from the same shoe-rental desk.

"I had to leave," I tell him. "My parents didn't make me come here. They've never made me go anywhere. I told you I run away, and I do. Because I had to. I couldn't handle it anymore."

I don't look at him. Even though I can't see him in the darkness, I feel like he can see me. My shame burns bright enough to fill the space.

"Do you want to tell me why?" he asks.

"Not really."

"You don't have to tell me, then. Just tell me when you're ready. It won't change anything. I promise."

"Can I have a cigarette?" He hands me one and I light it, but I don't smoke. I don't like the taste of it, but I want something to hold me here. Something to focus on while I dive down into these things I don't want anyone to know.

"I'm not . . ." How do you tell someone that you're a liar? That the person they've spent an entire day with is just a story?

"You don't have to tell me," he repeats.

I watch the cigarette burn. I watch the red glow travel closer to my fingers until eventually I have to stub it out on the ground to protect myself from being burned.

I've only said the words to Heath. After all this time, I've never said the words aloud except in therapy. I can't even say Scott's name, but I need to tell Marcus. I need him to know. I can't keep sitting here, or in his apartment, kissing him and pretending I'm someone I'm not. It's not fair to him, even though I know it will ruin this.

"I told you I had a brother," I say.

"Yeah," he says, the wariness in his voice digging its way into my skull.

"Well, I still have a brother. I just don't see him because . . . I can't be near my family. I keep running away because my brother . . ."

"It's okay, Lexi."

I shake my head. "No. It's really not. My brother . . . he killed someone. He killed three people, actually."

"Jesus."

I'm surprised I can say it. I'm surprised the words feel

so easy. I try not to think too much about it, and I continue. "It's . . . It wasn't an accident. He's a murderer."

"Wow. But, I mean, you didn't have anything to do with it, right?"

"No. I mean, not really. He was supposed to come get me. I was at school. I had to walk home and he wasn't there. I didn't do it, but maybe . . . but no. He did it by himself."

I see it all again, and I try to find Marcus's eyes in the darkness. Try not to end up back in that fall afternoon. Try not to hear the sirens. See the blood everywhere.

"He murdered our neighbor and her kids," I say, the words scratching my throat as they leave. As they fill the universe with their awfulness. "Stabbed them. When he was fifteen. The kids . . . they were little. Just little kids. We didn't even know them. They were just the people next door."

I pull my knees up to my body and tuck my head into my legs. "It was years ago. I was only twelve and it's been a while, but I just keep running away. Because I can't . . . Nobody here knows yet. I shouldn't have told you. I just didn't want you to find out from someone else."

"I'm sorry," he says. "Holy shit, I'm so sorry." But instead of leaving me here, like he should, he moves closer and holds me, wrapping himself around the ball I've turned myself into. I don't deserve it. I don't deserve to be touched.

"Everyone said it was something in him. They said that I had it, too. I couldn't go anywhere. The way they all looked at me." I pull myself tighter into a ball. "I'm diseased. I'm rotten, Marcus. I'm wrong, just like he was, and I've always been wrong. I should never have let you kiss me. I should never have let you believe me."

"That's bullshit," he says, clutching my hand. "It's messed up. It's horrible, but horrible things happen. These things might be a part of you, but they don't define you. You aren't accountable for someone else's actions. You're still you, Lexi. You're not your brother."

I shake my head. "They were right, though. Because I couldn't see it, you know. They said all these things. They called him a psycho. They said I was just like him, but you don't get it. I wanted to be just like him." I pause. "Well, not just like him, because I didn't want to hurt someone. But he was . . . he was everything I thought was good. I loved him. I still love him. Or part of him. The part I knew."

Marcus is quiet, and I imagine what he's thinking. I bet he's wondering how he chose so poorly. Why he spent the afternoon making out with a girl who has this poison inside her.

"Scott. His name's Scott," I say. "I'm sorry I didn't tell you. I'm sorry I lied. I'm sorry this is who I am."

"No," he says, pulling me tighter against him. "Don't tell me you're sorry, Lexi."

"But I am."

"No. I mean it. That's not who you are." He kisses me, and he tastes like my tears. "You're a separate person from Scott, no matter how much he's hurt you."

"No one has ever believed that before," I say.

"Well, I do."

"But it doesn't matter, does it? If I still love him? If I still see him as the big brother I admired? Something must be wrong with me, Marcus. Something has to be, if I can't see him for everything he is. If I can somehow find a way to care for him still."

"I told you about my dad," he says. "How he left because it was hard. Because he couldn't stand it. My father left my dying mom and me because he was annoyed that she kept him up all night. He was sick of her being sick. He thought cancer was annoying. He left me with nothing but a box of DVDs. That was all he could give me of himself, because he was too inconvenienced by my mom dying. But, shit, Lexi. He's my dad. I don't hear from him at all anymore, but if he came back . . . I still dream every night that he'll come back."

"What do you mean?"

"I love my father. No matter what kind of person he is. He's shit, but I love him." He picks up his phone and tries to get the flashlight working, but the battery is dead. "I don't think you're rotten. I don't think you're screwed up because you love your brother. Honestly? I'd find it harder to under-stand if you didn't."

"But after what he did . . ."

"Yeah, well, that's what sucks about letting people into your life, doesn't it?" Marcus says. "Once they're there, they're there, and you're fucked. You're fucked because you're dying inside every single day while they just go on being shitty people and you can't stop loving them anyway."

I can't believe he's not running away. I've carried five years of secrets. Five years of hurt. And I shouldn't have told him, but I did, and he's still here. He's here with all his own hurt, and the past is the past. But for the first time, I wonder if maybe that's not all there is. If maybe there's still the pos-sibility of a now. Not Lexi Lawlor and her fake world where the past isn't real, but a true and honest now where the past just is and maybe it's okay that it is.

"I haven't seen him since," I say. "No one expected me to visit him. No one thought I needed to talk to him. But sometimes I wish they had. I wish they'd pushed me harder. Made me see him. I wish they hadn't made it so easy to pre-tend it wasn't real."

"Where is he now?"

"Out by Boston. He'll be twenty-one soon. I have to go and talk to someone. Well, I don't *have* to, but I said I would. I have to go there and tell them about Scott. What I know about him. The thing is, I don't know what they want. I mean, I guess they want me to tell them if I think there's hope for him."

"They're not seriously letting him out?"

"No. Of course not. Nothing like that. But they're trying to decide if he's . . . well, I guess there are people they invest in. Like, try to fix. Try to hope that maybe they can do something. Someday. That maybe they don't need to die in there, never becoming something else. I guess they want to know if there's something left inside him. And they want my opinion on that."

"That's a lot. What are you planning to say?"

"I don't know. It is a lot. You're right. It's everything, right? I mean, I'm not solely responsible or anything, but they want to talk to people who know him. The thing is . . . I don't. How am I supposed to tell them what he has left? I don't know my brother anymore. I sometimes wonder if I ever did."

I try to sob quietly, but in the silence of the empty space, every breath echoes.

"Hey, let's head back," Marcus says, and he helps me to my feet.

We leave the bowling alley behind, tucking the key back into the abandoned truck before we go. It's not much for security, but I guess this isn't a place that needs it. They can't convince anyone to come here.

Outside it's almost winter. It just gets colder and colder with the minutes ticking down a day.

It's always amazing to me. I sometimes wish my parents

had sent me outside the Northeast to run away. There was Virginia, but they had fall and winter, too. I'd love to experience the world in a place where the seasons don't change much. Where they don't remind you repeatedly of how little in your life is permanent. It was cold last week, but it was still fall. Now there's frost forming on the grass, and the wind cuts deep into us as we walk.

Nothing lasts.

I try not to think about it as I walk with Marcus, holding his hand. I try to hope some things survive. I try to believe that maybe some people are stronger than winter.

Chapter Twenty-One

It's quiet in Marcus's room. We lie on his bed, wrapped in a blanket he dug out of his closet. I'm warm against him, and it seems like winter and the cold night and the stories we shared in the bowling alley might stay outside forever. Until he speaks.

"I heard a rumor about you," he says.

I hate those words. They're the sound of my life unfolding again.

"Did you?"

"Nothing bad. I just heard you were with some guy from the drama club."

I think of Ryan. Of his kindness and his secrets. I can't tell Marcus about him, but I don't know if I should feel guilty. If I'm lying to either of them or both of them. While it's not real with Ryan, if Marcus has heard about him, what's to stop this from getting back to Ryan? And what does that mean for his normal?

"It's . . . it's not really my place to say what that's about," I say. "But it's complicated. Not in a way that interferes with us. We're . . . It's not at all . . . It's not this."

Marcus nods, his face tickling mine. "But you're not? I mean, I don't need to worry?"

"No. You don't have to worry. I am, but I'm not, and it's complicated. I can . . . I'm not . . ."

"Honestly, it doesn't matter. I don't need to know. You're here. You're not with some guy from the drama club tonight, and I'm just gonna assume there's something in that."

"There's definitely something in this. This is more than what you've heard about me. But if you can keep that between us . . ."

"Yeah, I really don't care what anyone at school says. I'm not worried about who thinks what, or what the story people believe is. I just wanted to know. As long as I know," he says. "But since maybe I wasn't clear or maybe I hadn't asked the right way . . . I'd kind of like . . . well, I'd be happier if you weren't involved with some guy from the drama club. For purely selfish reasons."

I roll over so I'm almost on top of him. "It's just a story. It's a story, and it's only partly mine to tell, or I'd tell you everything. But it's nothing but a story. And you're . . . this . . ."

"You don't have to say it. As long as we're both clear."

"We're clear," I say, kissing him and then settling back into the space between his arm and his body. "I've only had one boyfriend. Real boyfriend, anyway. I guess I kind of have a fake boyfriend right now, but there's only been one guy I've kind of liked before."

"What happened?" Marcus asks.

"We had a glorious two weeks. Until someone found out about my brother, and he couldn't deal with it."

"I'm sorry."

"No, it's okay. It wasn't real anyway. You know, I worried about that with you. I wanted to tell you, because I wanted it to be real. If there was anything, I didn't want it to be just a story with you."

"I'm happy you're here," he says. "That's the only story I need to be true."

Still wrapped in the blanket, we stare at his ceiling. The wind shakes the windows, and the chill hints at the edges of the blanket, but we just push closer together.

It's weird how someone can take up space beside you and it feels like that space was always empty before. How the space was just waiting. I never felt this kind of emptiness before, because I never knew what it was like for the space to be full. I'm scared of tonight, but he knows my truth now. And he's still here.

"Listen, Lexi Lawlor—" Marcus starts.

"Stewart," I say.

"What?"

"It's Lexi Stewart. Lawlor is my aunt's name. My mom's maiden name. My real name is Lexi Stewart."

A name. Just letters assigned to you at birth. But in speaking it, I feel five years of myself shatter. I feel everything else start to fade.

Letting someone into your life is hard, but you don't let many people into the all of you. I never have—no one besides my family and the therapist we paid to listen to my secrets, because I needed to get them out of me. But in saying something as simple as a name, I realize what I've done. I've opened myself to Marcus in a way you can't take back.

"Okay, Lexi Stewart," he says. "I'm going to tell you something I shouldn't tell you now."

"Should I be worried?"

"I don't know."

But he doesn't tell me. He doesn't say anything. He merely lifts himself up and kisses me, and then the blanket lands on the floor and we're tangled in his sheets.

It makes sense what happens next. The physical act of being with someone—especially the first time—is supposed to be a defining moment. You're supposed to plan it and think about it endlessly, but I haven't. Not really. And when it happens, it's not something I feel needed to be planned. For me, it's a natural step.

Marcus knows my name. He has something of me no one else has except the few people who should. My family. Heath. But Marcus is the first person I chose to bring into my story. So the rest just makes sense.

"Are you sure?" he asks, right before it happens.

I nod. "Yes."

It's about so much more than sex, though. Sure, that's a part of it, but it's also security. Being with him is what it's like to love someone. It's forgiveness. This is me realizing who I am. There's no running away from here anymore. I can't hide in another girl's life now. Marcus Cotero knows everything I am. And even though there are still a million pieces we don't have to the puzzle of each other, it's too late to go back.

After, I press myself against his skin, leaning over and bringing the blanket back onto the bed. I pull it tight against us, although I don't need the warmth of it anymore.

"Alexia Stewart," Marcus says, his eyes closed, "you're beautiful, you know."

"You don't need to flatter me anymore," I tease. "Besides, you're not even looking at me."

"I don't need to."

I always told myself not to fall in love, because the universe wouldn't let me have that. But as I start to fall asleep beside Marcus, I promise myself this will be different.

I decide, before I fade into sleep, that I will forgive the universe after all. Maybe it wasn't trying to hurt me. Maybe it only wanted me to remember. Maybe it just wanted to remind me who I am.

Chapter Twenty-Two

Fake-breaking up with a person you're fake-dating feels way more complex than it should. I told myself it was the right thing to do, but once I get on the bus and I see Ryan, I feel sick. He sits beside me and holds my hand, and I'm grateful Marcus gets a ride. He knows, but knowing something theoretically is different from seeing it and wondering how complicated it really is.

"Are you okay?" Ryan asks. "I've been worried about you all weekend. I thought about coming to see you yesterday to see how you were. What's up with your mom?"

"Nothing. I mean, it's not important. I'm okay." I try not to feel guilty. *He's not really your boyfriend. You didn't do anything wrong,* my brain reminds me in a rare instance of not hating me.

"Well, I'm glad. I really was thinking about you."

I certainly wasn't thinking about him last night when I was lying in Marcus's bed.

"Do you have time to talk later?" I ask.

"What? You don't want to talk about it here?"

As if to demonstrate the point, Eric pushes Ryan further into the seat so he's nearly sitting on top of me. "Hey, listen, I was thinking," Eric says. "It's almost Thanksgiving, and you know what that means, right?"

"No. Unless you're suddenly a huge fan of turkey dinners," Ryan says.

"I'm always a fan of any dinner. It's like you don't even know me, man."

"So you came over here to tell us about a meal that happens every year?"

"No. I mean, it's almost Thanksgiving, which means it's almost Christmas. And Christmas brings shopping. In particular, it brings massively overpriced electronics at almost reasonable prices."

"Do you have a point?"

"It's the first year I've been able to drive for such things. We need to go. Just think of the shit we can buy."

"You have a car and a license. We're still broke as fuck."

Eric looks at me. "You in on this?"

I shrug. I don't want to tell them what I'm really doing for Thanksgiving weekend, but Eric isn't listening anyway. "I'm broker than the both of you. I don't even have a car or a license."

"We're going," Eric tells Ryan, and then he leaves with absolutely nothing accomplished by the conversation.

"So you were saying you wanted to talk?" Ryan asks.

"We're starting something new in calculus. What about second period? Auditorium?"

"Shouldn't you maybe go for the first day of something new in calculus?"

"New things mean two weeks of the teacher realizing how hopeless we all are. I won't miss anything."

"Okay, yeah. Second period. I'll meet you on the stage?"

I nod but don't get to say much else, because the bus arrives at school and we're suddenly caught up in the same group of people we spend every morning with—Eric, Lauren, Chloe, and Rory. The show's over, but we're on to the next play and planning the breakdown of the set, and everyone just moves forward. No one asks why I missed the party.

I spend all of first period trying to figure out how to tell Ryan. *What* to tell Ryan. I haven't told Marcus anything about Ryan, but do I tell Ryan about Marcus? And what loyalty am I supposed to have to my fake boyfriend or my sort-of boyfriend I slept with but haven't officially decided is a boyfriend?

"You're quiet," Lauren says toward the end of class. "Sorry you couldn't go to Rory's on Saturday. It was pretty ridiculous."

"I'm glad it was fun. I just had shit to deal with at home."

She shrugs. "There will be another party. Is everything okay?"

I look over at her. I don't know her well enough to tell her anything, but maybe she has some insight into my mess. "Have you ever been in the middle of something that doesn't make a whole lot of sense, but you feel like it's probably bad for everyone?"

"That's a bit vague."

"Okay, let's say . . . let's say there are a couple of people you care about. And you care about them in different ways. But everyone *thinks* you care about one person a way you don't, because you care about someone else that way. But you don't want to hurt the first person by making them feel bad. . . ."

Lauren pulls her desk closer to mine. "There's another guy?"

I sigh. "It's complicated." If I don't wear a sticker that says HELLO, MY NAME IS SORRY, I can definitely get one that says HELLO, MY NAME IS IT'S COMPLICATED.

"Does Ryan know?" she asks. I shake my head. "But you want to tell him, except you're afraid of hurting him, because you do like him. Just not as much as Pablo or whatever."

"Pablo?"

"I don't know. It sounded random. And better than Guy Two."

"I like him differently than I like Pablo."

"Does Pablo know about Ryan?"

"He does. Well, sort of."

"It really *is* complicated."

I put my head on my desk, which prompts our teacher, who has not paid attention to us for the last ten minutes, to yell at me.

"I hate everything," I tell Lauren.

"Well, Ryan's a good guy. He'll understand. Just tell him. It's not very nice to keep secrets from people you care about."

I ignore my teacher's yelling and keep my head down until the bell rings. I'm tempted to go home sick, but I don't think being called out for keeping secrets counts as a legitimate illness.

Ryan and I don't talk during our walk from the guidance office to the auditorium. I run through hypothetical conversations in my mind, all of which end in a lot of crying and everyone hating me. I don't know what Ryan does. He walks next to me. Maybe he's thinking of his own fears, or maybe he's just thinking about lunch.

"What's up?" he asks when we're finally inside the auditorium. "You sounded worried."

I turn on the light that we used for the balcony scene in the play and lean against the back stage wall. "I'm always worried. That's my sound."

Ryan laughs. "Okay, fine. But you sounded maybe specifically worried? Is that a thing?"

"I don't know," I say, picking at splinters of wood on a piece of a set. It's a random piece that doesn't belong to anything we still have, but I guess you can always use spare plywood.

Ryan sits on the floral couch from our first day back here and puts his feet on a gold coffee table. I imagine a person trying to make a home from all this furniture, decades and aesthetics mixing until there's so little left of real life that everything becomes spectacle.

"It's about us," I tell him.

"We're an us? I thought—"

"Fine. Fake us. It's about fake us." I sink to the floor and pull my legs into my body. "I just can't do it anymore."

Ryan nods and gets up, grabbing a can of soda before returning to the couch. "I see. After our whirlwind week together, you have finally decided it's too much and that you must instead run away with your lover?"

I think of Marcus's skin, warm against me under his blanket.

"I'm really sorry," I say, guilt pulling at my brain.

"Why? We weren't really a couple."

"I know, but I promised. I was supposed to be your normal, and I went and screwed it all up. I wish . . ."

He moves over to where I am and hands me his unopened soda. "L, I really don't care. Unless we can't be friends anymore. Then I care. Is your secret lover the jealous type?"

"Marcus," I say, taking the soda. I don't open it, but I pick at the pull tab, letting the sound of it hitting the top of the can echo across the empty stage. "You're right. There's another guy, and his name's Marcus. He's on our bus. Except, well, he doesn't take the bus."

"Ah, I see, then. So you really have left me for a much more interesting man. One who doesn't require transportation via large orange vehicles."

"It's not . . . I'm sorry, Ryan."

"I'm fucking with you, L. I'm totally on board with you and Marcus. He's the brooding one, right? Always sits in the back when he does take the bus?"

"Yeah. I mean, he's not brooding all the time."

"Girls always go for the brooding guy. It's inevitable."

I sigh and rest my head on my knees. "What happens to you, though? I can keep lying to everyone. Marcus knows—"

"Wait, you told him about me?" His smile disappears, and I recognize that instant fear that turns your entire body cold.

"No, just that we were kind of together, but not really. He'd heard I had a boyfriend before we . . . I wanted him to know I didn't have a boyfriend."

Ryan exhales, the sound of it louder than the echo of the aluminum pull tab against the can. "I don't want anyone else to know about me. As long as you promise not to tell anyone, we're good."

"That's your story. I don't have that right."

"Well then, you don't need to keep lying about us. People break up. I suppose I can fake some sporadic jealousy of Marcus?"

"Are you sure, though? I can keep pretending. I lasted a week. I'm so sorry. I don't want you—"

He rubs my knee, like you would with a sibling. It hurts when I realize how much he reminds me of Scott.

"How do we tell people?" I ask, looking down, hurting from the memory of my brother and everything he'll never be.

"I guess we just have to do it officially somehow?"

"Is there a form we fill out? Maybe a notary that's needed?"

"From what I've gathered, I'm pretty sure it requires the sacrifice of your firstborn or something."

"Probably," I say.

He adjusts until he's sitting beside me, and then he wraps his arm around my shoulders, pulling me into him. "Are you really okay, though?" he asks. "Do you want to talk about what happened Saturday?"

"No, it's nothing."

"Are you sure? We were all worried."

"Were you?"

He nods. "Of course. You're our friend."

I wonder how true that is. How much they really worried. I can't imagine they sat around Rory's cast party talking about me. Wondering what happened to me. Maybe Ryan did. Maybe even Rory or Lauren asked. But I feel like most people didn't care. Or if they did, I have a feeling it wasn't pure concern that drove them.

"I'm fine," I say, because it's not Ryan's fault that people are people. "Are you sure we're okay, though?"

"Yeah, we're okay. Still friends?"

"Always."

The bell rings, forcing us to leave. It's anticlimactic, but I guess there's no real drama associated with a fake breakup.

I still feel like something's missing between us, though, which bugs me. It bothers me all day—in the rest of my classes, at lunch, and at drama after school when we start breaking down the set as we brainstorm show ideas for winter. I know it's partly because Ryan's friends with someone else—a girl who's only a part of me, but there's more than that. When people come up and talk to me or when I hear them comforting Ryan about our breakup, I wonder if there's a place for Lexi Stewart in this group. I wonder if the only reason I belong is because this version of me is someone they can like. I can't help wondering if the place I have is so tenuous that it would explode if the real me touched it.

"Lexi Lawlor, you're a heartbreaker," Eric yells across the auditorium. "My buddy's wasting away from the pain. He can't even think about dinner right now."

"That's because he already ate the rest of the concessions," Lauren yells back. She turns to me. "Don't worry—I get it. Ryan will be okay. You did the right thing."

"Ignore him," Ryan yells, and I kind of wish we could continue discussing my relationships in closer proximity, rather than shouting about them for the entire drama club to hear. "I told him we're friends. Right, L?"

I nod and Eric looks at me, shaking his head. Rueful? I don't think that's an accurate description of Eric, but I think it's probably a good summation of my existence.

___

Chapter Twenty-Three

When I get home from drama, I go to Marcus's apartment first.

"Hey," I say when he opens the door. "I broke up with the guy I wasn't dating."

"There's a story."

"No kidding."

He stands awkwardly in the doorframe, his hands in his pockets, and moves from side to side. "So . . ."

"So . . ."

"Does that mean you're on the market?" he asks.

"Ew. You make me sound like a sandwich."

Marcus shrugs. "I like sandwiches."

"Do you want to come over?"

"Are you asking as a friend or as a girlfriend?"

"Does it matter?"

"Nah. I'm just trying to ask you out, and I suck at it."

He grabs a coat and his keys, taking my hand once we're outside, and then he awkwardly kisses me. He misses my lips by half an inch, but it's kind of cute in how nonsensical it is. I slept with him yesterday, and here we are, trying to figure out what words to use to define ourselves and forgetting how to kiss.

"Do you think this is always going to be weird?" he asks as we make our way to my apartment.

"Well, given my vast lifetime of experience, I'd say . . . maybe?"

"Excellent."

Once we get to my place, I show him around the kitchen. "Make yourself a sandwich, since you're such a fan. I have to call home real quick."

My room is still a blank box, but there's some comfort in hearing Marcus rustling about in my kitchen through the tie-dyed fabric that separates us. Like it's a real place for real people.

I grab my phone and call home.

"I scheduled your visit on Friday—right after Thanksgiving," my mom says in lieu of hello.

"Okay. Heath, too?"

"First thing in the morning with Heath and then . . ." She pauses. "Are you sure you can do this, Alexia? I think it would look worse if—"

"I can do it," I say, even though I already feel sick picturing it.

"They said you can spend time with Scott before or after. Whichever you want," she continues.

I try to imagine my brother. I try to picture myself there, in that place, with him. I try to see him as someone he isn't, try to erase all the things I remember and imagine a real person—an adult now—in his place. But all I can see is a twelve-year-old boy rummaging for loose change above our fridge or a seven-year-old trying to convince me to eat dirt because it was good for me. I can only remember summer and a brother who didn't hate the world this much.

"What do you think is better?" I ask my mom.

"It's really up to you."

I wish she wouldn't ask me to decide. I wish she'd listen and hear how hard it is for me. Would consider that it hurts me to try to remember and it hurts me to process these thoughts. I know if I go, if I see Scott before I have to talk about him, if I visit with him and realize how much he's not my brother anymore, I'll never be able to say whatever it is they want me to say. But then I think about trying to talk about him when he's nothing but a memory.

"I don't know," I admit.

"How about after?" she suggests. "You'll have more time that way."

"That sounds good. And—"

"Hey, Lexi, do you have mustard?" Marcus asks from my doorway.

I cover the phone. "On the top shelf of the fridge—behind the fruit punch."

"Thanks. Sorry. I didn't realize you were already on the phone."

I uncover the phone and go back to my mom, who's buzzing to my dad about something, but I can't hear her because she's muffled.

"What time am I seeing Heath again?" I ask, to let her know I'm back.

"Who was that?"

"Who was what?"

"There was a voice," she says. "A boy. Please tell me you don't have a boy over, Alexia."

I want to laugh. To point out the absurdity of it all. But I hate that the way she says it reminds me of all the conversations we should have had. The ones we'll never have, because those are conversations normal girls get. Girls like me just have to figure it all out and hope they survive.

"We're not doing this."

"Alexia, given the troubles you've had over the years, I really don't think it's appropriate that you—"

"I told him," I say. "About Scott, I mean."

"And about you? Does he knows what happens . . . Does he know how hard it can get?"

"Some. Enough. He knows who I am. He sees me, Mom. Like, really sees me."

"You're only seventeen," she reminds me. "I'm not sure I'm comfortable with you having a boy over when your aunt's not home. Maybe I should talk to Susie about this."

I clutch my phone. "No," I say. "I'm sorry, but no. You don't get to do this to me. You don't get to pretend we're normal or that you have any say in what I do. You don't get to pretend you're responsible for me."

"That's not fair. I just don't know if you can handle that, given everything else."

"It's also not fair to pretend you know anything about what I can and can't handle." I regret it as soon as I've said it. "I've had to make my own choices for five years now, Mom."

"And how well have those choices gone for you?"

She's going to call Aunt Susie anyway. I'll have to deal with that. I'll have to try to pretend to be a typical high school senior sneaking boys into her room, as if sex is the worst thing that could happen in my life. I'll have to go home in a few weeks and listen to my parents lecture me about how I'm still just a kid, when I haven't been a kid since my brother destroyed any semblance of a childhood I had left.

I could sit here and fight with my mom in the meantime, or I could go to the kitchen and eat whatever Marcus was trying to put mustard on and worry about it later.

So I hang up and go to the kitchen.

"What're you making?" I ask. He's sitting at the table with all the condiments we own spread out in front of him.

"Sandwiches."

"What kind?"

I stand in the doorway, trying to figure out how to get from here to there. It's not just about the few yards to the table. It's about the distance between my real life and this world I've built that I want to disappear in—and about how Marcus seems to teeter right in between the two.

"I wasn't sure what you liked. So . . . all of them?" He holds up a plate with a stack of sandwiches.

"I'm not actually hungry," I tell him. "I ate before drama."

He looks at the sandwiches in his hand. "Huh. Well . . . um . . ."

I grab the box of tinfoil from the cabinet closest to the doorway and help him wrap up his efforts. We put them in the fridge before heading to my room, sans food.

Once we sit down, neither of us moves. My cot is small. It's a cot; it's not meant to hold two people, and it's certainly seen better days. We both hang on to opposite sides of it, trying to decide what the expectation is now.

It's weird how you do something and you think it's supposed to be a big deal and it isn't, but then later you realize you don't know what comes after that. Not to mention all the other things swirling through my brain.

I'm surprised my cot has room for the two of us and a lifetime of my thoughts.

"So, I don't . . . ," Marcus starts, but his voice drifts off. He looks over at me, then looks back at the floor on his side of the cot. "There was one girl. A long time ago. I was a freshman. It was at a party and . . ."

"It's okay."

"I mean, I just want you to know it's not like I do this all the time. And I don't really expect it. I don't know how yesterday happened."

"Well, you see, when a man and a woman love each other very much . . ."

He laughs. "Shut up. I was trying to be sensitive."

"It's really okay," I tell him. "You don't have to explain. It's not like it's something I do every day, either. You're only the third guy I've kissed. Or fourth, I guess, if you count my fake boyfriend."

"Scandalous," Marcus says.

"Yeah, I'm a regular Jezebel."

He looks over at me again. "So how were your parents?"

I get up and open my shades. Not because I need light, but because I need something to do. Anything but talk about my family. Anything but lose the little bit of fiction I've created here.

"Lexi?" he asks.

"Eh. They're my parents."

"Point taken." He waits for me to say more about them or to change the subject, but neither of us knows what to say.

"Can I ask you something?" I lean against my window, the way he did the first time we were at his apartment. The glass is cold on my back.

"No. Absolutely not," he says. "I am one hundred percent opposed to being asked things."

"Seriously."

"Of course." He turns himself on my cot so he's on my side of it now, his legs draped over the edge.

"Do you think it will always be like this?"

"Like what?"

"Like, we'll both be sitting here not sure what to say. I'll be wondering if there's something I still need to tell you or if it'll change things. You'll be trying to make it normal, and I'll be messing it all up—"

"You're not messing anything up," he says. "I'm the farthest thing from normal anyway, remember? They even have me in special classes to make sure everyone knows it."

I sigh and press my shoulder blades against the chill of the window. I don't have the right to Marcus. And he deserves better than my life mixed up with his.

"There's all this. Like, this big stuff, right?" I say. "And I'm thinking about it, yeah, but I'm also . . . I mean, I wonder if I'll always be wondering if it's wrong that I don't really feel like talking. That I really want to kiss you a whole lot, but that seems kind of shallow. Since we should be dealing with everything else."

"I don't know. Everything else is kind of a nightmare. Kissing you isn't a nightmare. I'm definitely okay with kissing you and letting the rest figure itself out," he says, starting to get up.

I put out a hand to stop him. "It's just . . . I feel so . . . I don't know. Both normal and not? Like, I guess it's normal to be thinking about that when you have a hot guy sitting on your bed, but I have so many other things that should matter more."

"You think I'm hot?" he asks.

"You're seriously impossible."

"I don't know how it goes, Lexi. I don't know what the rules are. But I'm honestly happy to figure them out with you. Whatever they are."

"How was it with the girl before? Was it weird?"

"We didn't really see each other after the one night," he admits. "And I didn't miss her when she wasn't around. It happened, and I didn't really think about it much after it did."

"Do you miss me when I'm not around?"

"I thought that was obvious."

He moves over on the bed again, adjusting so he's on his side but also making room for me. I join him.

I wonder if you get to a point when you can be around someone without this between you. Half of me feels like we should be talking, but the other half just wants a repeat of last night. I love the way I forgot everything except him kissing me. And then I hate myself for being so pathetic that I love that.

"Please don't think less of me for this," I say as I pull him down on top of me.

"I could never think less of you. But so you know . . . I am totally fine with just eating sandwiches or whatever. I made a huge stack of them."

"Really? You're talking sandwiches?"

"I'm just saying. We don't have to, I mean."

"Yeah, sandwiches can definitely wait," I tell him.

. . .

I don't want to make Marcus leave, but as it gets late, I'm worried about my aunt finding him in my bedroom. In my bed. With all the lights in the apartment off and our clothes in a pile by the door.

"Maybe we should move to the living room," I suggest. "My mom's already planning to call my aunt. To discuss my having a boy over."

"You really are a scandal, aren't you?"

We get dressed and turn on some lights. I grab the plate of sandwiches he made from the fridge and stick it on the coffee table. We sit in the living room with the TV on, even if we aren't paying attention to it.

"I saw your aunt a few weeks ago, actually," he says. "I said hi, but she looked away."

"She's worried about me. She doesn't think it's a good idea for me to get involved with guys. And now . . . ugh. My mom is going to make a big deal about it."

"Is it you she's worried about? Or me?"

I shrug. "It's not you. Not really. Although I don't know. I guess that makes things more complicated."

"Always complicated."

"No kidding."

"Is it . . . has your aunt told you why?" he asks.

"Why what?"

"Why she's nervous about you being around me?"

"It's not you—" I start to say.

"It is. I know. I just wonder how much she's said."

"I . . ." I pause and look at him. "She's just heard a bunch of nonsense. It doesn't matter. I'll be eighteen in the spring, and she can deal."

"What kind of nonsense do people say?"

"Nothing really. Just some gossipy women saying you're, like, a drug dealer or something."

I take a drink of water, partly because my throat is dry

but mostly because I don't want to talk about this. I don't want to tell Marcus what they've said. I hate the feeling of having to defend yourself against people, of having to hear how the world sees you, when you just want to be allowed to live in it without being told where you fit.

"I did," he says. "I don't anymore, but they're not wrong. I used to."

"Used to what?"

"After my dad left, things were tough for a while. My mom's getting help now, but we didn't have any money, and I was still too young for a job, and we needed stuff. And it wasn't hard to find people who could get me into it. So . . . those women—they're not wrong. About the dealing. I don't do it anymore, but . . . I hope you don't hate me. I hope it doesn't make you think I'm a liar."

"I think we all do what we've gotta do," I say, which is the only way I know how to respond. I don't necessarily approve of it, but what other solutions were there? And it doesn't matter anyway what he did years ago. That's not who he is now.

"It wasn't a good time. Things were really bad. Things are still shitty, but not as much anymore." Marcus pauses. "Or maybe they are, but I just don't dwell on it. I don't know."

"I'm glad you survived. I'm glad you were here, and I don't really care what it took to get you here."

"You get the irony in that, right?"

"What do you mean?"

He runs his fingers over my knuckles, tracing patterns along the bones. "You so easily forgive me, but you won't forgive yourself. It doesn't make sense. How can I be okay, but you still think you're somehow not?"

"What happened to you *happened* to you. I chose to end up here," I argue.

"Not really. Maybe physically, sure. But what's the difference? I didn't choose to have a shitty dad, and you didn't choose what your brother did. I didn't choose my mom's cancer or being poor and needing to sell drugs so I could afford her bills, but you didn't choose the way people treated you, either. All you've chosen was to say 'enough.' You tried to start over. You tried to give people the opportunity to see you, beyond the things people around you did or were. I don't think that's anything to be ashamed of."

My aunt interrupts us, coming in with bags of groceries, and I'm grateful. I love the way Marcus gets me and sees me, but I also hate how he makes me feel hope. I don't like the idea of hope, and I don't like how it sneaks into my brain. I don't like the thoughts that try crowding it out, either. All the memories of the other times I thought that it would be different. That things would be okay. I don't want to think about what could still happen.

After the groceries are put away, I walk home with Marcus. We get to his apartment, and he kisses me under the porch light. A random moth that seems to have misunderstood that it's November flies under the light. The moth won't live through tomorrow, but it's trying to find warmth in what little life it has left.

Chapter Twenty-Four

In the days that pass between my fake breakup and the beginning of my new relationship, a shadow grows larger. As I think more and more about going home, about seeing Scott, reality settles in. Along with all the fear of what could happen because of it.

I spend hours thinking about it. Imagining it. And then I think about coming back afterward. About how long it'll be until someone finds out. I think about all the ways they could. Of what they'll say. I think about how it's happened in the past, of the precautions I've taken, but also of how secrets never stay secret for long.

I stopped counting the days left before graduation, and I wonder if that was my first mistake. I grew complacent, and now I'm just over two weeks from Thanksgiving, and that countdown is even worse. I know for sure something awful waits at the end of it.

Maybe it's the feeling of the inevitable looming over me that leads to the decision I make. Or to the possibility of the decision that I consider making.

"I need your advice," I tell Marcus while we're lying on his bed.

"Investments are a bad idea. Too risky," he says.

"Thanks, but I'm serious."

"Okay."

"So, I have an idea. I think. Maybe. I mean, I have an idea, but maybe it's a bad idea, or I'm not sleeping well enough or something."

"You're selling me hard on it," he says, rolling over onto his side.

"I know. Okay . . . So after Thanksgiving . . ." I pause. "You know there's a chance everyone finds out. I mean, they could not, but there's a chance they do, right?"

"I guess there's probably always a chance."

"Right. So I've known for a while that there's this possibility. There's this whole thing waiting to happen. And with having to visit and everything . . . It's just . . . the rest of the year . . . I don't know. I mean, winter is long."

"What are you saying?" he asks.

"I hate thinking about it constantly. Worrying about it. Wondering what might happen." I run the idea through my brain again to make sure I really want to say it. I know it's just between us, but I feel like once it's out there, it's a serious option, and I don't know if I really want it to be.

"Lexi?"

"I'm thinking of telling people. Like not making a formal schoolwide announcement or anything, but drama people."

"Really?"

"It's just . . . So, every time this happens, someone finds out and they tell everyone and then even the people I thought cared turn out to be awful. They're usually awful in different ways, but every year ends up the same: They find out, it's horrible, and I leave. But the thing is . . . I've never told them. So maybe it's partly on me? Like, if I told them first, maybe they wouldn't hate me for lying? Because I'd be the one telling them?"

"I don't know," Marcus says. "Yeah, it makes sense, but . . . I don't know. That requires more faith in people than I generally have, and . . . I don't want you to . . ."

Inside my head, I see two paths. I can go home, visit my brother, and then come back afterward and keep lying, all while I spend the rest of the year hoping no one finds out. I can still be with Marcus, and he can hold my secrets for me. We can continue in a suspended reality that's only part of what I am.

Or I can tell everyone. I can tell them who I am, and then I can be who I am fully. With Marcus. With Ryan. With myself. And if I tell them myself, it would be the first time. Whatever happens after telling them would be a consequence of *my* choice.

"There's some control in it," I say. "I've never had that. I'm always trying so hard to control time, to control what I wear, to control how I think. . . . But with other people . . . Like, you can't control them."

"No, but you can control how much you let them in."

"Eventually they're going to find out, or I'm going to run away. I don't know how it will happen, or what it will be like. But if I tell them, if I control how it happens, I know when it does. I know when they know."

"And that matters? I mean, sure, I get that it matters . . . but . . ."

"It does, because the anticipation makes it hard for me to be fully here. To actually be present with you, around anyone. To be myself. I'm always afraid. Always waiting and looking behind me. So if I told them instead, I'd be free of that. I'd be actually living, maybe. For the first time."

"Have you ever told anyone before?" he asks.

"Besides you? No. Only my parents and my therapist know anything about me. And now you."

"I'm flattered. But . . . your therapist—Heath, right?"

"Yeah, Heath."

"What does he think?" Marcus asks. "Does he think it's a good idea?"

I shrug. "I asked you first."

"Damn, Lexi. That's a hell of a lot of pressure."

"I know, and I'm sorry. I guess I just wanted to put it out there. To see how it felt to say it to someone."

"How does it feel?"

"Good," I admit. "It actually feels right."

Marcus moves again so he's lying on his back. His shirt rides up a little over his belt, and I tell myself to stop looking. I have no idea what's wrong with me. This moment is important. This decision is important. And here I am, staring at the little bit of Marcus's stomach I can see.

"Do you mind giving me a sort of rundown of what's happened?" he asks. "I mean, I know you move a lot. And I know people suck and all that. But I guess I don't know what's happened, and I don't know how you handled it. I don't want to tell you what I think, when I don't know what it might do."

I tuck myself into the space between his body and his arm. "Which time?"

"Start from the beginning," he says. "That's usually a good place to start."

"Well, the beginning was back home. Stonebridge. Before it happened, Scott was . . . We were really close. He was my best friend. My only true friend, really. We spent all our time together in the summers, because my parents were always off doing something for their research, or they'd taken on summer courses."

"I'm sorry. It's hard to lose someone who isn't really gone."

"Someone who's just let you down?" I ask. He nods. "Yeah. It really is."

I want to remember Scott *before*, but that's not the point, and Marcus is right. It's nearly impossible. The pain of missing someone who's there but who isn't the person you thought they were is unbearable.

"After, though . . . It happened in the fall of seventh grade. Everyone stared at me. They talked about me all the time—kids, adults, strangers. People left things in our mailbox. They threatened me. It was all really bad, and I started . . ." I look down at my arms, where the memories of their words are only faded white and red lines on my skin now. "I used to keep a record of what they said. The names they called me."

Marcus leans over and runs his fingers over the scars. "I noticed. I just didn't want to say anything. I figured you'd tell me when you were ready."

"That was when Heath suggested starting over. New place. New name. Whatever. So for eighth grade, my parents sent me to live with my cousin. And it did help at first. It even helped with the cutting. But people there found out about Scott, and then I had to leave again."

"What did they do?" he asks.

"Nothing, really. I mean, it wasn't big. Nothing major, I

guess. But it hurt, you know? It hurt to think I could move on, that maybe there was a version of me that wasn't linked to Scott. And they refused to let that be possible. They just kept reminding me. If they weren't harassing me and calling me names, they were asking a million questions. Just making sure it was all of who I was, instead of something that happened. Just one part of who I was supposed to be."

He looks at my arms, at the words they used. "When did you stop . . . with the . . ."

"The cutting? At the end of the following year. After boarding school in ninth grade. When I was there . . . well, my roommate . . ."

I stop, remembering her. Grace Cohen. She was my best friend. We told each other so many secrets at night after the dorm chaperones came by and made us turn out the lights. She trusted me with everything, and I trusted her, too. Well, with almost everything. But even that was asking too much of her, I guess.

"She saw the scars," I tell Marcus. "I had gotten smarter about it. My arms were too obvious. People asked questions, so—" He runs his hand under my shirt and traces the lines along my stomach and torso, as if he has them memorized. He's not looking, but he knows where the ugly parts of me are. "Exactly. So one night we were getting ready and we were in the showers and she saw them."

"The idea of girls all standing around naked in showers together isn't just some fantasy concocted by . . . well, me?" he asks, laughing.

I smack his shoulder lightly. "Gross. But no, it's not like it happens all the time. We just happened to be in the shower area, and she noticed while I was putting on my shirt."

"What happened?"

"Nothing, really. She asked and I told her. I told her as much as I could without telling her exactly what had happened. I told her the things people had said, that I'd needed to leave, that my family had secrets and I was trying to get away from them. I thought she was my friend. She even listened like she was my friend."

I remember Grace. I remember crying to her, and her hugging me, telling me it would be okay. "And then she filled in the rest herself," I say. "She made a point to dig, to fill in what I hadn't told her, and then she told everyone what I hadn't said. Along with what I had."

"What kind of person asks about something like that and then uses it against someone?" Marcus asks.

"Grace, apparently. I trusted her. And she pretended she got it. That she understood. I went to sleep trusting her, feeling like I had made some kind of progress. And the next day everyone knew. They knew everything. So I left. Again."

"Why would . . . They didn't even know those people. They only knew you, so why . . . ?"

"Why would they hate me for it?"

"Yeah. I mean, I guess people are just shitty, but I don't get it."

"It's weird. Some of them thrive on drama, I suppose. When Grace started with the newspapers on my door, when she started saying she was terrified in her own room, people got really into it. I don't think they cared what the real story was. I think they just liked being part of something."

"Is that always what it's like?"

"Pretty much. Sometimes it's different. Not better, but different. Like last year . . . at first, people weren't horrible at all. They were nice, but it wasn't real. It was a weird nice. They were nice because they wanted more. They needed to know details. There was this one group . . . They were obsessed with it. They wouldn't stop asking me questions. They'd get mad when I said I didn't want to talk about it. At first most people were more curious than mean. But when I started shutting them out because I couldn't handle it, that's when they got cruel. It didn't matter, because . . . well, as soon as everyone found out . . . My boyfriend . . . He couldn't stand the way it was all people talked about. How they kept asking him what I was really like. How they asked him things like what kind of knife my brother used or if I knew what bands he liked."

"That's random."

"People were fascinated by it," I explain. "I think they thought my brother was some kind of celebrity. Like they were walking the same halls as someone who knew Charles Manson. And they wanted it to wear off on them, whatever it was."

"Man, people are fucked up." Marcus pauses. "Well, if you haven't told people, but all this happened . . . what makes you think—?"

"That Ryan and Lauren and Rory and them are any different?"

"Exactly."

"Nothing. I don't know if they're different. I want to hope they are. Also I think maybe . . . maybe it's time. Maybe *I'm* different. So if they're not . . . if they can't handle it, I think I can. I *think* I can move forward."

"Are you sure?" he asks.

"Not remotely," I admit. "But I'm really tired, you know? It's hard to be scared of everything all the time. It's hard to obsess over what you wear, because that's the only thing that stops you from dragging a razor over your skin again. It's just exhausting to be someone else constantly."

"I don't know what to tell you," Marcus says. "But

whatever you decide . . . it doesn't matter. It doesn't change anything, all right?"

"You don't need to tell me what to do. I don't want you to be responsible for that. I just needed to say it. To see how it felt. To see how *I* felt."

We don't move or speak for a while, with only the noise of traffic fading outside to let us know time is passing. Eventually I turn over and look at him.

"Can we just stay here?" I ask. "Like, forever? I changed my mind. I don't have to tell anyone anything, and the whole world can just disappear, and this can be everything there is."

"I do have a giant tub of pretzels," he says. "It can hold us for a while."

"Perfect. You, me, some pretzels. That's pretty much my life goal anyway."

"It's a solid goal."

I sigh. "I wish that was possible. But . . . I think I need to do this."

"When do you think you'll tell them?"

"There's a drama meeting tomorrow. I could tell them after that?"

Marcus nods and sits up. "Okay. And after that . . . I'll be here. Regardless. And if things don't go well . . ."

"They might not. I hate thinking it, but I need to admit that. It could be horrible. Right now I don't think it will. Right now I think I'll be okay even if they're not, but . . ."

"I know. But I'm still here either way, okay?"

Since it's getting late, I get up to leave, hugging him before I go. I try to hold on to the way his arms reach around me. The way he smells. How his head feels resting against mine. Wanting to remember him. Regardless of what happens, I know it won't affect him at school, because he doesn't really know any of the same people I do, but what if I do it only to realize I can't handle what comes next? What if I think this is fine, and then suddenly it's not, and I do what I always do, leaving the pieces of whatever this is behind?

"If things don't work out, there's always a lifetime of pretzels, right?" I ask, pretending not to feel as anxious as I do.

"Nothing they say changes you, Lexi. Remember that. No matter what, nothing that comes next is about you. It's on them."

I cling to him, knowing I should get back to my aunt's. Knowing I should be stronger than I am.

This is my choice, I tell myself. And I can still change my mind. But being here with Marcus makes me even more sure I *need* to do this.

I need to face the truth of myself if I ever want to move forward. Even if it turns out like it always has in the past, I need to stop hiding.

Chapter Twenty-Five

t's hard knowing something is coming and letting it sit inside you all day. I spend the afternoon before the drama meeting talking myself through everything I need to say, playing out the ways it could go. There are so many possibilities, and by the time we get to the auditorium, I'm mostly desperate to see what happens.

I can't keep living in a million versions of could-be.

Heath would warn me that I'm trying to control time. That's what he says when I make rash decisions. I know he'd have plenty to say about this in general, but I think of all the times he's also told me I should be an active participant rather than a spectator in my life. For the first time I feel like I get what he was saying. You don't get more active than dumping truth at people's feet and seeing what they do with it.

It won't be a big deal, I tell myself. It can't be. Sure, maybe it will be to Chloe, who already hates me, but Lauren is nice.

She's not the type to get wrapped up in what other people say. Ryan will understand because he knows what it feels like to have to deny who you are to people. And Rory will probably create T-shirts or something, turning me into her newest pet cause.

I tell myself it will be fine. That there has to be good left in people.

You're okay, I repeat in my head over and over for about an hour.

When the meeting ends, everyone leaves except Ryan, Rory, Lauren, and Chloe. The auditorium is too vast to hold the five of us and everything I need to say, and I start feeling it close in on me. I tell myself to remember everything Heath has taught me over the years. I talk myself into the moment, rationalizing away all my thoughts.

"Can I talk to you all about something?" I ask.

"Sure. What's up?" Lauren asks.

"Well . . ." I try to figure out how to start. "So . . . I guess the first thing is that my real name isn't Lexi Lawlor. It's Stewart. Alexia Stewart."

They all look at me, not reacting, and I continue. "I didn't move here for school. I mean, my GPA is fine. It's always fine. But I had to move here. I had to move this year because I move every year. Because I've been running away from something my whole life."

"You can tell us, whatever it is," Ryan says. "We're your friends."

"Definitely, Lexi. You'll always be safe here," Rory agrees.

I take a deep breath. "When I was growing up . . . my brother and I were always close. But he's . . . My brother, Scott, isn't the person he was then. At fifteen . . . when I was twelve . . ."

They're all silent, and their faces reveal nothing as I tell them everything. They don't gasp or start talking. They just nod and shake their heads to show understanding or sympathy. I let the words spill out, like they did with Marcus. It's not the same, though, and I find myself yearning to feel the same way I did when I told him. Still, I fight through it. Everyone's in a different aisle from me, and I suddenly feel how small the auditorium is getting, and I try not to remember the blood on the stage and the feeling of the cold on my back when I was on the floor.

When it's over, it's quiet, and this huge open space just sits, waiting for something. I can hear the buzzing of the stage lights as the voices in my head start up again:

You shouldn't have said anything. They're going to make it hell for you. You couldn't do it. Of course you couldn't fucking do it. You are such a failure.

I bite down on my lip, trying to distract myself with pain.

Finally Lauren says, "Well, I don't care what your name is. You're still Elaine to me."

"She's right," Rory says, getting up and sitting beside me. "It's something we hadn't talked about, but it doesn't change things. Everyone has skeletons, right? At least now we know your real name."

Ryan nods, but he's quiet. Chloe simply stares at me.

"I'm sorry I lied," I say.

Rory smiles. "I get it. I mean, that's a lot to deal with. I can't even imagine how hard that was for you. I think you're really brave to tell us. I'm so glad you trusted us with something like that."

"You have no idea how relieved I am to hear that," I tell her. "I was so scared—"

"Our ride's here," Chloe interrupts. "I'm sure we can hear

all about it tomorrow at lunch. I'm sure we'll all be dying to know more."

"Chloe!... God," Rory snaps as she stands up.

"What?"

"'Dying to know more'? What the hell is wrong with you?" Rory whispers, but her voice is loud enough that I catch it. While Chloe pretty much acted like I expected, I'm relieved that Rory and Lauren understand. They both hug me before they leave with Chloe.

When it's just me and Ryan, I collapse back into my seat. "I was so scared that wouldn't go well."

He doesn't respond. He won't even look at me. "Hey. What's up? Are you okay?"

"I wish you would've told me," he says.

"I did. I literally just told you."

"No, I wish you would've told *me*. Before you told them."

"Why? What does it matter? It's out. I've been carrying that for years, Ryan. And I needed to let it go." I pause, looking at him. He keeps staring at the ground. "You're not upset with me, are you?"

He shakes his head. "No. It's not you. It's just... I really hope it's fine."

"Why wouldn't it be?"

Finally he looks at me, his eyes dark. "We've all got secrets. Sometimes it's better not to trust certain people with them. I wouldn't have cared. I mean, I don't care. Not about your past or your brother. I don't know... I'm sorry. Forget it."

But no one has ever been able to forget it when someone says that. It's like the worst phrase possible if you really want someone to forget something.

"I can't when you say it like that."

Ryan sighs. "So I've told you most of the things about me you'd need to know. And there are, like, layers of those things, right?"

"How so?" I ask.

"I told you about the lawn ornaments because they're just lawn ornaments. Most of the people in drama who know me know about that. They're only a silly hobby. But even then, I don't tell everyone."

"I don't . . ." I can't finish, because I'm not sure what's happening.

"It's not easy for me, L. Until a couple of years ago, I was afraid to even come to school, okay? And now I'm not, but not because it's changed. Not because people suddenly understand and are different. I'm only okay now because I spend a lot of time being someone I'm not."

"What do you mean? You're you. I don't understand," I say.

"No, I'm not myself. Not really. I'm not really outgoing. I pretend I am, but mostly I worry constantly about what people think. I can't even tell people I make fucking lawn ornaments. And the real stuff . . . who I really am . . . I told you the other thing. . . ." He looks away.

"When we were outside? About Chloe and why you lied about us?" I ask.

"Yeah. I told you that, but nobody else knows. I don't want them to know."

"I'm honored you trusted me."

"I guess," he says. "Except you're not the person I thought you were that night, and now you have that information and—"

"Whoa. Hold on. First of all, I am *still* the person I was that night. It's only been a few weeks. Second, there's no way

192

in hell I'm ever going to use that against you. I don't care what happens. That's not who I am, and I'd think, regardless of what you thought my last name was, you'd have figured that out. Especially before you told me something like that."

Ryan stands up and paces the aisle, not saying anything and not looking at me. I'm half hurt and half angry. He's my friend. Probably my closest friend here. Maybe even a closer friend than Marcus, really. When Ryan offered his secrets to me, I held them and I kept them safe. It hurts that he thinks he can't trust me to keep doing that.

"I'm not gonna tell anyone you're not interested in sex," I tell him. "Not that it matters, because Rory would be all over being your advocate. That's, like, her thing."

He turns around from where he's pacing and faces me, the stage lights a halo around him. Because of the lights, he's nothing but shadow. I can't see his expression or his eyes.

"Maybe I don't want a goddamn advocate," he says. "Maybe I just want to get through fucking high school."

It's funny how sometimes things make so much sense at the worst possible times. Suddenly, under the glare of the stage lights, I see it all. I see myself in Ryan. I remember how it feels. Spending your days as a person wrapped in secrets. Needing to hide, and then having that safety stripped away by someone else. I remember five years of it. How I hated even going to the grocery store.

I told Ryan how important it is to believe in the fiction of yourself that you create, and suddenly I realize what I've done.

"I'm sorry. I am so sorry," I say.

"I don't know what happens next."

"I don't, either. But no matter what, I won't tell anyone about you. You can trust me, Ryan."

"That's not the point, though, is it?" he asks. "If this stuff about you gets out . . . if more people know . . . it's not something that people forget, you know? And if they know that, and if I'm around you . . . it just draws attention to me. You get that, right? You're my friend. My ex-girlfriend, as far as they're concerned. If they find out . . . they'll start to look at me, Lexi. Really look. Don't you get how badly I want to avoid them looking at me?"

I nod, because of course I do. Of course I know how hard it is to stay out of the glare of your own shame. "I do. But . . . you don't have a reason to be afraid of people. Nothing's wrong with you."

"That doesn't matter to people. You have to know that. I mean, when was the last time people went after someone because something was actually wrong with them?"

I wish I had an answer for him, but I remember the things they've said about me. I remember my parents. My mom crying in the kitchen because everywhere felt different. I remember Ben last year and how he started to avoid me. How Grace told people she felt unsafe around me. That she was sure I was only a moment away from snapping.

I think of Marcus and the drugs and the stories people tell. And how the truth has never mattered at all.

"They're not going to turn on you," I tell Ryan. "It doesn't have to be like that, because they won't find out. And even if they do, anyone who knows you won't turn on you."

I know I'm lying to him. I know how people are, but I hate myself for not thinking of him. For putting him here. I lie to him because I can't accept what I might have done.

"How do you know that?" he asks. "How can you act like it's that easy? Maybe you're suddenly comfortable walking around and wearing your secrets for everyone to see, but I needed this. I needed to hide in whatever idea they had of me, whatever idea made them stop treating me the way they used to. I really needed to be okay."

"Yeah, I get that. I've lived that way for five years."

He leans against the stage and runs his hands through his hair. I want to go to him and tell him it will be okay. At the same time, I want to run away. I want to go home for Thanksgiving, do what I have to with Scott, and never come back here. I want to take back the words I said, but not for any of the reasons I was scared of. I just don't want Ryan to feel like I have, and I especially don't want to be the reason he does.

"When they were talking about me . . . after that one rehearsal, you said it didn't matter," I remind him. "You said you didn't care what people think."

"I know. But there's pointless high school stuff and then there's . . ." He doesn't finish.

Ryan's secret isn't even bad, but it's his secret. It's something he's protected because that was what he needed to do to feel safe. What he needed to do to survive. And if it gets out, once it's out there, there's nothing anyone can do to put it back.

There are things you don't get to escape. There are things people won't let you forget. No matter how much you tell yourself it's okay. No matter how much you want to believe there's a tomorrow where yesterday isn't always looming. There are some things that shape every minute of forever.

"I'm sorry. I wasn't thinking. I didn't think."

"I want so badly to be your friend, L," he says. "I can't even explain it. I just feel normal with you. But . . ."

"Yeah. I know. But maybe it's not what you think. Maybe nothing will have to change."

"You don't really know Rory and them. They're amazing. Until they're not. We never really talked about everything that happened before you came here, but trust me: They're my friends now, but I didn't forget how things used to be with them."

"Well, you're still my friend. No matter what happens. And I won't betray you. But I understand . . . I get it. It'll hurt like hell if that's the way it goes, but yeah, I get it."

"I'm sorry. I'm so sorry I'm not a better friend or a better person, but I have another year and a half left. I can't survive on the wrong end of it."

"I know."

I try not to cry. I try not to make him feel worse, because I really do understand. And I hate myself more for it. I hate myself for not even thinking about Ryan. Not once since my parents showed up for lunch did I consider what I might be doing to him as collateral damage.

"I hope I'm wrong. Maybe they changed. Maybe it's not . . ." He pauses and hugs me. "I really hope I'm wrong."

"Me too."

Chapter Twenty-Six

Ryan isn't wrong.

I'm lying on Marcus's bed, trying to do homework. After the drama meeting and my talk with Ryan, I came to Marcus's apartment, still crying. The worst is that I couldn't tell him why. I couldn't betray Ryan just because it hurt, so we sat for a while in Marcus's room, neither of us talking, before I eventually got up and grabbed my books. You can only spend so much time thinking of what-ifs. Even when you're me.

Now he's working on something on his laptop, and I'm trying to focus on Supreme Court cases.

"Can I ask you something?" he asks, breaking the quiet for the first time in nearly an hour.

"Obviously."

"If someone said something about you—something bad—would you want to find out from hearing it around or would you want me to tell you?"

"Who said something?"

"You didn't answer my question," he says.

I close my government textbook and sit up on the bed, pressing my feet against the floor. "I'd want you to tell me."

He swivels in his chair so he's facing me and hands me his computer, resting it on my lap with the screen open.

"Where'd you get this? What is it?" I ask.

"It was sent out with the student newsletter."

"Oh. I don't get that. I never gave them my email." This factoid seems relevant or important. I don't know why. Marcus doesn't care, and it doesn't change what everyone who *has* given their email to the student government sees.

On Marcus's laptop screen are pictures of Lucy and Miles Cabot. The same pictures that graced the internet postings, TV, social media, newspapers, even national magazines for a time. The same pictures I tried to forget, to block out. To leave in the past, because I can't bring the Cabots back. I used to sit awake at night, shaking, begging God to bring them back. But God didn't listen, and it doesn't work that way.

I know their faces because I used to dream about them. Until I made a conscious choice to forget them. Heath said the forgetting was a defense mechanism. It absolutely is, because as soon as I see them again, I can't breathe. All I can think of is how I used to be afraid to sleep. Of how when I finally did fall asleep, I woke up later, sweating, with their faces hovering over me in the darkness.

"Why would they do this?" I ask. "*Who* would do this?"

I close my eyes, and it's like time folds itself up and resets. I'm there again. That night. The weeks that followed. I'm in my dorm in Virginia. I'm at my grandparents' house, trying to avoid Facebook and Twitter and even email while trying to pass classes online. I'm everywhere else, and I wonder what I was thinking. Why I thought anyone could be different. Why I thought I'd gotten better.

"I shouldn't have shown you," Marcus says. He sits on the floor in front of me, his hands on my knees, trying to keep me steady. I feel him lift the laptop away, but I can't see him. I can't open my eyes. I don't want to look at him.

I thought it would be okay, but seeing Lucy and Miles there, bringing them into this room—it takes apart everything I built up inside myself to stay safe. I thought if my real world exploded into this one, it would be okay. That the pieces could come together and create something different. Something new. But this is just more of the same destruction my world always creates. Scar tissue of the things I'd thought could be possible. All the things that died five years ago. With the kids whose faces are still in front of me, even with my eyes closed.

"Lexi," Marcus says, trying to bring me back to now. "I'm so sorry. I shouldn't have . . ."

"I'm glad you did. I wouldn't have wanted anyone else to tell me. I don't understand, though. I mean, I only told four people. It's only been a few hours. They were okay. I mean, they wouldn't . . ."

And yet they did.

"I'm sorry," he says again.

I think of her smirk. I think of everything she's said. Of how she told me that day by the prop room exactly what she'd do. I think of how much she hates me, and I hate myself for not listening.

"It was Chloe," I say. "Right? It had to be Chloe."

Marcus doesn't respond, and I reach for the computer. To see if there's some sign of who sent it. To see her name there, showing me what kind of person she is. Proving me right. I shouldn't have told her. I should have asked her to leave, or told Rory I needed Chloe not to be there. Three of them were my friends, but Chloe was just waiting for this.

I should have known.

Marcus moves the computer out of reach. "It doesn't matter, Lexi."

"Of course it does. Let me see it."

"I don't think you want to."

"Don't tell me what I want," I snap. I feel instantly guilty, but it doesn't stop me from reaching for the laptop again.

"This isn't going to make it better," he says, but he gives in. What else can he do?

But it's not what I expect. It's not Chloe's name. The name isn't even a secret. It's there on the screen, and I don't understand. If I were planning to ruin someone, I'd probably try to cover up my part in it. I wouldn't want everyone to know I did it. And yet, there it is. A name. An email address.

"Rory?" I ask. Her name feels like a foreign word in my mouth. Or like poison. Something that doesn't feel right. Something wrong.

She added her own note when she forwarded the article:

It's on all of us to protect our school—and our community—from monsters.

Marcus takes the computer back and hugs my legs. "It doesn't matter, Lexi."

"I don't understand. Why? She was always nice. She cares about people. She makes it a point to care about people. Why would she do this?"

He shakes his head. "Sometimes people are kinder in theory than in real life."

"No, it just doesn't make sense. Like, Rory is the first person to defend anyone from anything. She spends more time online fighting for people she's never met than she does doing her damn homework, but she still does fine in school because even teachers love that about her. She wouldn't. It doesn't make sense."

But her name's there. And no one else would dare use Rory's name.

I know what Heath would say. He'd tell me I'm separating truth from my perception, but this time it's reversed. Usually he tells me that when I become convinced everyone's talking about me. When I used to sit in his office, crying and shaking because I said something weird, and I was positive everyone was still making fun of me for it. That I imagined people coming together just to talk about how wrong I was. He'd tell me that was only my reality. That it wasn't the same as something being real.

"I don't . . . I don't know what I'm going to do tomorrow," I say. "I'm gonna be sick." I want to escape. To hide. To forget all of this. To pretend I never came to Westbrook. I think about my arms, my torso. The scars. I wonder if I have anything in my apartment. Anything to make the hurt stop hurting. To make it bleed out from my skin and let the poison spill from my flesh.

Marcus holds me and rubs my shoulders. "You can do this. You're okay. You're going to be okay."

But I can't. I can't do this. I can't walk into school tomorrow and see them. To go into the cafeteria at lunch and know what she did. I don't know if she'll admit it to my face—or, worse, if she'll pretend, like she did earlier, that everything is fine. If she'll call me brave while she plans to ruin me.

I can't get on the bus and see Ryan and Eric. Ryan, who's so wrapped up in his own fears of the things people say that he won't be able to handle my stuff, too. And Eric, who I don't even know that well but has always been nice to me. Everyone will stare, but they won't be able to see me. They'll only see Miles and Lucy and the crime scene photos, and I will never escape it. No matter how far I go or how many names I use or what I do to change it, I will never get away from this.

I will never be allowed to exist.

"Lexi," Marcus says. He's holding me, and I don't know when he joined me on the bed, but he keeps holding me and rocking me while I try to hang on to something.

I knew this could happen. I did this to myself. Now that it's here, now that it's happened, I need to keep going. I can't fall apart. I made this choice.

I just didn't think she'd do it this way.

I didn't think it would be her.

"I don't want to go back there tomorrow," I tell Marcus.

"So don't. You can take a day off."

"But they'll all be talking about me. I can't sit at home and wonder what they're saying."

"Then you go."

"Everyone will stare. They'll whisper. I won't be able to breathe. They'll all be looking at me."

"Maybe they will," he admits. "But you don't have to listen to it."

"I do."

"Don't go tomorrow. Don't go this week. Talk to guidance about tutoring or something. Go home for Thanksgiving and maybe stay a little longer than you're supposed to. Take as long as you need before you go back. Let them find something else to distract them first," he says.

I shake my head. "I can't. That will be worse. I'll just be imagining what they're saying. And the longer I wait, the worse it will be. The more I'll imagine what was said. The more every whisper and smile and laugh will break me into a million pieces. I'll create a reality in my head, and I'll never come back if I run away."

"I wish I could be there. At school. It's so hard knowing I'm right there and I still can't be there for you."

"They'd just make it worse for you. At least you don't have to be caught up in it all."

"I can go on the bus tomorrow," he offers. "I can sit with you."

"No. Thank you, but no. I like that there's something they can't get to. I like this. Being with you is the safest I've felt in forever."

Chapter Twenty-Seven

decide to have my aunt bring me to school in the morning. That's my concession. I can't face Ryan's disappointment first. I'll have to see him at some point, especially since I have to take the bus home, but it's small victories that keep me grounded.

I'm not surprised to find the picture of Miles and Lucy taped to my locker. Or to see the words *psycho bitch* written on the bottom of it. I'm impressed someone got here early enough to make sure it was printed and ready for me, but I guess people have a lot of motivation when it comes to making another person want to die. It's like a national pastime these days. Baseball, then destroying every bit of hope another human being has. Because, I mean, otherwise life gets dull.

When I get to my first class, most of the other students are sitting around in a circle, staring at their phones. When

I enter, they instantly become a cone of silence, but they don't stop texting. I try not to imagine what they're saying. I already know. I've seen the comments so many times before.

At least they're quiet about it. It's one of the luxuries of high school. In middle school we couldn't have our phones out, and so everyone said aloud what they were thinking. Now they say it to one another right near me, but I don't have to know what they think.

Lauren comes in and pulls a chair up to my desk. "Hey, I'm really sorry."

"You didn't do it. And you should be careful. They'll start texting about you next."

She looks over my shoulder at the throng of people and shrugs. "I'm nowhere near as interesting as you."

"*Interesting* isn't really the word you want," I say. "I think you meant . . . what was it Rory called me? I think it was . . . *monster.* That was it, right?"

Lauren taps her fingers on my desk and stares down the people who are texting, but they're so wrapped up in their phones that they don't even see her. I don't need to turn around to know this. I can tell by the disappointment that falls over her glare.

"So, I guess you saw it?" she asks.

"I did."

"I didn't know. I hope you know that. I had no idea she would do that."

"Can I ask you why? I mean, you've known her forever. Why would she do it?"

Lauren sighs. "It's . . . complicated."

"Isn't it always?" I ask, thinking back to my first day of school. The day I met Marcus. Oddly, that morning feels more distant than the day Scott killed our neighbors. I guess it's because no one puts pictures on your locker of the cute boy who lives in your neighborhood and treats you like you're human. No one hunts you down to tell you're okay.

"The thing with Rory," Lauren says, "is that she's really sure of what's right. And she feels this need to make certain she sets right anything she thinks is wrong."

"So I'm wrong?"

Lauren bites her lip. She doesn't want to defend Rory, but she doesn't want to say anything bad about her, either. "It's not that you're wrong, but I guess . . . Well, it's just that . . ."

"Just say it. Honestly, just say it. I'm not gonna hate you for telling me you think I'm fucked up. I *am* fucked up. I'm just not a monster. I didn't kill anyone. But yeah, it sucks, and it's part of who I am, and I live with it every day. Plus, I lied to you, and that's a dick move, and, well, I don't know. I guess I deserve it."

"You don't," she says. "I know that. But . . . it's hard, because I kinda get what Rory's saying. I don't totally agree, and I really don't feel right about how she did it, but I kinda get it, too."

"What's she saying? What do you get?"

"Just that you should feel worse about it, you know? I mean, you were kinda chill about the whole thing. Even when you were telling us. You seemed sorta . . . I don't know. But I mean . . . Like, those were people. Kids, Lexi. Your brother butchered little kids, and you don't seem all that broken up about that part of it."

I look at my desk. Jonathan Groves sucks dick, I guess. At least that's what someone who shares my English desk

206

wants me to think. I wonder if Jonathan Groves knows this is here. I wonder if he cares.

"It's been a long time," I try to explain.

"Like, five years. That's not that long in the grand scheme of things. . . . And something like this? It just feels like it should hurt more," she says.

I think of Miles. He'd be eleven now. And Lucy. She had this wild red hair, which made no sense because everyone else in the family looked the same. The rest of them were blond and summery and always out of place in Massachusetts, where summer is way too short. But then there was Lucy with her hair right out of autumn.

I spent more than a year obsessing over them. I used to write them letters. I cried every single night for kids I didn't even know. I felt worse because I didn't know them. I knew their names, how old they were, what they looked like, but that was it. I ended up learning more about them during the trial and through the media. It turns out that Lucy was exceptionally smart and loved space. She wanted to be an astronaut. And Miles loved jazz music and had begged his parents for a saxophone. They'd already ordered one for him for Christmas that year. I had to think about Mr. Cabot calling and canceling the order. Having to tell them why. I used to wake up imagining that phone call.

There were nights I could almost hear the ghost of the music that Miles loved. I imagined he was there with me, playing the saxophone his parents never got to give him. I would look up at the night sky and tell myself Lucy was up there, traveling around the galaxy.

But you can only hold that kind of pain inside yourself for so long. Eventually you start to fall apart a bit. You start hearing phantom jazz at the grocery store, and suddenly you can't walk or speak, and everyone's crowded around you, worried. Until they realize who you are, and then they almost hope you don't survive the panic attack.

There's little that makes you feel more vulnerable than losing your mind in public and knowing everyone's waiting for you to give in to it. I hate feeling that vulnerable, so I tucked Miles and Lucy away in a place I don't go to anymore. But at least now I can go to the store without ending up on the floor in a sweat.

"I did care," I tell Lauren. "I do. You can't even begin to know how much I care. How much it hurts. But I didn't kill them. And I can't keep hurting for them and crying for my brother and hating myself. I can't do all these things and still function. I just can't. There's only so much I can handle."

"So you chose your brother?" she asks. "You chose him over the little kids he killed? Don't you get why Rory feels like she does?"

"I didn't choose my brother. I didn't pick him over them. I just couldn't keep hurting over something I couldn't fix." I pause and look at her, although I know she can't understand. Not really. I know it's pointless to try to explain, but I do anyway. "I didn't choose him. I chose myself. I chose surviving."

...

I end up skipping lunch, sitting inside a bathroom stall and counting the minutes until it ends. People come in and out of the bathroom, but I stay silent, hoping they won't notice me.

No one's talking about me yet. Not really. A couple girls

mention "that crazy new chick with the psycho brother," and one admits she thinks Scott's "kinda sexy in a bad-boy way." It makes me want to throw up. Not because he's my brother and because I don't want anyone thinking about him that way, but because who finds a murderer attractive? It's not like she ran into him at speed dating while he was out on parole and they hit it off and then she found out. She literally only knows he exists because he killed three people, and that's what she thinks of. Worse, she even goes so far as to say it.

Some people amaze me. And then I'm more amazed that I'm still surprised by them.

The part of the day I'm dreading most is my last class. It's actually a study hall, which is even worse, because there's no teacher talking and keeping the focus on some subject we need to learn. It's just people stuck in a room with nothing to do but look at one another and judge.

And Chloe is in my study hall.

I head toward the back. Usually I sit up front because I kind of like having the time to, you know, study, but today I'm hoping I can fade right out the back wall.

It's a small group, too. There are only ten of us in total, and that includes Mike Jeffries, who skips school more than he attends.

When Chloe comes in, she looks right at me and stands in the doorway, blocking the entrance for everyone else.

"Get out of the way," Mike Jeffries says from behind her as the bell rings and most of the people in study hall enter. I guess today was one of Mike's on days.

I wait for the attack. I wait for her to say something obnoxious, but she doesn't. She stays in the front and doesn't turn around for most of the period. Mike Jeffries and some freshman named Wayne sit near me, stabbing each other in the arm with pencils.

The minutes pass and no one says anything. I've dreaded it all day, and yet it's the most peace I've had since I told the drama kids about Scott. No one acknowledges I'm here.

But then, with ten minutes left of study hall, the teacher leaves to go make copies or something. The teachers aren't really supposed to leave us unattended, but they do it all the time. And besides possible lead poisoning from Mike Jeffries, there's no reason they shouldn't. We don't do much. They like to think we're out-of-control hormones and destruction contained only by a middle-aged guy in a plaid button-down shirt reading us Shakespeare, but we're just people. And we're bored people. Boredom worries them, but all it does is drain us of the will to live. Especially in study hall when there are ten minutes left in the school day.

Chloe comes over to my desk after the teacher leaves. I'm sure my expression isn't welcoming, because she pauses halfway between sitting and standing.

"I can't do this right now," I tell her. "Can you save it for tomorrow?"

"Can I sit?" she asks.

I pack up my stuff and gesture to the desk next to me. Clearly, she's incapable of basic instruction.

"Just say it, then. Since you can't wait."

She actually makes eye contact, which is bold, since most people look away when they tell me what a terrible person I am.

"I know we don't exactly get along."

"Mostly because you've been horrible to me since my first day here," I point out.

"Yeah, I know. And the thing is . . . I don't really like you that much."

"This is a charming way to start a conversation."

She shifts in her seat but doesn't look away from me. "Look, I'm just being honest. I don't expect us to be friends. I don't think we're really . . . I don't like you much, like I said. But I wanted you to know . . . I'm not okay with everything."

"What do you mean?"

"What Rory did. I'm not okay with it. Sure, I'll admit it. I felt a little validated by your confession yesterday. It was like proof I was right all along."

"Right about what?"

"I didn't like you and I didn't trust you. And yesterday I felt like I had a reason."

"But you didn't. You only hated me because you like Ryan and he's not interested in you."

Now she looks away. "Yeah, okay. That's a huge part of it. I do like him, and he made me feel like shit last year. I thought we were good together, and he just . . . gave up. And it hurt like hell that he didn't even know you, that you just showed up and he acted like you were somehow special. I've cried for more than a year over him, you know."

I could tell her. I could let her know it's not her. In some ways I want to tell her, because I hate knowing she hurts. No matter how horrible she's been to me. Ryan doesn't want her to hurt, either, and I could make that go away in an instant.

But that's Ryan's story to tell, and I won't do that to him. I know, more than anyone, about keeping yourself safe by lying.

So I shrug instead. I have to let Chloe keep hurting to protect Ryan, and he has to let me hurt to protect himself, and it's a cycle of self-preservation through the pain of someone else.

"We broke up," I tell Chloe. "We weren't even together that long. And it's really not cool that you hate me because he liked me."

"I know. But whatever. That's not why I wanted to talk to you. I wanted you to know that it's not okay what Rory did. No, I don't think we'll ever be friends. I don't even know if I want to be. I barely know you, and we never really tried, and now . . . I don't know." She pauses. "But you're still a person, and you don't deserve this. And I just wanted to say that . . . as far as I'm concerned . . . things are still the same with us."

"So, horribly awkward and uncomfortable?" I ask.

She laughs. "Yeah, I guess. But not *because* of what you told us. Just . . ."

"Because."

It's not a friendship. It's barely tolerance of each other. She's right. We won't ever get along. There's a giant gap between us that's been there since we met, and it's mostly on her that it exists. I won't even admit to her now that she made me feel better; she's made me feel bad too many other times in the last few months. But she's right: I'd rather we don't get along for reasons unrelated to my brother.

"So, I'll see ya," Chloe says as the bell rings.

"Yeah. See ya."

I head to the bus, where I'm going to have to face Ryan and where Marcus won't be. I walk slowly and consider how far it would be to walk home. A few miles? Through most of town? I think about running and seeing how far I can get. How long until I don't need to run anymore.

I know I made a choice, and this is what came of it. I can either leave and give up, or I can face what my life is now. I can take reality for what it is.

If I decide to leave—if I run—I have to keep running. I can't turn around and change my mind later.

Run, my brain tells me.

But I don't. I head to the bus because my feet are tired. My body is tired and my mind is tired. I'm tired of everything.

And I'm so damn tired of running.

Chapter Twenty-Eight

Ryan isn't on the bus after all. Eric is, although he just says hi and moves to his seat like it's a typical day. We weren't really close in the first place, so I didn't expect much to change with him. We were mostly friends through Ryan, but I still thought maybe he'd be uncomfortable. That he would say something. Would maybe ask about it. But Eric acts like he doesn't even know, although I can't imagine that's true. Rory made sure everyone knew.

This is proven when some freshman girl I've never spoken to comes up to the front of the bus and sits behind me.

"So I hear you get off on killing kids," she says.

"No, just freshmen," I reply.

"I wouldn't joke about shit like that. Given your history."

I turn around in my seat. She's leaning forward, so I almost kiss her when I do.

She's one of those people you look at and you can tell she

worries about what everyone thinks of her. Her hair is perfectly put together, and she wears just enough makeup to look like she's not wearing makeup but also to appear flawless. Her clothes look like she walked right out of a Fashion Week layout. But her eyes are empty. It's something I've grown to recognize in people over time. Some people burn inside themselves. They're more soul than body. And some, like this girl whose name I don't know and don't plan to remember, are merely a shell.

"What history is that?" I ask.

"Like I said, killing kids."

"You do know that people are individuals, correct? That you're not every single person on this bus, for instance? So, like, if I were to punch you in the face right now, you can't go blaming him." I point to some random guy across the aisle, who's too far away to hear what we're saying but looks nervous about being involved in any discussion we're having.

"Blood is thicker than water," she says.

"That literally makes no sense."

"He was your brother. I'm sure you knew. You were probably in on it."

"Yeah, totally. The cops just never caught me, because I'm that fucking wily."

"You're a bitch."

"Say hello to the kettle," I say, and turn around. She huffs from behind me, but I hear her shuffle back to wherever she came from.

I don't want to do this for another however many days or months it's going to be. I don't want to pretend it's a joke, to dig up snarky retorts to hide how much every single word hurts. I don't want to sit on the bus and have people look at me. To go into class and wonder if people are texting about me, to worry about what they're saying. I don't want to find pictures on my locker or see Ryan in school and know I can't even say hi.

But I don't have much of a choice unless I leave Westbrook. Go back home. Head back for Thanksgiving and admit I messed up again. Since I don't want to do that, this is basically what I have to look forward to.

Still, I decide that I'll see if I can at least stop taking the bus.

I'm a freaking senior. I shouldn't be taking the damn bus anyway.

Marcus isn't around when I get home. I have homework to do, so I just go to Aunt Susie's apartment. There are several texts from my parents waiting for me, but I ignore them. I'm not in the mood to fill my parents in on the latest drama. I can't tolerate my mom's *I told you so* disguised as worry.

"You're home," my aunt says when she comes in from work. "That's new."

"I told everyone about Scott yesterday," I tell her in response.

She nods. "So you'll be home a lot more, I guess."

"At least I'm an excellent cook." I'm not, but it makes her laugh.

Aunt Susie sits on my bed. "Do you want to talk about it?"

"Pretty much want to talk about nothing less."

"Well, that's a relief. I'm really not good at the parent thing."

I put my homework away and tuck my legs under myself. "Hey, don't be so hard on yourself. You've been plenty good at keeping my shit together."

"I should probably tell you to watch your language. Thing is . . . I don't give a fuck."

I think we're both relieved in a way that it's out there. Aunt Susie's always been my favorite aunt, but she's not great at making sure I follow my parents' rules or trying to worry about me like they want her to worry. I don't know if she doesn't agree with their rules or if she just doesn't know how to be a parent, but this is the first time since I got here that I remember the aunt I was excited to live with for a year. She was last on the list because my parents didn't think she was reliable, but I'm really glad right now she's the one who's here.

"Let's order takeout," she says after a while. "And do nothing."

"You're a bad influence. What if I had hours of home-work?" I ask, putting my bag by my nightstand.

"Do you?"

I shrug. "Nothing that can't wait. I'll meet you out there. I just need to—"

"Invite him if you want. He's not a bad guy. I was worried about you getting caught up in the rumors, and I didn't want you to deal with that. But I guess you've managed to do that yourself. So there's nothing to protect you from anymore."

"That's okay. We can see each other tomorrow. I just want to let him know."

She goes out to the kitchen to riffle through menus, and I call Marcus. It's the first time we've talked on the phone, and I know it seems silly and small, but it's a big deal. He has my number now. He has my name and he knows every-thing about me, and he still answers the phone.

"Today sucked," I tell him when he picks up.

"I'm sure. Do you want me to come over?"

"I do, but . . . no, my aunt and I are going to hang out. It's really hard not seeing you, but I should . . . I haven't really spent much time with her."

"Of course. I can see you when you're free."

"You know what I can't do, though?"

"What's that?" he asks.

"I can't do this bus thing anymore."

He laughs. "Yeah, well, there's a reason I gave up on that."

"Can I get a ride with you? Can you ask whoever takes you?"

"I will. I'm sure we can figure it out."

There's quiet on the line for a few minutes. I want to see him. I want to run to him and hide in his room and kiss him and eat pretzels and not think about Rory or Scott or school or anything. But that wasn't the plan, and Heath would say I didn't decide to tell people only to hide again. He would tell me I can't create a cocoon in Marcus's life, because it's no better than shaping new realities of myself every year and then giving up on them.

I love how I've spent so much time in therapy that I don't even need to go to know exactly what Heath would tell me. In his bullshit lingo and all.

"I wish I could see you," Marcus says, breaking the silence. "But it's probably good. My mom could use some company anyway. She's not feeling well lately."

"I'm sorry."

"Don't be. It's just a part of who I am. I'm not sorry I'm me."

"That sounds like some kind of lesson," I say.

"It might be. But I'll let you figure it out."

"It's been, like, a day . . . and this is absolutely vapid . . .

but I kind of miss you. I know I just said I couldn't see you, and I know I just saw you last night, but I do."

"I miss you, too, if it makes you feel better. But don't you worry. This jug of pretzels is infinite. It can wait a day."

"All right. Well, I'm going to head out because my aunt is yelling about Thai food and mispronouncing everything. I think I should help."

"I'll text you later and I'll figure out your ride for tomorrow, okay?"

"Okay. And . . . uh, hey . . . I know I haven't said it yet but, um. . . ."

I've never told anyone besides my family. And I don't know how it works in real life, like in relationships. I'm not sure what happens when you say it, but we've had sex. We're clearly together. He's carrying all the weight I needed to let go of, and I'm carrying his, and yet I still haven't told him. I feel like I'm supposed to tell him. That he should hear the words, even if he probably knows they're there.

"I know," he says. "And I'll hold you to that conversation tomorrow or next week or whenever it makes sense, but it can wait. Like pretzels, some things take ages to expire, okay?"

I hang up, smiling to myself.

I know I'm not better because of Marcus. I'm not better at all. The thoughts are still there. The pain is still there. There's still a whole mess of confrontation waiting, too. I haven't even allowed myself to think about what it's going to be like talking about Scott. What it will be like to see him. About Thanksgiving and what Heath will say and how easy it will seem to just stay there with my parents and to let Rory do her worst while I'm in another state and I don't have to hear it.

I have another half a year or more of high school to survive. I've lost Ryan and drama club and the only other friends I had here. I've lost a lot, and I'm still hurting from so much more. But in the small moments with Marcus, there's still something to look forward to. And there's got to be something in that.

Chapter Twenty-Nine

knew Rory wasn't done with me, but I'd hoped she would wait. That it would happen after Thanksgiving, so I'd have at least a moment to breathe. Time to process it. To work through everything else first, but of course things don't work out that way.

Instead it happens on the Monday morning before Thanksgiving, just in time to make sure I go home knowing exactly what will be waiting for me after the break.

I wish she could've waited until Wednesday. Or at least until the afternoon. Because 7:10 a.m. is way too early for this.

She's standing at my locker with a stack of flyers in her arms. I don't need to look at them to know they're somehow about me. About some cause she's championing that's essentially about letting everyone know how horrible I am. Because that's how she cares. She cares by hurting people she deems unworthy of caring. The hypocrisy is amazing.

"I'm doing some work with victims' families," she says as a means of introduction.

I put my stuff in my locker and pretend she's not there.

"Like, to help people understand why people like your brother should never be allowed out."

"Well, you've got about thirty years before that happens," I say, wishing as soon as I do that I'd kept pretending she wasn't there.

"Is this a joke to you?"

I lean forward, pressing my forehead into my locker, feeling the metal on each side of my face carving marks into my skin. I wish I could make myself small enough to hide in here. I wish I could physically become as small as Rory makes me feel.

"You're incredible," she says. "You come here and you pretend to be this girl who lives in public housing. You act like you've got all these issues, with your clothes and your drama and your phony freak-outs during rehearsals."

I remember feeling like I was dying during that rehearsal. I think of how I still can't sleep if I don't do laundry beforehand, because I can't worry about not having the clothes I need. I think of how I want to dress up to see Marcus sometimes, but I can't on certain days because I don't have anything pretty in those colors. I think of all the hurt and the fear and the anxiety and how I sometimes wish I could disappear. But I don't say anything to Rory, because there's no point. She won't get it.

Telling them about Scott was just one thing. It doesn't change anything else. It doesn't make the scars on my skin fade. It doesn't make me get up in the morning and not panic when I realize the only yellow T-shirt I own has a hole in it now and I don't want to wear a dress. How I stand in my room crying because I can either skip school or wear something uncomfortable, because I can't simply wear something else.

"You are the epitome of privilege," Rory says. "Hiding and dumping your problems on everyone else because you can't handle them. Rather than facing what you are."

I feel like I'll die here in this locker, but eventually, when I don't respond, she leaves. After shoving one of her flyers over my head into my locker.

I pull away from the locker and look at the flyer. It's got pictures of Miles and Lucy on it, along with a note that reads *For the Ones People Seem So Quick to Forget*.

I crumple the paper and toss it into the trash can at the end of the block of lockers.

All day I think about what she said. Am I privileged?

Maybe she's right. I already know I'm hiding in a life Marcus never had a choice about. He grew up at Castle Estates, but I just hid there like I had a right to it.

I think of Ryan and his secret. How he's scared of sharing something that makes him who he is, and of how unfair it is that he should be afraid of that. I think of the night on the bleachers when I promised to be his normal and of how I let him down. Not that he'd want to fake-date the sister of a killer now, but I think of how I abandoned Ryan, even though he welcomed me on the first day of school. I slept with Marcus not even a week after I promised Ryan I'd be there for him. Then I told everyone about me and Scott without considering what that might mean for Ryan as well. That's privilege, right? Thinking I'm entitled to what I want rather than thinking of anyone else.

But then I think of my physics teacher and how she won't look at me anymore. How she makes sure to pass out papers so she never has to come near my desk—and I sit in the front row. I think of cross-country two years ago. How much I loved running in the fall. How the woods felt like opportunity and how I sometimes slowed my pace just to live in that moment a little longer. How after the season ended I was part of something, and then, right before track season, some stranger sent them a message because they'd seen my picture on Instagram with the team and they felt like they owed the team a warning. How quickly I was left behind.

It's not easy to know what's right. I lied to everyone for years. I was able to run away and hide, and maybe that's wrong. Maybe that makes what happens now my penance.

At the same time, I've had to disappear because they never listened. They never took a moment to see me beyond Scott. To know that he hurt me, too. I didn't show them the pain on my body that was a testament to what had happened, but they could see it elsewhere. They could see how I color-coded my wardrobe. How I stayed quiet whenever there was conflict. They saw all this, but no one ever asked if I was okay.

Because they didn't care. Because it's easier to hate someone than to understand them.

It's my aunt's day off, so even though she was supposed to pick me up at the end of the day, I skip lunch and head to the nurse. I fake sick, and since the nurse doesn't want to be here any more than I do, she calls my aunt and tells her to come get me.

"I talked to your mom this morning," Aunt Susie says once we leave the school.

"Yeah?"

"I talked to her about what's been happening. She's worried about you, but not like you thought. She doesn't want you to feel like you failed. She does want you home, though."

"I wish you hadn't told her."

"I know, but they're worried. And I wanted them to know what happened in case you changed your mind about Friday. I wanted them to remember what you deal with every day, too."

"I feel like in three months you've noticed more than they have since I was twelve."

"Don't say that. They're trying, Lexi. I promise."

"Do you want me to go back there?" I ask. "To move back in with them?"

She shakes her head. "Of course not. But your parents want you to know you're welcome. That you're wanted. You can go home if that's what you decide is best."

"What about school? I can't just stop school."

"Your mom said she talked to someone at the university, and I guess they know someone who does private tutoring. They can work with you for the rest of the year."

"It kind of sounds like you think I should. You've worked out all the details already."

"That's not it," my aunt says. "But I don't know. Maybe it would be better for you. I just want you to be somewhere you feel okay."

I know Rory won't stop. There will be more flyers and more causes. I think of drama and the auditions scheduled for the week before Christmas. I think of Ryan and how much easier it would be for him if I never came back. How he can fade again, and everyone will get distracted by the next play and forget he dated the girl I was.

And there's Scott. With his birthday coming up, it's important that I'm home and that I'm there for my parents and for my brother right now. There's no reason to stay here to be miserable, when other people somewhere else need me.

"It would be easier," I admit to Aunt Susie.

"I'd miss you, but we could probably make it happen this week. Or if not, you can stay here and we can coordinate something online for the next few weeks until Christmas. It doesn't have to be chaotic."

I consider it, but then I remember Marcus and how he asked me not to leave.

"I don't know," I say. "It really would be easier. I can picture it, and it sounds great. I could take classes in the living room, and I wouldn't have to deal with any of it anymore. But I don't know. I guess I kind of want to finish this year. Here. I want to know I tried to make something work, even when it seemed impossible. Does that make sense?"

"It does, but I can't come get you every time something happens. With work and—"

"I know. And I really don't think it's smart to stay. I probably shouldn't stay. There are a million reasons to go home. It's ridiculous not to."

"Is this about Marcus?" Aunt Susie asks.

I shake my head. "Not really. I mean, sure, I like having him around, but that wouldn't be enough. It's only a few hours, and we don't see each other at school anyway. We could make it work if it's meant to work. I can't stay here just for him."

"But you want to stay?"

I nod. "Yeah. I feel like I need to. I need to stop running away every time."

"It's going to be hard, isn't it?"

"Probably impossible. But I can't go home. Maybe it's

226

because I'll always feel like I gave up. I'll always know I never survived anything if I run away again."

"You've survived plenty, Lexi," my aunt says. "I'm happy having you here. But if it's too much . . . you don't need to fight for this. Sometimes there's nothing to win by fighting."

"No," I agree, "but there's still so much more to lose."

Chapter Thirty

When I head home for Thanksgiving, I remember how confusing it always is to come back. Part of it's because it's not home anymore. Just a place where my parents live with a vague room I stay in a few months a year.

There's also the fact that I ended up on my own earlier than I should have. I suppose this is how I would've felt coming home from college someday, but it's different. Everyone else still lives a normal life with parents and siblings and friends and rules and curfews. And a home. Meanwhile, I float among family members who never know what to make of me.

Being home feels strange because that word lost all meaning some time ago.

Since it's Thanksgiving, my mom is making way too much food for three of us. I asked Aunt Susie to come, but she has to work on Black Friday, and besides, she's smart enough to stay out of it as much as she can. Her entire parenting experience has been warning me about Marcus because of the women at work, giving up on that when I fell for him anyway, and then reminding me to use condoms after the night she came home to find him in the apartment.

As soon as we get back from Connecticut, my dad puts my stuff in the room where I sleep. He didn't talk to me during the entire drive from my aunt's place—all two and a half hours of it.

I remember when my dad and I were close. When he would sit with me and talk to me about a story he was teaching. When I asked him about tragedy and feminism and he brought home a copy of *Tess of the D'Urbervilles* for me, even though I was nine and I couldn't get interested in Tess. I remember all the things we were—and now none of us are any of those things. We're just memories of other people trying to figure out how to continue in this state of unbeing.

While I watch my dad carry my bags upstairs and listen to my mom run down the list of foods she's prepared, I realize how the time has passed for them, too. I've spent so much of the last few years worrying about myself, never thinking about how it must have been for my parents.

I wonder how my mother must feel every day at the university—seeing students barely older than me and wondering what my day was like but not being able to come home and ask me herself. I wonder if she sits down at dinner sometimes and wishes she could argue with me about clothes or boys or my grades. Did she have a visceral reaction to hearing Marcus on the other end of the phone? The recognition of the fact that she was supposed to worry, but worrying didn't make sense because *we* don't make sense?

What about my dad? Does he miss what we were, too?

I head to the bathroom because it's too much to think about. But the bathroom isn't an escape. My mom makes a big deal out of holidays. I know she's trying to compensate for something that isn't really anyone's fault. But it's exhausting.

The hand towels are embroidered with pilgrim hats, the soap dish is shaped like a cornucopia, and turkeys sit on the top of the toilet. I imagine my mom buying these decorations in some big-box store, hoping I'd come home and forget what we are. Not knowing they'd only serve to remind me that normal people have holidays. They remind me that normal people don't make dinner and wonder what kinds of questions people at the prison will ask them tomorrow about their brother and why he murdered a woman and two children.

For the first time I feel anger rising in me, but not at strangers on TV, or at myself, or at people at school, or at my parents for not being able to help me. I'm not angry at Heath for another of his catchphrases.

I'm angry at Scott. Because not only did he destroy the Cabots, but he also destroyed us. He took away all the things we could have been. *Should* have been.

"I made pie, too," my mom tells me when I get back to the kitchen and sit at the table. I fight back tears, thinking of her buying hand towels and knowing we'll never have a normal holiday again.

"Traffic was light," my dad says. He pours three glasses of cider, setting them up on the table. We used to drink lemonade whenever we were all together for meals, but, well, none of us drink lemonade anymore.

"That's good. How's the construction on the highway?" my mom asks.

"Not bad. Surprising with the holiday, since it's usually terrible. I guess they finally remembered what a headache it is, so they tried to clear as much as they could before today."

He sips his cider and my mom turns to me. "Tomorrow you'll be meeting with Heath first, then we have the other meeting, and after that we've arranged for Scott to visit with you for up to an hour. Usually they only do about twenty minutes, but they're making an exception."

"Since it's been a while," my dad adds, like Scott was on vacation or we just missed each other on holidays.

"Okay."

"I ironed something for you to wear," my mom continues. "And I made sure it was yellow."

"Okay."

We go on this way for a while. She recites the logistics of the weekend ahead, all while preparing a family dinner for three people who haven't known how to be a family since I was twelve. My dad interjects every so often with random tidbits of irrelevant information. And I just nod and say everything's okay.

"I also got Scott a card, if you want to sign it," my mom says. "For his birthday."

Suddenly I can't speak.

Nothing happened. Not really. Nothing bigger or more important than anything else. And yet it's all darkness in an instant.

I can't make sense of this. I hate how one minute life is a series of moments and reflections, and the next it's chaos and hurt and I'm surrounded by words and ideas and memories. I hate how my brain works—or doesn't—and I hate that I can't explain it to anyone. When I try, they just slap on phrases like *cognitive dissonance* or *trauma response*. I hate that everything is words in a textbook, but there is still no guide for navigating it.

"I need to lie down," I say.

"But the potatoes will be ready in twenty minutes," my mom says, freezing in place, because what are we going to do with all those potatoes?

"I'll be down for the potatoes. Just call me when they're ready."

I run upstairs, to the second floor of their condo, away from them and from the multicolored corn on the sliding door to their porch and from my mom's schedule for visiting my brother in prison.

I collapse on the bed and take out my phone. Marcus texted while I was in the car, but I didn't have a chance to respond. He sent me an emoji of a chicken and an explanation.

I can't find the turkey.

I text him back the turkey emoji with no comment.

How's home? he replies.

Not home. I hate the holidays.

Me too. Wish you were here. My mom's trying to make sense of a vegan turkey.

Don't you eat meat?

Yeah, but she forgot to shop for groceries until almost midnight last night and this was all they had left. So Happy Lentil Loaf Day.

He follows the text with an emoji of a jalapeño.

That's a jalapeño, not a lentil. I smile even though I'm still crying. Because I'm a fucking mess and my brain doesn't know what it's doing.

What's a lentil look like?

I don't know. But not a jalapeño.

Prove it, he texts back.

I'm so grateful for him, which is fitting on Thanksgiving. He distracts me from all the things that have been running through my head for the last few hours by sending me on a Google image search for a lentil. And I almost forget. I almost believe I'm a girl who misses her boyfriend and just finds her parents' weird mealtime chats uncomfortable.

I almost let Rory and her flyers fade into someone else's world.

I'm almost okay.

Almost. Until my mom calls up to me that the potatoes are ready.

And follows with, "Grab your brother's birthday card off my nightstand. You can sign it while we eat."

Chapter Thirty-One

Heath hasn't changed much in the time I've known him. I come back to see him a couple times a year, even though I don't change, either. I suppose our money could go to better uses, since five years have accomplished nothing, but then again, I don't need more change than is necessary.

I sit in the lobby of his office, which may as well be an accountant's office for all its drab colors, until he finishes with his previous appointment and comes to get me.

He's too tan to be a therapist. Too tan and too blond. He has a beard, but it's too neat. Everything about him is too *too*. He looks like he should be on a billboard for underwear or cologne or ties or something, not meeting with me to talk about my anxieties.

"How goes it, Lexicon?" He thinks this nickname is cute.

"Off the goddamn rails."

"I'm sorry to hear that. Come on in and let's talk about what's been happening."

I follow him to his office, which is as tan as he is. It's not literally tan, although there are too many brown tones, and it continues the accounting vibe, but it feels like an office would feel if tanned surfers were offices. Maybe that doesn't make sense, but that's exactly what it looks like.

"So tell me what's going on," he says, sitting and crossing his legs and looking . . . well, like a tan guy named Heath in designer pants.

"Why'd you become a therapist?" I ask.

"Is that relevant to what's been happening with you?"

"Maybe? It just seems like you don't really know much about me or what it might be like to be me."

He reaches for his tea and sips it, placing the cup down after a moment. "We're not here to discuss me. Let me ask you: How does it make you feel when people assume things about you based on news stories about Scott?"

"It sucks."

"Yes, it does. It does suck when people think they know you based on something superficial or something outside your control."

Score one for Heath, but he's still too tan.

I sit back on his couch, picking at the threads on the blanket he keeps draped across it. "The thing that's the worst is that I literally don't know how I'm going to feel from one minute to the next. Like, I come in here and I'm angry and snarky and that's okay, but I could start crying any second, and I won't even know why."

"You've been through a great deal," he says. "Trauma can make it very hard to understand what's real. It doesn't really let go of you, either. So even when you feel like you're breaking past it, it's still there, waiting."

"That's exactly what it's like. I'll be happy and laughing and things are okay, and then . . . they aren't and I hate it. I look like a mess."

"I notice you often use phrasing like that. That you *look like* something or another. Do you think there's anything in that?"

"Isn't that why my parents pay you? To tell me if there's anything in that?"

He smiles and sips his tea again. I think he's waiting for me.

"Fine. Okay," I say. "Yes, I say those things because . . . what? Because my focus is on other people?" More sipping, but his smile extends past the edges of the teacup. "Look, I *know* that. I know I worry too much about what people think and how they judge me, but that doesn't make it hurt less. It doesn't make me *stop* worrying."

"But they don't know you. They don't know who you are truly. No matter how much they do or do not know about your situation, they don't take the time to get to know who Alexia is. They only know a version you want them to know, or they know their own perceptions, so their opinions aren't valid. What good does worrying do?" he asks.

"Yeah, if I knew that, and if I knew how to have this rational conversation with myself every time it happened, would I be here right now?"

"You can try having that conversation. Have you tried?"

"Nope. I've never tried something as simple as trying to get better. I just thought it was grand to be miserable all the time."

He leans toward me, looking pensive. "I need you to

understand something, okay? I'm not totally sure it would matter if you didn't have a brother."

"What do you mean?"

"People are people. Some are going to amaze you. Some make every day a memory. Others . . . maybe even what feels like a majority some days . . . they're not like that. Some people search out weakness. When they sense it, they find those cracks, the places you hurt, and they dig at them. They're only happy when other people are in pieces, because they don't know wholeness themselves."

"I don't understand," I say. "I mean, I get that and I agree, but why wouldn't it change if Scott hadn't . . . if I didn't have a brother?"

"If it wasn't Scott, you'd still have cracks. They'd just be in different places and would've been caused by something else. Maybe the same people wouldn't care about those cracks, but I'm sure a new group of people would find them instead. That's how people are, sadly."

"So you're saying it's hopeless?" I ask.

"I'm saying it's human."

"What do I do about it, though?"

"I don't know if there's anything to do about other people. I think there's only what you can do for *you*."

"This is all too reasonable and meta for the morning after Thanksgiving when you're seventeen, you know."

"I don't think so," Heath says. "I think you're far more capable of appreciating what I'm saying than you pretend. And I think you need me a lot less than anyone thinks."

"I never pretended to need you. I tell you all the time this is pointless." He nods and waits. "And yet I'm here, right? I'm sitting here because I want to believe it? That's what you're saying? So this is all basically the point? That it's about what

I think will happen and self-fulfilling prophecies and all that?"

Heath hands me a bowl full of mints, taking one out and unwrapping it for himself first. "How's the new school?" he asks.

"It's . . . a school."

"It's more than a building."

I sigh and look out the window. It's snowing, but only kind of. It's that lazy early-winter reminder of what's to come. A few flakes, a gust of wind, and maybe a brush of white on the lawns, but nothing that we even notice unless we stop and focus for a moment.

"I joined the drama club," I tell him. "And I was in the play."

"That's amazing."

"It is. It was."

"That doesn't sound good."

"At first it was weird. There were some people . . . they didn't really like me. They talked about me when I wasn't around, and I tried not to care, but I did. And I worried because I wondered what would happen if they found out."

"You don't worry about that anymore?" Heath asks.

"I told them."

He pauses. "Did you?"

"There's . . ." I don't know how to explain it.

The snow's picking up, but it's still not sticking to the pavement. "I told them because . . . I don't know. I thought you'd think it was a good idea."

"Why's that?"

"You're always talking about choice. About empowering myself. Defining myself. They would have found out eventually. If not because I visited Scott, something else would have happened. It always does. So I . . . I didn't want to keep waiting for it to happen."

"And? How did it go?" he asks.

"It was awful," I admit. "It might even be worse now than it's ever been. There's this one girl. Rory. I thought she was my friend. She's always defending people. Like, she's constantly on her phone or online or ranting in class. There's always some injustice she's upset about, and she said I was brave for telling them. She promised I was always safe with her."

Heath takes another sip of his tea. "Let me guess. Turns out those injustices are easier to define when she's dealing with abstract people rather than the flawed and complex morality of real people?"

"Let's just say she's the worst."

"I don't think you were wrong," he says. "I think the idea had a lot of merit, even if it was hard. Even if it didn't turn out how you'd hoped. There's a great sense of pride in owning your pain. It's a form of controlling the outflow."

"I hate when you talk like that."

"Like what?" he asks.

"Clinical. I hate when you make me sound like a science experiment."

He doesn't respond to that, but he makes a note. I'm sure it's something else with a name. Some symptom of being me.

"Also—and it's not really related—but there's a guy. Well, two guys, actually."

Heath nods. "I guess we've never talked about what this kind of complication might do to everything else you're dealing with. Do you want to talk about him—or them?"

"Well, one isn't . . . He's not that kind of guy. I mean, he is, but not for me. Which is good because he doesn't feel like that about me, either, but everyone expected us to be together and . . ." I pause. "I'm not explaining this right."

"Is this situation with the guy making you more or less anxious?" Heath asks.

"I don't know. Both? At first it was fine. But now it's not, because he was my friend. I really cared about him, and it was nice having this friend I connected to. And he has this thing . . . It's his thing, and it doesn't affect me, so let's just leave it at that. But now he doesn't want me around because of the stuff people are saying, and he doesn't want this spotlight on him, but it means I lose. Again. I always have to lose what matters."

"How are you feeling about . . . Have you considered reverting back to old coping mechanisms because of this?"

"No," I say. "I'm not cutting again."

"And how is the environment with your aunt? Is it stable, would you say?"

I nod. "It's actually good. I like being there. Except this school stuff."

"Have you considered finishing here? You're almost done with high school and—"

"I think about it constantly. But I don't want to give up. If I give up now, isn't that basically saying the last five years were a waste? That it was some kind of failed experiment and I should've stayed here all along, because I can't function on my own?"

"You're still young," Heath says. "You don't need to function on your own yet."

"I want to, though. I've given up so much these last few years. I want it to count for something."

"So what's preventing you from getting through the year there? Is it what happened?"

240

I shake my head. "Not really. It is, but . . . I'm not upset about the right things."

"What are the right things?" he asks.

"I don't know. I wish I could explain. Like Scott. I have this whole thing today to deal with, but all I'm thinking about is some people I've known for a few months and worrying about what they think of me. I try not to care. And it works . . . until I do. And when I do care, I lose it. I can't make sense of things, and there's no steep slope where I slide down and end up in that place. Instead it's like I'm just walking along and then the ground's gone and I'm in this pit and everyone's looking down this endless cavern at me and I can't get out. And they're all talking about it and judging me and I can't get rid of the things they say and think about me. I know none of it matters, but I can't stop my thoughts."

Heath nods. "I know you didn't want to try medication before, but—"

"No. I still don't. Like, I get it. I know what you're trying to say. And yes, I know it's probably often the best solution. But it's not the best solution for me. Because I'll know, and it will make it worse, you know? Like, I'll always be waiting for the ground to disappear, and when it doesn't, I'll know it's only because I'm being suspended. I'll know the ground still isn't there. Because you didn't fix the ground. You just gave me a parachute."

"That's okay," he says. "You don't have to. I don't want it to make you feel worse. But it's something to consider. If you're feeling like it's hard to go on, I don't think you need to worry about asking for help. It's okay to take the parachute sometimes. And once the ground comes back, we can take it away again. It doesn't have to be permanent."

"Fine," I agree. "If it gets to that point, fine."

"Message received."

"So all these thoughts are there . . . and it's hard to figure out what to choose to focus on. And then there's this other thing, too."

"Does the other thing have a name?" he asks. "Is this the other guy?"

"How'd you know?"

He laughs. "That's why your parents are paying me, remember?"

"Touché."

"He has a name. Marcus."

"I imagine he's aware of everything with your brother, too. If you told everyone?"

"I told him first."

"How did that go?"

"Good. It's kind of like you promised years ago. He can look at me and he doesn't hate me because of it."

"It sounds like you've made serious progress this year, Alexia."

"I think so. But then . . . none of it goes away. Like I'm good and then I'm not. Sometimes I kind of want to come home and pretend this year didn't happen. But then I think of the good stuff. Like having friends before they hated me. Drama club. Marcus. And it's all reason to fight for myself, but then . . . then my brain does what it does, and the world becomes chaos and confusion, and I can't do it anymore. I just wish I was doing it right."

"How do you imagine 'doing it' looks? If you did it right?"

"I don't know. I think if I knew that, I'd be able to figure out where I'm going wrong."

He nods. "How are you feeling about today? About seeing Scott?"

"Do you think that's why I still can't put things together right?" I ask.

"Maybe. I think it could help to talk about it."

"I can't, though. I don't know how to talk about it. Like, it's there, in my head, all the time, but I can't find the words. They don't exist. I *want* to talk about it. I want you to understand. But I literally can't."

"Are you angry?" he asks.

"I was yesterday. I was really angry."

"Who were you angry with yesterday?"

"Scott. For the first time I was really angry at him."

"Why's that?"

"Because it's not fair. He took so much from us, and now I have to go there today and do something for him, but it's not right. What about me? When will my life not be about this anymore?"

"Is that what you want most? If you could change any one thing, is that what it would be?" Heath asks.

"No. I'd stop being angry at myself if I could change something," I admit.

"Why are you angry with yourself?"

"I don't know. I guess . . . I wish I could remember. I wish I could make sense of it all, and because I can't, I feel like I'm somehow to blame. I'm angry at Scott, but I still love him, and I feel like I shouldn't. I should feel more for Mrs. Cabot and her kids. I shouldn't lie. I should face my past. But *should* is just a word. It's a direction from someone else. And I'm angry I can't do what I should, but I'm also angry that there's even that expectation."

"This is a defense mechanism, Alexia. It's a healthy response to trauma. But to move on with your life, we need to find a way to make it not the only thing going on."

"Do I deserve to move on with my life?" I ask.

"Why wouldn't you?"

"What about everyone Scott hurt? Not just the people he killed, but everyone? Mr. Cabot? People in town? My parents? Me? How do I have the right to act like everything is normal? I don't get to live a normal life. That's my penance."

Heath leans back in his chair. It's a rocking chair, and it looks absurd when he leans back like that, because he looks like a hipster uncle with designer taste.

"I want you to think about this, and I don't want an answer today," he says. "I want you to think about it, and when you come home again around the holidays, we can talk then."

"Think about what?"

"I want you to think about why you feel you need penance. I want to know why you think you're in any way to blame."

"Rory . . . that girl . . . She said I was privileged. Am I?"

"I think that's a word that requires a great deal of unpacking, and I think you have other things to process first. I think there are levels of what we experience, and I think people on the outside only see some of those, which allows them to feel that they can understand the layers they can't see."

I look around his office and start to cry. "I'm so scared."

"Of what?"

"Of today. I'm afraid of what he'll be. Scott. I'm so scared of reconciling him with what I remember. Of him being nothing like my memory. Of him being exactly like he was. I don't know which would be worse."

We sit in silence, although time's up. Time's been up for a while now, but Heath doesn't push me to leave. Eventually my dad knocks on the office door. He looks sheepish, and I know he spent ten minutes sitting in the car, talking himself into coming in. He doesn't want to pull me away from this place just to make me face the one thing I've kept avoiding.

Heath gives me some tissues and I dry my eyes, trying to put myself together. My dad goes back to the car after checking on me, and I schedule an appointment for after Christmas.

"I'll see you in a few weeks, okay?" Heath says as I grab my coat. "And don't forget what I asked you to think about."

I nod and leave the office with two words running through my mind: *Penance. Blame.*

I used to cut the words people said into my skin. Now I don't hurt myself anymore. At least not where it's visible. Instead of remembering on my flesh, I take their words and I play them over and over in my mind every day. Every hour. Every second.

But I've never asked myself why. I've never stopped to wonder where their words end, where they belong to them and don't serve as an extension of me.

As my dad drives us toward the prison, I stare out the window. The snow's passed completely, and there's almost no remnant of it. Except in what used to be flowers alongside the bland buildings. Now they're just death with a dusting of winter.

Chapter Thirty-Two

When you avoid something, you never really escape it. You just put it somewhere in your head, but it's always there, reminding you that you're trying to pretend it isn't.

I've thought about Scott every day since he was arrested, and I always tried to imagine him in prison. What a prison even looked like. But all I had to go off was movies and TV, so I've created this entire world for my brother to live in that looks nothing like the real thing.

Except for the barbed wire around the place. That's right out of my nightmares.

"I thought people didn't work today," I say to my mom as we cross the parking lot. It feels too bland for a parking lot at a place like this. We could be at Walmart.

"They made an exception. I wasn't about to pull you out of school if I could avoid it."

My dad coughs from my left side. It's weird having my parents flank me on my way into a prison.

Inside, the lobby looks like Heath's office building—with the addition of a row of metal detectors, a security team, and countless cameras. Little red eyes watch me from every direction. I think this must be the worst part of all—the way you can't escape notice. You're forced to be reminded of what you did all day every day, because the cameras and the eyes behind them won't let you forget. It's a worse punishment than probably anything within these walls.

Or at least I would think so, but what do I know? I'm a seventeen-year-old girl afraid of herself.

I don't like how the security guards look at me. They make me feel guilty. They look at me like I'm a criminal, and I hate that I feel ashamed of something I didn't do.

I take out my wallet and put it in the little plastic bin, sliding it down the belt to be scanned. I don't like the way everyone can see inside it. I'm not even sure why I brought it in. Maybe I thought there was a gift shop.

My mom goes into one of the other lanes, and they go through her purse. Then they open Scott's birthday card and read it. Once I've passed through the security area and met my dad on the other side, we head to where my mom is, waiting while a guard reads the card aloud to another guard.

"I think it's copacetic," the guard reading it says. "Nothing odd?"

"Why are they doing that?" I ask my dad.

He shrugs. "Potential for codes, I guess."

"Codes? Like in a spy movie?"

"No, it's . . . There's a hierarchy inside here, Lexi. And it reaches outside."

"And they think Mom's part of it?" I want to laugh, but he's not smiling.

"Never underestimate what people will do for someone they love. Even if that person deserves to be here."

Once the card is cleared and it's determined my family isn't part of some secret society helping with a massive prison break or whatever, they lead us down a hallway, through several doors with alarms, until we reach a dank room. The only light comes from a small line of windows on the very top of the rear wall, but the windows are grimy. Lights come through an opaque curtain of time.

A guard grunts in the direction of a table against the back wall, with five brown folding chairs around it, waiting for a conference. My parents each take one, familiar with this place and its procedures. They leave a space for me between them, where I sit and stare up at the ceiling. Several ceiling fans spin, but barely.

The two people who join us at the table are wearing suits, but they're the suits of people who work for the state. The man's doesn't fit right; it's too tight in the shoulders, but the sleeves go to his fingertips. Hers fits fine, but there's something wrong about it. I'm no expert on fashion, as clearly noted by my yellow skirt and blouse that my mom picked out, but this woman's suit is old. Someone probably wore it, and wore it at least a decade before I was born.

"We're glad we're finally getting a chance to meet you, Alexia," the woman says as she tries to sit on the folding chair. She rocks back and forth, and her skirt rides up when she sits. She doesn't cover the fact that she's uncomfortable. In this place. In that suit. In general.

"Yes, it's a delight," I reply.

"Alexia," my mother growls in my ear.

"Sorry," I mumble.

The woman pretends not to notice and takes out a legal pad and a tape recorder, along with a small bag of pens. All from an oversized black bag. It feels so rehearsed. I hate it. I hate that my brother and my life are just notes jotted on a piece of paper, the same paper she'll use when she goes to jot down someone else's life.

"Have your parents explained the purpose of this meeting?" the man asks. He's bored. Probably angry he's even here. I imagine his wife and kids at home, tired after a long Thanksgiving of running around between relatives' houses and then late-night shopping for bargains. I create an entire world for him because his world is more interesting than this room.

I nod.

"For the purposes of this session, can you confirm that aloud?" the woman asks.

"Yes, I understand why I'm here."

This isn't an ideal time to have an existential breakdown. But when I say it, I start wondering if I do understand. Not just today, but why here? Why me? Why that day? I feel like I'll never know why Scott did it. Why he couldn't have just come to pick me up and we could be somewhere else right now. This man in the ill-fitting suit could be at home, napping with his family after hitting the Black Friday sales. This woman could be doing anything else, so she wouldn't have to keep pulling at her skirt. My parents could be writing yet another book about the importance of meter in Anglo-Saxon poetry, or whatever they're into now. All these things could have been avoided. Scott just needed to come get me like he did every other day.

And that starts me on the path that I live on. How it's my

fault. If I'd been sick that day and he hadn't needed to come get me, he wouldn't have been able to go there, because I would have been home. If I'd walked home sooner instead of waiting for him.

If I'd . . .

If I'd . . .

"Miss?" the man in the suit says, but my brain doesn't want to hear him. It doesn't want to be in this room, on this chair, in the dim light of winter. It's pulling me back to that October afternoon and I'm sitting in front of the school and I'm texting Scott and he's not answering and I can't breathe and I can't stop it and . . .

"Lexi, we're here," my dad says, putting his hand on my shoulder.

I nod again, but it's through the space of five years. The walls of the room are also the trees in front of my middle school, and we're sitting around another table, but this time it's with a detective and Scott's already been taken and the bloody clothes are being placed in a bag and the detective is asking me about Mrs. Cabot and what I know about her.

"Does she need a minute?" the man in the suit asks my mom.

I want to say no, and I shake my head, but I can't see his face. He's the detective, not this man in the suit, and my parents are watching me, but they're in two places as well.

"I'm sorry," I say, and then it's an echo. *Sorry. Sorry. Sorry.*

"Maybe we should try another day," the woman says, and I see her reach for the tape recorder, but it's also the glass of water my mom gave the detective that day.

"No!" I cry out, but I still can't find my way to this room and to now.

"Perhaps you could give us a moment," my mom suggests. I'm aware of the two people in the suits leaving, taking the notepad and the tape recorder and even the pens, and then it's me with my parents and the ceiling fans.

"Alexia," my mom says, but she's not sure what to say. "Should I call Heath?"

I'm crying. Because I don't want to be here, but I can't not be here. I want to be at drama club, and I want Chloe to be mad at me because Ryan gave me a ride somewhere, and I want that to be all.

I want a new reality.

I shake my head. "I just don't know what they want me to know."

"What do you mean, sweetheart?" my dad asks, talking to me like he did when I was a kid, and I wish I could curl up and be that girl again. I imagined seventeen being so different.

"I don't know why he did it," I say. "I don't even know who he is. How am I supposed to—?"

My mom cuts me off. "Alexia, I don't think you understand."

"What do you mean?"

"No one's asking you to pretend it didn't happen. No one expects you to think Scott's something he's not. All they want to know is what you know him to be."

"But I don't know. That's just it, right? How could I? I haven't seen him since that day. I mean, except in court, and that . . ."

I only went to one day of the trial. There shouldn't have even been a trial, since Scott confessed, but the attorney wanted to argue that he was innocent. He had to sit there and say the words *not guilty* after he'd already told the police what he'd done. The trial didn't last very long. Even my brother didn't want to fight for himself.

I remember going, seeing all the reporters, watching Scott sit up front with his attorney. Heath thought it might be good for me to face it, but then I went back to school afterward and everyone had seen me on TV somehow as my parents tried shielding me from the media when we walked to the car. It was only supposed to be one day, and it was supposed to be safe. Heath thought I might be able to find solace in it, but all I found was more of the same.

"Lexi, everyone already knows what your brother did. All they care about now is what you remember," my dad says.

"And if I say the wrong thing?" I ask.

"You're not responsible for your brother's life. You're only responsible for yours. We didn't ask you to do this because Scott's future is dependent on you."

"Why'd you ask me to do this, then?"

My dad looks at my mother and then back to me. I remember loving my father. I remember being a family, and it hurts to see the echo of it now. I still love them, but they're almost strangers because of how much time we've been apart.

My dad gets up and hugs me to him, and I disappear into the comfort of it.

"Lexi, you need to live your life. You need to close this chapter with Scott." He pulls away and looks at me, his eyes wet. "We didn't ask you to do this for him. Today isn't about your brother's future, honey. It's about yours."

Chapter Thirty-Three

When the people in the suits come back, I tell them what I remember.

"So your brother loved comic books?" the woman asks.

"He loved stories. And the best part of it was that he taught me to love them," I say. "I didn't care about superheroes or teams of mutants. I cared about being normal. Scott never did. He used to tell me that it didn't matter. That all the normal people were really just hiding who they were. I don't know. He got the metaphor of superheroes way before I did."

"Were those the only comics he read?"

I shake my head. "He read everything. Well, everything we were allowed to read. My parents were really strict about making sure everything was age-appropriate or whatever, but he read a bunch of different things. He liked this one . . .

It was about a samurai rabbit. I forget the name. But it was all in black and white, and there were all these animals. Like ninjas and bounty hunters. It wasn't cute, though, you know? Like it was serious stuff, but they just happened to be animals."

The people in the suits nod. I don't know how useful any of this is, but I can't help feeling lightened by it. I've barely mentioned my brother since I was twelve. I couldn't talk about him when I was trying to disappear. And even with Heath and my parents, we talked about the murder and how Scott had affected me. But we didn't talk about *Scott.* Who he used to be. We never remembered.

I like remembering, even if nothing I say helps right now.

"I love my brother," I tell them. "But he did this horrible thing. I know he did. He didn't even deny it. And I know that's part of who he is, and I'm gonna have to live with that for the rest of my life. Worse, I'm gonna have to live with the fact that he's never going to be only that person. Because the guy you know, the one who's a file, the one who sits in this place, he's only a part of the person. Inside that guy there's still the boy who read comic books with me and taught me the alphabet and burned grilled cheese sandwiches."

I laugh and shake my head, remembering how ashamed he'd look when he'd hand me my lunch. "For the few years before it happened, our parents let us stay home without a babysitter during the summers, because it was only for a few hours. My dad spent hours teaching Scott how to cook before they allowed it. Hours. And Scott could cook just fine. Except I only ever wanted grilled cheese, and Scott couldn't make a grilled cheese without burning it. Every single one tasted like char."

My dad squeezes my hand under the table, and I smile at him.

"Do you think your brother is capable of rehabilitation?" the man in the suit asks. He doesn't care about grilled cheese or about what I remember. But I'm glad I get to remember.

"I don't know. I'm seventeen. I don't know what happened that day, but I can tell you there wasn't a reason. It was what it was. He murdered three people because he felt like it. That's inside of him. That's who he is."

"And the boy you just described?" the woman asks, packing up her pens because they're done with me. I didn't give them anything useful, but it felt good to say what I said anyway.

"That's who he is, too."

"We really appreciate your insight, Miss Stewart," the man says, and they talk to my parents for a few minutes. Policies and timelines. What to expect. It'll likely be after Christmas before we get an answer. It won't really matter, but maybe my parents will feel better if Scott goes someplace where people talk of hope.

I wait, wondering how far away he is. Wondering what he looks like. I'm sure they made him cut his hair. He used to chew on it when he got nervous. I try picturing him as an adult. Grown up. But I can't.

A guard comes into the room to escort us to where Scott will be.

"Are you all coming?" he asks.

My mom looks at me as the suit people sneak past the guard and out into the world, taking my memories and my secrets with them. To pile them up with all the memories and secrets of the other people they see.

"It's up to Alexia," my mom says.

I don't want to be alone. I don't want to sit with Scott

and try to pretend neither of us is hurt. I don't want to visit him and act like it's normal that I showed up today, as if this were common. But at the same time, I don't want to sit on the side, an observer. I don't want my parents to dominate the moment and leave me still detached from him.

I shake my head. "You'll be close, though?"

"We'll be right through the door," my dad says.

I follow the guard out into the hall, through more doors, even farther from the light and from freedom, to face my brother for the first time since that afternoon a lifetime ago.

Chapter Thirty-Four

notice his hands first. Everything about him is so much larger than it was the last time I saw him. He's gotten taller, but he's expanded outward, too. Into muscle and sinew. Tough. He looks like he belongs here, and it's terrifying. But then he lifts a hand to grab the phone, and I see his fingernails. He still bites them. He always did when he was nervous, and they're bitten to almost nothing now.

I lift the phone on my side, too. It's so surreal. Sitting here like someone in a movie. My brother behind glass.

No, not my brother. This *man*. This man who's swallowed the brother I knew.

"I always wondered if I'd see you again," he says as an introduction.

"Hi."

"So they asked you if I could get better, huh?"

I nod, clutching the phone to my ear. My palms are sweating, and the hard plastic of it feels like liquid.

"I won't ask what you said."

"I told them I didn't know. I told them what I remembered."

Scott nods and stands up. I wonder if he's done with me already, but I realize he's trying to look at me, to see as much of me as he can despite the glass and the setup. I stand for a moment and then sit back down, not sure if I feel ashamed. I hate that this is how I feel near my brother.

"You look like sunshine," he says. "I don't see that much in here."

I don't know what to say. I just watch him. This person who looks like a memory. But a memory that's changed while you've tried to forget it.

His head is shaved nearly bald. None of the kid I remember remains. My brother was scrawny, although always athletic, but now he fills the space between the two walls that make this cube.

"Mom and Dad said you live with Aunt Susie now," he says.

"This year."

"How's that?"

"It's okay. Do you remember when I was seven and you were ten? She came to Christmas with that guy she was dating? I think his name was Aaron? He was a magician?"

"And he kept trying to show us card tricks, but he messed them all up?" Scott answers. "Like even the most basic ones. And you tried to help him and you'd lie about which card you picked, hoping he'd feel less embarrassed?"

"Yeah," I say. "That was him."

"Are they still together?" Scott asks.

"No, she's single now. I can't say it's surprising."

He laughs, and it shatters me through the phone. It's the same laugh I hear still. The one I can sometimes hear across time. The one that filled my life until I was twelve. It's so unfair he can still laugh the same way. I can't remember the last time I felt able to laugh so freely.

I must flinch, because he stops abruptly.

"I'm so sorry, Lexi. I never meant to hurt you."

"But what about them? You killed them. You meant to hurt them."

"I know."

"Why?"

It's amazing how three letters can sum up a lifetime. Everything rests in those three letters. I need to understand. I need him to give me a reason.

"I don't know," Scott says. "I'm sorry, but I don't know."

I try to remember Mrs. Cabot. Lucy. Miles. I know their faces so well from the media, but I still can't really remember anything about them. Nothing that matters. They're only names and faces and scattered visions of things I might have known. I hate myself because I can't remember something this important. I feel like it's the least I can do. I should have memorized everything they were. Kept a record of what my brother erased.

"Please," I beg. "I need to know why."

"There was no why. That's just it. I don't remember anything about that day. Before it, I mean. I came home and I wasn't angry. I wasn't upset. I wasn't anything. That's what I remember. Feeling nothing. I don't know what happened. I don't know why I didn't feel anything."

"Even after?"

He shakes his head. "Not until I saw you. I remember wanting to cry because I'd hurt you."

"They said in the newspapers that you showed no remorse," I tell him. "That you were calculated. That was the word they used. I hated that word. I couldn't even sit through fucking math class anymore because of it. All I could see was your face and hear the things people called me." I pause. He won't make eye contact with me anymore. "Has Mom ever told you what they did? How hard it was for us?"

"No, but I can imagine."

"Can you?" I ask. "Can you really? Can you understand what it's like to know you can't have friends? To only have friends if you lie to them about who you are? I've moved every year because people hated me. They didn't want to be near me, like I was contagious."

"I'm sorry."

"But you're not. That's just it. You're not sorry. You don't even know why you did it, so how can you be sorry?"

"Lexi . . ."

"You're not sorry to Mr. Cabot, are you?" I ask. "He moved away, too. Right after the trial. He almost stayed. He was going to keep living there, if you can believe it. But then he met someone. Some woman from a counseling group or whatever. He should have been allowed to be happy, but he brought her home one night and some journalist saw it and people wouldn't let him forget. Someone wrote something online. They claimed he hired you. That you were paid to do it so he could be rid of his family. For this other woman. The one he only met because he had to go to a group for people who were falling apart."

"That's bullshit, but I can't say it surprises me."

"Well, it surprised me," I say. "It surprised the hell out of me to watch everyone mourn for him for all that time. To bring him casseroles and Christmas presents and cry with him at the funeral. And then they suddenly changed their minds. They started talking and then they thought they had the right . . . Once they started talking, it was impossible, you know. It was impossible for him."

"What do you want me to say?" Scott asks, and this time he looks at me. His eyes shimmer with tears, but he won't cry. Not here. Because it's a waste of time to cry here.

"I want you to tell him you're sorry."

"I don't think he wants to hear from me," he says.

The metal chair under me is uncomfortable. Scott probably lives in a room with a chair like this and some kind of cot. I'm sure it's nothing like his room at home, with his video games and his comics and the things he cared about.

I'm kind of glad he lost all that. I'm kind of glad he has to spend the rest of his life sitting on chairs like this.

"Tell me you wish you could take it back," I say. "That you would take it back if you could. I know you can't, but tell me you'd give anything to take it back. Tell me you wouldn't do it again if we could reset time."

"I can't say that."

"Why not? Why can't you do that for me? After everything you've stolen, why can't you give me that?"

"Because it's not true. Not totally. Yes, I would take it back knowing what I do now. I would absolutely take it back to make it so you wouldn't have to sit here, looking like sunlight in a place that forgot sunlight before either of us was born. But if I hadn't done it? I don't know. I don't know if I can say I wouldn't do it again."

He pauses and lifts his hand to the glass, but I don't press my hand against it. I hold myself as small as I can on the chair and wait for my brother to tell me it's not true. I never realized how badly I wanted it to be a mistake. I knew it wasn't, but I guess I still wished it was.

"Honestly?" Scott continues. "I can't say it, because I probably still would have done it if I hadn't done it that day. Maybe not them. Maybe someone else. Maybe it wouldn't have even happened yet, and your life would be different, but I don't know. I don't know why I did it, and because I don't know that, I can't say what I would have done. I just think this is inside me. I don't think you can change what's inside you."

"Everyone says the same thing is inside me," I tell him.

"I don't believe that."

I don't know how to have this conversation. I love my brother, but it's real here. Suddenly it's all real, and it's a new feeling, because I've always put it outside me. Like it happened, but only in a bad dream or in a movie. But he's here and it's real and the Cabots were real, too, and I can't even remember them properly.

"I'm sorry," Scott says yet again.

"You should be. Do you know what it's been like for Mom and Dad? For all of us? We don't live in the same house. We can't. I don't have a home anymore. I go from place to place because nothing feels real. I try to be someone, but I'm nothing but an idea. I'm a memory of summers and a brother who saved me from spiders and all the things that were supposed to happen. I'm not even alive, Scott."

"I know, Lexi, and I'm sorry. I promise, it hasn't been easy here, either."

"No. Fuck you. Absolutely not. Don't compare us. Don't try to make this about you," I say. "You put yourself here. How dare you sit there and tell me how hard it's been for you? How dare you pretend it's anything like it's been for me?"

I try to figure out how to say it all. How to turn all the memories and the could-have-beens and the things people thought about me into something I can explain.

"I was supposed to go to prom last year," I tell him. "I spent days flipping through magazines, looking at dresses. I wanted to tell Mom, to have her take me shopping, but I was afraid of giving her hope and having things go wrong. I wanted to be a normal girl, but I didn't get to be. Do you know what happened at prom?" Scott shakes his head. "Yeah, well, neither do I, because when people at school found out about what you'd done, my date changed his mind. So I'm glad I didn't tell Mom after all, because she would've had to live it all over again. To hurt for all the things she'll never experience. She'll never take me to look for dresses, because I'll never be the girl who gets to have those things. Or if she does, it'll be as a stranger, because I haven't lived with her and Dad in five years."

"Lexi—"

"I was sixteen last year. I was a junior in high school, and I wanted to go to prom. That's what you do at sixteen. Not me, though. I don't get to do those things. Because of you." I pause. "I can't talk to Mom about prom or things I care about, because I can't disappoint her when they never work out. I have to plan how I function around what will hurt everyone least. I shouldn't have to think about these kinds of things, Scott."

"Lexi—" he tries again.

"I'm not finished," I tell him. "This year I met a guy. I really like him. And sometimes when I'm around him, I can almost forget. He makes me feel okay. So I decided that because he can make me feel okay, then maybe enough time had gone by. I thought maybe . . . I had friends. I thought they were really my friends. And I started to think that maybe, finally, they liked me. That people would like me in spite of everything."

I pause, feeling the tears dropping onto the little desk in front of me, but I don't take my eyes off my brother. I don't even move, because I'm afraid it isn't real and I can't say these things a second time.

"I thought things had changed," I continue. "So I told my friends about you. You said you weren't surprised about how people treated Mr. Cabot, so I doubt you'll be surprised this time, either, but I was. I was devastated when I realized that they're not really my friends. They can't be. Of course they can't, right? Because I can't have friends, can I? I can't have anything. Because of what *you* did. You've done this to my life, and you sit there and you can't even give me a reason? You can't even tell me why you've taken so much from me?"

"I thought it would be better if I told you the truth," he says. "I thought you'd be better off if I didn't lie and tell you I knew why I did it."

I pull up my sleeves, pressing my skin against the glass, and I show him the scars along my arms. Raised white and pink lines. Scar tissue spelling out my story.

Psycho. Freak. Evil.

I show him the words, show him what he did to me. What he created for me.

"Do you see that?" I ask. "These are the things they've said about me. I kept a diary of everything I remember. Of everything people said because of you. Do you see what you left me? These are the things I am, Scott. These are the things you made me."

"I'm sorry. I'm so sorry, Lexi."

"Yeah, me too. I'm sorry you weren't there. I'm sorry that it took me this long to recognize this. I've hated myself for years. This morning before I came here, I had to go to yet another therapy session, and my therapist asked me to think about why I feel like I'm to blame. He asked me what I thought I did to deserve all this."

"It's not your fault," Scott says.

He reaches his hand up and touches where my arm still presses against the window. He places a finger along the word *Evil*, and I can almost feel his hands on my skin. I can almost remember him holding me when he'd push me on the swings. I can almost remember, and I almost let myself forget right now, but I fight it. Because I've spent five years surrounded by memories, letting them dim all the things I couldn't face.

I've spent five years trying to understand, and he doesn't even have an answer for me.

"You've taken everything from me," I tell my brother. "I grew up a shadow of a girl. I'm not a person anymore. I'm just leftover damage from you. You said I looked like sunlight, but that's a lie. I'm wearing yellow because I have to coordinate my clothes in solid shades so I can pretend I have control over any part of who I am. That I have a voice in my own life. I can't function without this, because it's the only way I know how to decide my own fate. It's all I can do to hold on."

I try to control the tears, but the entire world is a vacuum. Sounds and light and time are all fuzzy edges as Scott and I sit suspended on some kind of event horizon.

"It's not fair," I say. "You took away who I was and everything I was supposed to be. I don't know who I am anymore.

You're supposed to be my brother. You're supposed to have cared. Sure, I guess you owed me nothing, but I trusted you, Scott. I counted on you, and you were supposed to be there. You were supposed to protect me. And it turns out that you couldn't. You couldn't save me from my biggest threat, because that was you all along."

"I don't know what to say, Lexi. I don't know what to tell you except I'm sorry," Scott says.

"It's fine. There's nothing left to say. This is it. This is who we are."

I look at him one last time. Try to remember. Try to separate this man from the brother I loved. The one who believed in me. I try to isolate what it felt like to be happy from the girl I am now. All this fear. The anxiety. I try to find Scott through all these things, try to make them tangible. I assign all the painful thoughts to the parts of him that have changed. Rory and her flyers are my brother's shaved head. Being afraid of mixing colors in my wardrobe is the way his right eye doesn't open all the way anymore.

"I'm not coming back," I tell him. "At least not for a while. Maybe someday I will. Maybe someday when I figure out who I am outside of what you've done, I'll be a different person. Maybe I'll be able to forgive you, and the memories won't hurt so much that I can't breathe. But I can't do this again until I can figure that out. I miss my brother, but my brother isn't real. You're not him, just like I'm not the girl I was. None of us are the same anymore. That's what you did."

"I know."

I pause, debating whether I want to say more, but I can't. I just can't. I hang up the phone and he looks at me, but I can't meet his eyes. I don't want to be here anymore.

My parents go in after me, but we don't talk, and I have

the guard walk me outside so I can sit in the car. It's started to snow again, and this time it's sticking. The car is covered with white, and the sky's turned nearly black.

I open the door, crawl into the backseat, and go to sleep.

Chapter Thirty-Five

Nothing changes after Thanksgiving. My parents try to talk me into staying behind, but I can't. I don't want to be there. Not with their holiday-themed towels and the worry and the always-remembering-something-that-isn't-real-anymore.

There's no sudden freedom after seeing Scott, but there is relief at having said all those things aloud. At moving the voices from my head onto the person who earned them.

On his birthday I sit in the apartment, thinking about him. He's officially an adult now. I try to feel something about it. Try remembering in a way that doesn't hurt. A way that doesn't suffocate where we are now with some distorted nostalgia. But instead all I can think of are the realities that could have been. All the ways today could have gone if he'd only made a different choice.

I call Marcus and we go back to the bowling alley, walking the entire way in silence. It's a new silence, though. It's the quiet of knowing there are things that can't be said but are still understood.

The bowling alley is one of those places that should be depressing, but it's kind of comforting in how sad it is. I figure at least it's not another chain store. It's not anything, but it's better than being just another of something.

"It's Scott's birthday," I tell him when we get inside.

"I'm sorry."

"I know."

"My dad's birthday is the week after Christmas. It's unfair, isn't it?" he asks.

"What is?"

"We both fill Decembers with the memories of people who disappointed us. The holidays will never be like a Christmas card for us because either right before or right after, there's just the reminder of them."

We sit in one of the lanes this time. If I lean back, I'll end up in the gutter. I tell myself not to analyze that. *It's not a symbol,* I repeat in my head. *It's just a bowling alley.*

"I . . ." I realize I don't want to talk about Scott anymore. I don't want anything but to try to be here. To be now. I promised myself I'd make a conscious effort to be present instead of always seeing the world through the fabric of the past.

"Do you ever wonder if people change?" I ask.

Marcus shakes his head, the motion in silhouette thanks to the camping lantern behind him. "Not really. No. I don't think they do."

"So you don't think there's a chance? You don't think people like Rory grow up?"

"Some do, I guess. But I don't know. Most of them, I'd say

no. I think people are who they are. I think everyone has a person they wish they were, and they try to convince everyone else that's who they are, but most people are just themselves."

"And after high school? It's more of the same?"

"Well, I don't think there's this high school version of people and then suddenly, they graduate and they change. Yeah, I think a lot of people appear to change. Probably for a lot of reasons. Maybe it's not really anything different, but you're in a different place, and so you don't see it the same way. I think maybe you don't have to deal with Rory every day, so later you don't feel the same when you do see her, but that's not a difference in her."

"That's pretty cynical," I tell him. I don't mean to be critical. I don't mind his cynicism. I'm curious about it. Despite everything, I guess I've always clung to this idea that it was all temporary. But maybe he's right.

"Probably," he says. "I don't know. I guess I feel like I've seen enough of people to know you can't count on them to be anything but themselves."

The bowling alley is shadows and flashes of light from the lantern and the cars passing outside. I have no idea what's waiting on the other side of the glass doors. The world could be falling down around us, but in here it's fine. A little cold, but fine.

Marcus notices my shivering and takes out a blanket from a bag he brought. He wraps the blanket around me and tries to cover both of us with the ends of it, but it only reaches to his shoulders. His back is still out in the cold.

"I think some people can change," he says finally. "I know you want to hope for Scott, and I don't want you to think—"

"It's not that," I admit. "I think he's probably beyond that point. I don't know if I'll ever really forgive him, no matter who or what he becomes. Even if change is possible. But I guess I want to think that maybe someday people will remember me and feel sorry they said the things they did. It's selfish, I know. It just . . . it really fucking hurts. And I guess I like hoping that maybe someday someone will feel bad for making me feel like this."

Marcus pulls me closer, but still the blanket doesn't reach around him. "It's probably possible. I'm sorry I'm a cynic."

"I'm sorry I'm not. Sometimes I wish I listened to the voices in my head. You'd think after years of being hurt like this, I'd know better. Maybe I deserve it. Maybe I just don't know how to stop hoping."

"I don't think there's anything wrong with hoping. I just don't think it's worth expecting it. It's not worth how much it hurts."

We both lie back, wrapping the blanket around us. The lane is cold on my back, but between Marcus and the blanket, I don't mind it.

"After my dad left," he says, "for a while I lived in this fantasy. I told myself he'd come back. That he'd left the movies because they mattered to him. That they were some kind of code. That his note wasn't saying it was permanent. He was saying someday he'd be there to watch them, too. That he wanted me to know he was coming back. But he didn't. And eventually I kind of realized that's just people. He should've been better. He should've at least tried. But people don't do what they should. People disappoint you. You can hope they won't, and you can imagine them making different choices, but in the end they sometimes let you down. For no reason at all."

"I think that's what bugs me. The disappointment," I

say. "Because I keep hoping for more, and I'm always disappointed. And I hate how much it hurts, and yet I can't stop thinking it might be different. This year was one of the worst."

"Why?" Marcus asks.

"Probably because of Ryan. I mean, I get it. But he was better than the rest of them. With Rory, she's not who I thought she was. That's on me. I saw her as a different kind of person, but like you said, people disappoint you. Chloe and I weren't friends, so it didn't hurt with her. And she's been . . . I don't know. She surprises me. And then there's Lauren, but we didn't know each other well enough. She's still friendly, too, so there's no real absence there. But Ryan . . . he was my friend. My best friend here."

"I've never even met him. It's weird we live in these different realities, even when we're so close," Marcus says.

"It is. I wish you knew him. I wish I could explain. Because he's . . . he's honestly a good person. And that makes it harder. Because I understand. If I was him, if it was a year ago and we were in different situations, I would have done the same thing. I would've cut him out of my life, too."

"Really?"

I don't want to admit it. I want to tell Marcus I'm better than I am, but I imagine myself as Ryan. I imagine being in Maine last fall, becoming close to someone, and then having their secret lead people to mine. I imagine Ben having a secret that could have drawn attention to me, and I think about how I would have reacted.

"Yeah," I say. "Last year, if I'd been in the same place, I would've been scared. That doesn't mean it doesn't hurt, but I would have done the same thing."

"If you say so," Marcus says.

"I know you don't understand, because you don't know

the whole story, and I can't tell you. I won't do that to him. But trust me, it's all the same, really. Sometimes it's just about getting by."

"That's why your aunt worried about me. Because she was worried I'd make it harder for you."

"She never believed them, you know. She always liked you. Still does. She just . . . worried."

"I know. And it wasn't far from the truth. I mean, it was true. Once."

I turn onto my side and rest my arm across his body. "I think I'm gonna stay here," I tell him. "Not just for this year. Like, until I figure shit out."

"What do you mean?"

"Like . . . as long as I need to stay here. College or whatever. My parents wanted me to go home and take classes online for a while. But I'm not going to. I'm gonna stay here. I'll go to school locally somehow. I want to make this work."

"Are you sure?"

I nod. "Yeah. I need to stop leaving everything behind just because it gets hard. I mean, it's always gonna be tough, right? I can keep running away from it all, or I can start trying to live. I might as well start living."

Marcus sits up and lays the blanket across the lane, lying down on it and pulling me down beside him. We don't touch except for our fingertips.

"I want you to stay," he says. "I want to know you'll be here, but I don't want you to stay because of me."

"I'm not. It's a bonus. But I'm not. This is for me, I promise."

"I need to get a job. I want to go to school next year, too, but we can't afford it. And there aren't a lot of places excited about taking fuckups, especially on scholarship. I don't even take real classes."

"You could take a year off and then go," I say. "People do it all the time. And now I'll be here to annoy you about it."

He links his fingers with mine. Our hands glow in the unnatural light. A red-and-black shadow. It feels solid and real to hold his hand, but it looks like a dream.

"It's weird, isn't it?" I ask.

"What is?"

"There's an entire life waiting for us. Six months from now. A year from now. And I have no idea what that looks like. I don't know how to imagine it."

"Do you know what you want to do in school?"

"Not really. It's kinda unfair they want us to decide now, isn't it? I still don't even know who I am. How can I decide now who future me should be?"

"I get that," he says.

"What about you? Movies?"

Marcus shakes his head, staring up at the pipes and loose tiles on the ceiling. "Nah. That's just something I hold on to. For me. I don't want that to define me. I don't want . . . I think I need them to be something else. Something I don't share with people."

"So what do you want to do, then?"

"It's between two things. Maybe there's some happy medium in there between them both. I don't know. Maybe. But I've kind of always known. At least since my mom got sick. When she got sick, I decided I wanted to go into nursing. I want to be there for people like her. Not that it's going to be easy, since I only learn real things from the internet."

"That's still pretty amazing," I say. "What's the other thing? Please don't say, like, football star. That will really detract from this wonderful revelation that you have a deep heart."

"Hey, you didn't already know that?" he asks, laughing.

"I did, but don't prove me wrong with some nonsense."

"Well, first of all, I don't play football. I don't play any-thing. But if I did, it would be hockey."

"Really? Hockey? I never would've guessed that."

"I'm full of secrets and surprises."

"Okay, so you want to be a nurse or a hockey player."

His laugh bounces off the wood of the lane and the hollow space where the pins would be if this place still existed for any purpose. I love the sound of it. A memory of life in a place that thought it had been forgotten.

"No hockey," Marcus says. "I just meant if I was going to pick some sports fantasy, it would be hockey."

"Are you going to tell me, then?"

"I was, until you started with your twenty questions about my sports preferences."

"Go on," I say.

"I want to do something for people like my dad. Social work, maybe? I don't know. I don't know if there's even a title, but I want to be the person who finds people like him. People who can't handle the day-to-day shit of cancer. I want to help them handle it."

"That's really sweet. And even more amazing."

He sighs. "Please don't tell anyone I'm either of those things. I kind of like my total-fuckup image."

"Yeah, I'm pretty sure I'm done telling people anything."

...

It's the middle of the night when we leave the bowling alley. It's also snowing and has been for a while. There's at least two inches on the ground, and it's not stopping anytime soon.

"Maybe they'll give us a snow day tomorrow," I say.

"I hope so, because functioning on two hours of sleep is probably unhealthy."

"I seem to remember there was some sleeping in there."

"There was, but there was also a great deal of . . . not sleeping," Marcus says.

He stops and turns in the snow, kissing me as the flakes bear down on us.

"You know what?" I ask.

"What's that?"

"I like this reality," I tell him. "I've been trying so hard to find one I could stick to. There's the version of my life from before Scott happened. And the multiple forms it took over the past five years. Even this year there have been a few sort-of-close-but-not-totally-me versions of me. But with you I feel like this is the right one. I really like this one. I like this."

"I like it, too." He smiles, his eyes flickering. "You know what I think about a lot? Remember the first day of school? What if no one had put that dick on the knight?"

"Right? What would we have talked about? *Would* we have talked?"

"It's weird, isn't it?"

"It's weird," I agree. "So I guess in a way we have to be thankful for that graffiti artist. It's the best thing that's happened to me this year."

"Smart guy," he says.

I look over at him. "You didn't . . . ?"

He laughs. "No. First of all, I am god-awful at art, even spray-painted dicks. Secondly, I am not so amazing that I planned a night of wild graffiti chaos, all of which I foresaw would lead us here. I just think about it a lot. How weird things are. And how it's kind of lucky they are."

Marcus smokes in silence as we trudge home through the snow. It's impressive he can keep the cigarette lit in the storm, but I guess you can become an expert on slowly killing yourself.

When we get to the complex, we take the long way back to my apartment. It's late and we should hurry, but I don't want to go home yet.

"I'm really glad someone painted a dick on that sign," I tell him.

"I really am, too."

"It's funny, because if you'd told me we'd be here tonight—that you would be the only person standing here after everything—I don't know if I would've believed you."

"Why not?" he asks.

"I don't know. Not because I didn't want you to be, but for a while there I thought I had friends. I had drama. I didn't see you much after the sign and the ice cream."

"I'm sorry I'm the only one here," he says.

"That's okay. I'm glad you're here. It's just not how I would've expected things to go."

"Sometimes the people you expect to be there—the ones you trust the most—they're the first to leave." I know he's thinking about his dad. I wish I'd known him. I wish I could know him now. Could tell him what he gave up. "It's really too bad we couldn't get some kind of warranty on decency. Like, before we fall in love with someone, I wish we could we get a guarantee they'll be there when it counts."

When we reach my apartment, I stop only a few yards

from my door and face him. "I love you, you know. I don't come with a guarantee, but I do love you."

"I love you, too," Marcus says, kissing me under the security lights as they turn the snow into an explosion of starlight.

Chapter Thirty-Six

Just before winter break, Rory Winters reappears. I walk into school and find my locker covered with flyers. Some are for her victims' group or whatever, welcoming me to another Monday morning with the faces of dead kids staring back at me. The rest are for drama auditions, which are today. I'm not welcome in drama anymore, so they were left simply as a reminder of how much she hates me.

"Fuck you, Rory Winters," I say, pulling the flyers off the locker and tossing them into the trash.

"What's that, Alexia Stewart? I got your name right, didn't I? That's your name?" she asks from behind me.

I turn around to face her. "How petty can you be?"

"I just wanted to remind you about auditions. You are auditioning, right? It would be such a shame for you to miss out. I mean, we aren't doing *Macbeth*, so it might be hard for you to find a psycho-bitch character to relate to, but I'm sure you can figure something out. I'm sure you can pretend to be anyone you want to be, can't you, Lexi?"

I create an entire rant in my head about her use of the words *psycho* and *bitch*. About the irony of her self-righteousness. But words are wasted on someone like her, so I just smile.

"Oh yeah. Thanks so much for reminding me. I almost forgot. Well, see you at auditions," I say, walking away.

I have no intention of going, but I love knowing she'll spend all day wondering whether I was serious.

Lauren comes up to me in class right after that, which is how I know it worked. "I heard you're going to auditions?" she asks.

"I was thinking about it."

"Oh. Well, I mean, there aren't a ton of parts, but yeah . . . it would be nice to see you."

Throughout the day several other random drama kids ask me, tentatively, if I'm really auditioning. I love that it's so unreasonable that I might still feel like acting, just because everyone knows my real last name.

Even Chloe mentions it in study hall. We're currently existing in a strange in-between. We really don't like each other, but there's something in the quiet acceptance we've built. We try to remain civil because she hates me for things that have nothing to do with Scott, and I respect her begrudgingly for that.

"I actually think it's a great idea," she says, sitting next to me. The teacher keeps looking up at us, but she doesn't ask us to be quiet. Even the teachers don't care right now. There are only a few days left until break, and school's mostly for show. "You won't get a part, but I think it's basically the biggest 'fuck you' ever."

"You think it's a great idea because you're pretty much guaranteed a part this time," I say. "If you weren't, you'd try to talk me out of it. But this time there aren't enough people. Or so I've heard."

"So? You're still not getting one," Chloe says, and I laugh.

"You know what? I'm glad you're the worst."

"Yeah, well, it's mutual."

When the bell rings, I head toward the parking lot to meet Marcus and his friends, who drive us to and from school now. I really don't plan to audition, despite what I told people. On my way out I pass the auditorium, where everyone is starting to congregate. I don't let myself remember how it felt to belong for a moment. I ignore the memory of that first moment on the stage.

I tell myself not to think about the bleachers, either. About Ryan. That's not the truth of it all anymore. That's not real for me now.

I make it to the staircase that leads out to the parking lot. I'm almost outside. Almost free of it.

On the window of the door that leads outside, I see one of Rory's "Let's all point out what a terrible person Lexi is" flyers, and I stop. I see Miles and Lucy from the glass, and I can make out cars and people through their faces. I turn and look back down the hall, toward the auditorium, and then turn back, staring at the flyer and the world beyond it again.

In *Romeo and Juliet*, I had three lines and I played a nonexistent character. I got to wear clothes I chose, on the days I needed to, and I never had to feel uncomfortable. Being part of something was easy.

This won't be. If I go to auditions, I most likely won't get a part. But if I do, it will be revenge for Rory. She'll make it miserable. It will be the wrong role. Probably something that reaches into the things I hate most about myself. Something that will lead to a lot of nights of anxious tears with Marcus and Aunt Susie. I will absolutely have to wear something that will make me want to vomit. Maybe even red. They'll cast me in a part that makes me remember Scott every day at rehearsal. They won't let me forget.

I can walk away. I can go outside, can meet Marcus at the car, can head home and be done with it all. I won't benefit at all from auditioning. Either it will be humiliating in a simple way—no part for me, even though there aren't enough actors—or it will be hell for months.

But if I go outside and I don't audition today, Rory Winters wins. She breaks me.

I text Marcus and turn around.

The auditorium is full of all the same people. They stop what they're doing and look at me when I enter. I feel the doors whoosh closed. It's too cold inside, the fake air pumped through the vents making me shiver. I ignore it, and I ignore everyone's stares, looking straight ahead and focusing on the stage lights.

I stroll to the front of the auditorium, pick up a packet, and start preparing. I'll have to use the only monologue I've ever memorized, because I didn't plan to be here.

After I get my forms, I sit in the second row and fill out the papers while the silence turns to a quiet hum. People start talking, pretending they're not uncomfortable. A couple of girls stare at me and whisper, but I focus on filling out my details and I try not to hear them. I even include my phone number this time on my info sheet. They can do their worst.

Rory walks to the stage, and the auditorium settles into quiet. She glares at me while speaking.

"I'm really excited to see most of you here. It's nice to see the same faces. Clearly, we have to be open to all, and sometimes there are people we're not really expecting to see here, but I'm happy there are so many familiar faces. The important thing is to do your best. I know people assume I get every lead, but things can change." She smiles as if she believes it. "So let's get started, shall we? Any volunteers to be first?"

No one volunteers. No one wants to be first; the first person is like the practice audition. Whoever goes first sets the bar for everyone else, so it's usually someone new. They're chosen by Rory so they can set the bar low. That way everyone else feels good about themselves. Yeah, it's a pretty shitty way to do things, but it works and keeps most of the drama club members feeling good. One random person who will likely never try out again is a sacrifice Rory is more than willing to make.

I'm not at all surprised to hear my name called as the sacrifice today.

I don't really know why I'm doing this, I think as I walk up the aisle. I can't win. But I guess it's like I told my aunt: It's not about winning; it's about not losing anything else. It's about not letting Rory Winters have the last word.

I head onto the stage, feeling Rory's eyes on me. When I turn to face the audience, though, I can't see any of them. Just darkness against darkness because of the lights in my eyes.

I remind myself that Ryan is in here somewhere. I think of him. I think of all the things I promised him and how I let him down. He's who I hold on to when I speak.

Nothing hurts more beautifully than memory.

When I speak, I think of that evening with him on the bleachers. I try to make him remember.

Even after you think the scars have healed, they never, ever heal.

I promised I would be his normal. I still want that for us. I still want to be something to him. I realize as I speak these words about memory and pain that I love Ryan. I love him in a way that makes it ache not having him around. It's a different kind of love than romance. It's nothing like it is with Marcus, but I miss it so much.

I can continue. I can start over. Not a new beginning . . . but a different beginning. One that branches out from the old. That takes into account all that came before it.

I say someone else's words to Ryan, and I try to make him see. I try to show him what I'm missing without him. Friendship and trust and knowing you can bear your burden because you're happy to carry someone else's for them.

I tell him all this through the words of another person. Through a writer I don't know and through a character who isn't real. I try to tell him, and I try to let the words come from me instead. To let him see me.

Something will remind me. And that pain will still be there . . . but part of me welcomes it now.

After my audition I leave. I don't wait for feedback from Rory. I realized while I spoke, while I tried to tell Ryan what I wanted him to know, that it doesn't matter if I get cast.

I don't want to be a part of them anymore. I just wanted them to know I'm still here.

Chapter Thirty-Seven

'm in my room packing for winter break when my phone buzzes. My parents are on their way to come get me, and Marcus was just here, so I can't imagine who it could be.

Do you have a couple hours? the text says.

Who is this?

Oliver Queen.

I run through all the conversations I've ever had. The people I've met. I try to place the name and I can't.

Who?

I keep packing while I wait for a response. But as I fold my shirts and see the green corner of one on the bottom of the pile, I remember.

Ryan?

Green Arrow, he texts. *Remember?*

I do. How'd you get my number?

Drama form. Sorry you weren't cast.

I sit on my bed and close my suitcase. My parents will

be here in a few hours pending traffic, but I can probably find time. Worst case, they can talk to my aunt until I get back.

I didn't really want a part anyway.

I figured.

So I have some time now. A little.

Meet me outside.

When?

I'm already here.

I go outside as he's pulling into the driveway. I'm tempted to lecture him on texting and driving, especially in the snow, but I'm too surprised to say much of anything. I lean over and open the passenger door, peering inside.

"Hey," I say. "What if I hadn't answered?"

"I brought you a present. I was just going to leave it." He gestures to a red bag on the passenger seat.

"I didn't get you anything."

"That's okay. It's kind of crap anyway."

I laugh. "It's freezing. I'm going to get in."

"Please."

"Can I open it?" I ask once I'm in the car.

"It's really nothing," he says. I ignore him and pull the tissue from the bag. Inside is a ladybug lawn ornament with a Santa hat.

"It's the sibling to the one you bought," he explains. "Seasonal. I . . . I'm sorry. It's garbage."

"I love it. It's a festive delight."

"I just . . . I wanted you to know . . . I . . ."

I watch him struggling to find words, and I put the bag down by my feet. "So where are we going?" I ask, trying to distract him from what he doesn't want to—or can't—say.

"It's Christmas. Well, Christmas season. And where better to spend it than at the greatest comic-book store ever?"

The car is warm. He's been in here for a while, because it's that toasty warm that feels like its own memory of summer. A break from the chill outside. I love riding around in winter just because of the contrast. Sweating while the entire world outside becomes white.

"Sounds good to me," I say.

It's silent in the car for a while as the snow continues to fall all around us.

"Look, L," he says finally. "I don't know how to do this."

"Do what?"

"This. Us. Whatever. I miss you. I can't stand not seeing you. But I don't know how to have people look at me. I can't have them truly look at me."

"I want to tell you you're overreacting. I want to say you have nothing to worry about. But I can't. People . . ."

Ryan turns on the windshield wipers, pushing winter in arcs along the glass. "I'm sorry they're not . . . People change."

I think of everything Marcus said. "Do they? Sometimes I hope they can, but—"

"I don't mean in a good way," Ryan says. "I mean, sure, sometimes I guess people do. It's nice hoping they do anyway. But what I mean is that people change when you really see them. They're one way when it's easy. But they change when they're tested. When something makes them uncomfortable."

"She wasn't tested," I say. "Rory Winters has never been tested in any way."

We drive forward into warp speed, snow coming down faster as we go, the faint sounds of Christmas carols coming from his stereo.

"I don't know what would happen if they found out," he admits. "Maybe they'd think it's fine. But what if they didn't? I don't know what it would be like, but I know for sure that I can't survive a year and a half if it turns out like it did for you."

"You know I get it, right? You know it's all okay?"

"I'm not a good person. I should have been your friend. I was supposed to be your friend."

"Ryan, people get scared. You have a right to be scared. I was selfish. I should have thought about you, about the ripples of the things I was doing, before I went off and did something like that."

He shakes his head, clutching the steering wheel. "I'm an asshole. I don't want them in my life over you. They weren't there. They haven't been there. Two years ago when I wanted to die every day, where the fuck was Rory Winters? She was part of the problem, and I'm letting her do it again. It's just in a different way. You know I get that, right?"

"There's nothing wrong with you, you know," I tell him.

"I know. But . . . I just don't have the desire to explain it to them. To try to make them get it. If I told them I'm not into girls, everyone would assume I'm gay. Which would be fine, except I'm not. So if I said that, they'd tell me I'll find the right girl someday. Like everything is defined by who I end up with. I can't make them get it. And I don't feel like trying. I just want them to leave me alone."

"I can appreciate that. And for the record, I get it. I don't think you have to explain."

"I miss you," he says.

"Me too. I miss you constantly. I tried . . . during my audition, I tried to tell you. I wanted you to know I was talking to you. I really wish things were different."

"How do I be good for you and still be okay, L? Just tell me how."

I shrug. "I don't know. I guess we figure it out as we go. You know I don't need the world to know we're friends, right?

I don't care about any of that anymore. I just need you to know. I need to know you don't hate me."

"I never hated you," he says. "For the last month, I've hated me. I wanted to defend you. Whenever they'd start shit. Rory and her fucking flyers. At auditions. I wanted to be there. I *want* to be there for you."

"I thought about going back home," I tell him. "At first. I almost gave up when she started it."

"I'm glad you didn't, even if I don't have the right to feel that way."

We slow down and Ryan pulls up to a brick building with a gray sign. According to him, this is the world's most exciting comic book store. It looks like another accountant's office, but hey, what do I know? Maybe everything holds much more on the inside.

"I'm not leaving," I say. "I'm gonna stay here. I decided I'll stay here for a while after all. You know why?"

"Why?"

"Because on my first day of school here, I met two people. A boy I admit I've fallen pretty embarrassingly in love with."

"See? What kind of friend am I that I haven't even been there for that?" Ryan asks.

"Don't worry. I will be happy to regale you with all the stories. Maybe at the next regional craft fair. In between fighting off the hordes, of course."

"It's January third. They don't even give people time to put away all the shit they got for Christmas that they didn't want."

"Well, I'll be there with bells on," I say. "Probably literally. You know, when in Rome . . ."

"Mildred is selling jingle bells. After Christmas. And don't worry. She'll sell out," he says.

"The corruption runs deep."

"It does. But I interrupted you. You said you met two people . . ."

"I did. Two boys, actually. I worried at first, I admit. I've read enough books to realize that meeting two boys on the first day of school is usually a bad sign. And one's probably a werewolf or something."

Ryan laughs. "Can you imagine how annoying it would be to have your relationships decided by hashtags and team names?"

"Seriously. I think I'm going to be nothing but #TeamMe."

"#TeamNope?"

"You're the worst distraction," I say, laughing. "I'm supposed to be telling you my feelings right now, you know."

"I think it's pretty clear. And so you know, I'm definitely on your team. I'm just . . ."

"Yeah, I know."

"So we're still friends? Even with the complications?" he asks.

"I told you before. We're always friends. I miss you, Ryan. I don't care if we're only friends at craft fairs and on secret snowy trips to this kind of shady brick building. I'd rather have you in my life than not."

"Galactic Empire is absolutely not shady. I am quite disturbed you'd say so," he says, turning off the car.

"Okay, except the sign is a gray rectangle with only the letter *M* still visible. It's not a good omen for the state of the company."

"Listen, L. Galactic Empire is such that it doesn't need signs. People *know* this place. They can sense it through time and space."

We both get out of the car, standing in the snow as it continues to dust the world.

"You'll see," Ryan says. "You'll come to know the wonders of Galactic Empire, and the world as you know it will never be the same."

He takes my arm as we walk. I lean on him because the snow makes the driveway slippery.

"What are you into for comics?" he asks. "You said a while back that you were kind of into them."

"That was a while ago," I say. "With my brother."

"Oh . . . is this . . . Are you okay?"

I nod. "Yeah. Yeah, you know what? I'm okay. I'm good, actually."

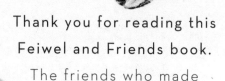